FEET OF CLAY

RUTH BIRMINGHAM

FEET OF
CLAY

THOMAS DUNNE BOOKS
ST. MARTIN'S MINOTAUR
NEW YORK

THOMAS DUNNE BOOKS.
An imprint of St. Martin's Press.

FEET OF CLAY. Copyright © 2006 by Ruth Birmingham. All rights reserved. Printed in the United States of America. No part of this book may be used or reproduced in any manner whatsoever without written permission except in the case of brief quotations embodied in critical articles or reviews. For information, address St. Martin's Press, 175 Fifth Avenue, New York, N.Y. 10010.

www.minotaurbooks.com

Library of Congress Cataloging-in-Publication Data

Birmingham, Ruth.
    Feet of clay / Ruth Birmingham.–1st ed.
        p. cm.
    ISBN 0-312-28424-1
    EAN 978-0-312-28424-4
    1. Childs, Sunny (Fictitious character)–Fiction. 2. Women private investigators–Georgia–Atlanta–Fiction. 3. Atlanta (Ga.)–Fiction. I. Title.
PS3569.O695F44 2006
813'.54–dc22

                                                            2006040165

10   9   8   7   6   5   4   3   2

FEET OF CLAY

PROLOGUE

When she saw what was inside the shed, Terri tried to run.

But it was no good. She was barefoot, naked, hands secured behind her back with duct tape. She made it thirty or forty yards across the bare slash of slippery white clay before her feet went out from under her. He grabbed her by the hair and dragged her back to the shed. She would have screamed, but the plastic gag made it pointless.

Around them was nothing but barren, trackless pine forest, pressing in against the bare white scar of ground.

They went inside the shed, an industrial building of some sort, and there it was again, the horrible thing, hanging like meat from a hook in the rafters. The *thing*—Terri tried to think of it that way. Not as a person. Not as her friend Brittany. More like a cocoon, dangling in the stifling heat.

He pushed her roughly to the ground, then grabbed her legs and looped duct tape around them four or five times. She struggled, tried to kick. But it was too late. He was faster, more powerful than he looked.

As she lay on the ground, she saw that there was some kind of hoist or pulley attached to the rafters, the sort of thing her brother Larry used to haul engines up out of the crappy old cars he was always buying and fixing up. At the end of the chain, hanging just inches from her face, was a blunt and rusting hook. The man spun her around, attached the chain to the loop around her ankles, then hauled on the hoist. She began to rise slowly, slowly into the air. The blood rushed into her head.

"Please!" she tried to scream. But through the gag, it came out as just a muffled whimper. "Please!"

The chain hoist rattled and clanked. She closed her eyes and prayed. When the chain finally stopped clanking, she opened her eyes. She was spinning. Very slowly. The shed revolved around her. Her friend Brittany hung only a few yards away. Brittany's face was covered by a black trash bag. But the tattoo on the small of her back—a huge red bird taking flight—it was impossible not to recognize.

Soon that would be her, too. A cocoon. That's all, just a cocoon. *Think of it that way,* Terri told herself.

Below her, the man spoke. "I'm sorry," he said. His voice was a monotone.

It was the first time he'd spoken since he'd gagged her half an hour earlier. She looked down and he was holding something in his left hand. A black trash bag. Over on a card table near the door lay a jumble of gleaming tools. He walked to the table, unbuttoned his cuff links, set them on the table, then rolled up his sleeves. He picked something up off the table—a screwdriver—and began walking briskly toward her. She decided she didn't want to see any more. She looked up and saw her feet hanging up there in the air. They were impossibly white. Weird, she thought. And then she realized. It was from the white clay that she'd stumbled through on her way to the shed.

It was the last thing she saw before the trash bag covered up her face. She felt a loop of tape going around her neck, securing the bag over her head. It wasn't tight enough to keep her from breathing, though. It just blinded her.

Then she heard footsteps walking away. Where was he going?

ONE
SIX YEARS LATER

"*Crack-up!*" Lee-Lee said. "How's that grab you, Sunny? Or maybe like, *Three Strikes, You're Dead*? Wait, wait, I know! *Rape Factory!*"

"You're serious?" I said. "You want to make a film about a convicted rapist and murderer?"

Lee-Lee nodded vigorously, her eyebrow ring flashing in the light of the bar where we were sitting.

I said, "Explain to me why this would be of interest to sane human beings. I mean, it's like sticking your camera into a train wreck."

Lee-Lee wrinkled her nose at me. "Exactly! That's the point, Sunny," she said. "Everybody wants to look at a train wreck."

I sighed. Everybody has a crazy cousin. Lee-Lee is mine. Her craziness manifests itself in the form of various obsessions, each of which inevitably leads her into some kind of ridiculous disaster. She then relies on her boundless naïveté and charm to get herself out of the inevitable disaster. Generally, she drags everybody she knows into the tragicomic storm that surrounds her, putting us all to great effort, pain, expense, or some combination thereof. At various times she has announced to us that she had decided to become: a professional bull rider, a painter, a swimwear designer, a banjo player, and a lot of other things. Her most recent mania was documentary filmmaking.

"So this guy is down at the death house at Jackson penitentiary?" I said.

"Germind Dale Weedlow," she said. "Convictions for assault, possession of stolen goods, got six months for receiving, and time served for possession of marijuana and drug paraphernalia. Then he got the big one."

"The big one."

"He got convicted of raping and killing two girls down in Flournoy County. Two death sentences: rape, murder, assault with a deadly weapon." She smiled. "He's a bad, bad, bad boy."

"Well, all I've got to say," I told her, "is don't get the idea that you're going to be the big crusader who proves this monster didn't do it."

"*Au contraire*, Sunny," she said. "I just want to, like, get inside this perv's mind, see what his deal is."

"How charming," I said. "Anyway, guys like this, they see some cute little sorority chickie like you, they're gonna be racking their sociopathic brains trying to figure out a million ways of using you, of abusing your trust."

Lee-Lee, more than anything else in the universe, hates being called a sorority chickie. These days, she's all nose rings and dyed black hair and tattoos. But she had spent about three weeks as a Tri Delt back when she was a freshman at UGA, and I've never let her forget it.

"Trust?" She laughed loudly, tossed a mug shot of a guy on the table. "You think I'd trust a guy like *that*?"

I looked at the guy in the picture; then I looked up at her. The contrast couldn't have been more stark. Weedlow had white-trash loser practically tattooed on his forehead. Small head, protuberant eyes, one tooth eaten away by decay, bad skin, a stringy mullet, a mulish expression in his eyes. Lee-Lee, on the other hand, is a child of privilege. I looked at her pretty dentistry, her flawless skin, her expensively dyed and disheveled hair, her nose ring, her eyebrow ring, the tattoo of Marilyn Manson on her shoulder—the whole sorority-girl-gone-wrong shtick—and I felt something cool move across my skin. She'd never had anything bad happen to her, didn't realize how ugly and how real a thing like this would turn out to be.

"You don't have a clue what you're getting into," I said. "You sit around up here in some coffeehouse in Atlanta with all your cynical hipster friends egging you on and you think, *Hey, great, this'll be fun!*" I shook my head. "I'm telling you, it ain't gonna be fun."

But she didn't listen. Lee-Lee's a sweet girl, but she never listens. Never ever. I've always been like her responsible big sister, the one who gives her good advice that she ignores. But then, I guess it's a family trait. Since when did I ever listen to anybody either?

"So when's he scheduled to get the needle?" I said. "Sometime in the next couple years?"

"Uh . . ." Lee-Lee said. "Actually, next Saturday."

I sighed loudly. "Germind?" I said. "This sicko's name is really Germind?"

"He goes by Dale. We can head down tonight."

"Tonight! Are you crazy?"

Lee-Lee smirked. "Tonight."

"No, Lee-Lee! Absolutely not."

"Oh, come on! Just for a day. Two at most."

"Lee-Lee," I said. "I've got a very big case I'm working on right now. If I go down there with you, all of a sudden you'll be convinced that this idiot got framed, that he's all innocent and everything. Next thing I know, I'll be wasting a week poking around down there in some jerkwater county full of inbred rednecks."

"Flournoy County is not that bad, Sunny!"

"Oh yes it is," I said. I drained the last of my beer. "Sorry, Lee-Lee. I can't."

TWO

The phone next to our bed rang at around four o'clock in the morning.

"I'll get it," Barrington mumbled. "It's probably for me."

My fiancé sat up, swung his feet out of bed, and grabbed the phone.

"Special Agent Cherry speaking," he said. He listened for a minute, then swore and slammed down the phone.

"What was it, Barrington?" I said.

"Collect call from prison," Barrington said. "What makes these idiots think I'd accept the charges?"

"Great."

"I don't even have any cases in Flournoy County."

"*Flournoy* County?" I said. The phone began to ring again.

•

Three hours later, I was walking in the front door of the Flournoy County Sheriff's Department in the somewhat grim-looking town of Pettigrew, Georgia. My brother Walter was two strides behind me. Walter is one of the top lawyers in Atlanta. He's not a criminal lawyer, but I figured whatever Lee-Lee had gotten herself into down here wouldn't require anything more than a simple stand-up-sit-down appearance by the lawyer.

"I'll handle this," I whispered to Walter. "I know how to handle these kind of people."

"Of course," he said.

"I don't really need you here," I said. "But I figured it might be handy to have someone with a bar card. Strictly as backup."

"Oh, sure," my brother said. "I understand."

The Sheriff's Department building in Flournoy County was newer than I might have expected. Flournoy County was truly out in the ass end of nowhere, but they had a nice modern facility with security cameras on the walls and a door you had to be buzzed through from the inside.

"Hi there," I said to the uniformed desk clerk behind the bulletproof glass. The clerk was a large meaty woman with dyed blond hair and a mouth full of gum. She was busy reading a magazine called *Personal Investor.* "My name's Sunny Childs. I'm a private investigator from Atlanta. A client of mine has recently been brought in. What do I need to do to get her out?"

I waited patiently for about three seconds while the clerk kept staring at the magazine. When my patience ran out, I rapped on the glass with the heavy silver ring I wear on my right thumb. "Hey!" I said. "Hello in there. Could I break you away from your stock portfolio for a minute?"

The clerk finally looked up. "What."

I repeated myself.

"You said, 'brought in,'" the clerk said. She had this truculent gleam in her eye, the kind of person who's going to make you work for everything. "What's that mean, 'brought in'?"

"Picked up. Arrested."

She kept chewing the gum for a while. "Name?" she said finally.

"Lee Edwards."

"Her. Yeah. Y'all wastin' y'all's time." The clerk made a show of looking at her investment magazine again.

"Meaning *what?*" I said.

She took her time, then looked up again. "Meaning, look like y'all drove down here for nothing. Here in Flournoy County, pleas and arraignments ain't till a week from Thursday. Judge'll set bail; y'all can get her out then."

"Bail!" I said. Lee-Lee's collect call had been cut off in the middle, so I hadn't gotten the full story on why she'd been arrested. I assumed she'd gotten pulled over for DWI or some other minor charge. You didn't get stuck in jail for a week and a half on a DWI. "What'd she get arrested for?"

"I believe it was ADW, resisting, speeding, reckless endangerment, violation of GCSA."

"Assault with a deadly weapon! Georgia Controlled Substances Act!" I said. "Notwithstanding her nose ring and her tattoos, I happen to know for a fact that Lee-Lee doesn't use drugs. This whole thing's total BS and you know it."

"Plus, I think we booked her for being a skinny, mouthy little complainer from Atlanta," the clerk said. "But then you wouldn't know nothing about that, would you?"

She smiled and looked back down at her magazine.

I started rapping on the glass again with my ring.

It took her a while, but finally she looked up again. "Y'all still here?" she said.

"I want to talk to the sheriff," I said.

"Okay," she said. She kept looking at me for a while, then finally shrugged and looked back down at her magazine.

"Hey!" I said. I rapped my ring on the window some more. "Get the sheriff out here right now."

She looked up again, turned her shoulder slightly, pointed a long red fingernail at the patch on her shoulder.

"What?" I said.

"I *am* the sheriff," she said. The patch read RENICE POWELL–SHERIFF FLOURNOY COUNTY. She gave me a big cool smile. "Now if you don't step your skinny shanks back, I'm gonna find some reason to lock you up, too."

I looked at my brother.

Walter smiled mildly back at me. " 'I know how to *handle* these kind of people'?" he said. "Wasn't that how you put it?"

I held my hands up in exasperation. "Hey, go for it."

Walter pulled out his cell phone, stepped a couple of paces away from me, and then had a brief conversation in a voice so low, I couldn't hear a word he said. When he was done, he walked back to the window and slid a business card through the slot. "Thank you for your assistance, Sheriff Powell. You can call me at that number."

"Why would I want to?" the sheriff said.

Walter just smiled mysteriously and said, "You have a nice morning, Sheriff."

I followed Walter outside and we sat down in my car. We sat in silence for a while. I knew Walter had just pulled some kind of shifty lawyer trick, and it irritated me. Because it would probably work, whatever it was. Everything Walter does works. If my brother weren't such a nice guy, I would hate him.

About ten minutes later, his phone rang. He flipped it open and said, "Walter Childs here. Mm-hm. Mm-hm. Awful kind of you to go to all that trouble, Sheriff. We'll meet you there."

He flipped the phone shut. "Let's go get her," he said.

We'd walked about halfway across the square, past the Confederate soldier, and up onto the marble steps of the old courthouse, and he still hadn't said anything.

"Well?" I said. "You gonna tell me?"

"I called the governor," he said. "Asked him to make a courtesy call."

"The governor."

"He owes me a favor. Got him out of a tight spot last year."

"You know," I said, "I knew there was a reason I brought you."

THREE

Five minutes later, we were sitting in the office of Judge Landers Calhoon, on the second floor of the Flournoy County courthouse. The office was paneled in dingy oak, with a ten-foot-high ceiling. An ancient fan hung above us, stirring the stuffy air.

"Pardon me if I don't get up, Mr. Childs," the judge said to my brother. "Busted my hip dove hunting last year, ain't been worth shooting since then." Judge Calhoon must have been ninety years old. He wore a bow tie and a seersucker suit and he kept licking his upper lip like he was afraid maybe he was drooling or something. "Normally, I do arraignments for major felonies every other Thursday, but the governor said he could only spare you down here for today, so I'ma get the appropriate parties up here and we'll get this young lady arraigned in camera."

"Thank you, Your Honor," my brother said. "The governor sure appreciates the accommodation."

The door opened at that moment and several more people entered the room. I recognized the sheriff. She was accompanied by a very large deputy, who propelled Lee-Lee into the room in front of him. Lee-Lee was wearing an orange jumpsuit, shackles, and yellow prison flip-flops. Finally, a pleasant-looking young man in a blue suit entered. He wore an enamel American flag pinned to his lapel and very neat hair.

"This is our district attorney, Dalton Cullihue," the judge said, pointing at the man in the blue suit. "I believe y'all met Sheriff

Powell? Sheriff, Dalton, this is Mr. Childs." He glanced at me. "Uh, hon, I didn't catch your name."

"Sunny Childs," I said.

"Oh, are you Mr. Childs's wife? You can step outside while we get this done."

"I'm his sister," I snapped. "I'm a private investigator."

The judge smiled. "Oh, isn't that nice for you. A lady private investigator! My land!"

"Your Honor, could I beg your indulgence for about thirty seconds and have a brief colloquy with my client?" Walter said.

"Oh, sure, sure," the judge said pleasantly. "I've got a conference room right next door. Y'all take all the time you need."

The sheriff snorted.

"You got something to say, Renice?" the judge said sharply. Suddenly, the benevolent old grandfather seemed to have disappeared, his bright blue eyes gone cold and hard.

"No, sir."

"Then how 'bout you contain yourself."

•

Lee-Lee, Walter, and I walked into the room next door.

"What a nightmare!" Lee-Lee said. "Thank you *so* much for coming."

"Tell me what happened," I said. "What did you do to get arrested?"

"Nothing!" she said.

"You had to have been doing something," I said.

"I swear to God!"

"Just tell us the whole story," Walter said.

Lee-Lee took a deep breath. "Well, you know I'm doing this film, right?"

"I already explained all of that to Walter," I said.

"So I've been in town here a couple of times already, talking to people about the case. Last night I came down, checked into the motel, started getting my gear together. I was planning to shoot an interview with a witness from Dale Weedlow's trial the next day. Middle of the night, there's a knock on the door. I open it and there's this black guy standing in the hallway. He kind of looks around and then he goes, 'You the one making that movie about that boy?' And I'm like, 'Yeah?' And he's like, 'I know somebody y'all need to talk to.'"

"Uh-huh," I said.

"Then he tells me to meet somebody out at this place out in the country."

"What place?" I said.

"Some kind of abandoned mine. Anyway, he's acting all nervous and he scoots before I can ask him anything else. But I figure, you know, it's worth a try. Even though it's getting kind of late by that time. So I get in my car, start driving. Next thing I know, I'm out in the middle of the country. I mean out in the middle of *nowhere*. And then—boom—suddenly there's blue lights in my rearview mirror."

"They drove up behind you?"

"Nah, it was like he just appeared. One second there's nothing there; then next second there's blue lights."

"So you pulled over."

"Sure. I'm getting out my driver's license and stuff and there's this knock on the window. I open it, and there's this big goon outside my door."

"The deputy who came over here with you and the sheriff?" I said.

She nodded. "That's him. Before he even says a word, he reaches through the window, turns off my car, pulls out the keys, and sticks them in his pocket. Doesn't say a word. Then he walks around back, writes down my license number. Taking his time, you know. Finally he comes back, says, 'Get out, Lee-Lee.' And I'm like, 'Dude, how'd you know my name?' He just says, 'Turn around, put your hands on the car.' And I'm like, 'Turn around, my ass. I haven't done shit.' Then I probably called him a few names."

"Nice," I said.

"Hey, Sunny, you're not exactly the queen of winning friends and influencing people yourself, huh?"

Walter said, "Let's stick to the story."

"So this deputy sheriff, he just grabs me, slams me up against the car, slaps a pair of cuffs on me, and then says, 'You don't got no idea what this is about, do you, hon?' And I'm like, 'I didn't do anything.' And he goes, 'Nah, see, that's the thing. You did do something.' And I go, 'What did I do?' And he goes, 'You're gonna be allowed to ponder that question in jail. When you figure it out, we might could see our way clear to lighten up on these charges.'"

"Wait, wait, wait," I said. "What charges?"

"That's what *I* said! And Deputy Goober's like, 'Oh, let's see, I think maybe we'll charge you with speeding first. Then I'm gonna detect what we call a distinct odor of beverage alcohol on your person and I'm gonna have to charge you with DWI. And when I do that, I'm gonna notice that big old reefer rolled up on the seat next to you.' And I go, 'There's no dope in my car.' And he reaches in his pocket, pulls out a big old spliff, tosses it on the seat, and goes, 'There is now.'" Lee-Lee broke off and looked out the window.

"What?" Walter said.

"Well, I'm getting a little pissed by that point, so I go, 'You forgot resisting arrest.' And he kind of looks at me like, 'Huh?'"

"Oh no, you didn't!" I said.

"Yeah," she said.

Walter looked at me, then at her. "What?"

"You know that I teach women's self-defense," I said.

Walter nodded.

"I took a few lessons from her," Lee-Lee said. "Her first lesson, Sunny teaches if you're getting hassled by some douche bag, the first thing you do is kick him in the jewels."

"Ouch," Walter said.

"What happened then?" I said.

"I tried to get back in the car. But I forgot that the deputy had taken the keys. I was like, 'Aw man!' Next thing I know, another deputy rolls up. Ten seconds later I'm in cuffs, lying on the ground with this dude's knee on my neck."

"What happened to your car?" I said.

"They must have towed it," Lee-Lee said. "I saw it just now, sitting in the lot behind the Sheriff's Department. You think you could go over there and make sure they didn't steal all my equipment? I had about ten grand worth of video cams and recording equipment sitting in the front seat."

Which gave me a sudden idea.

"Let me go check on that," I said.

Walter looked at me curiously. "Why?"

"I have an idea," I said.

He kept looking at me for a minute. Then suddenly one eyebrow went up. "You are a devious woman, Sunny," he said.

•

"All right," Judge Calhoon said. "Superior Court of Flournoy County is now in special session. We're holding a brief arraignment in the chambers of Judge Lander T. Calhoon. Present are the defendant, Ms. Lee Edwards. . . ."

He reeled off the rest of the names while I caught my breath. I had just run back from Lee-Lee's car, carrying two aluminum suitcases full of video and recording equipment.

"I would like the Court to note for the record," Walter said, "that my investigator, Ms. Sunny Childs, has just retrieved some recording equipment from the defendant's car."

"So noted."

"Now hold on," the district attorney said. "That vehicle has been impounded. I don't see that you have any right to—"

"That's a police matter, Mr. Cullihue," the judge snapped. "Sort it out later. Let's stick to the case at hand. Mr. Cullihue, call your case."

"Ah, yes, Your Honor."

It was obvious from the way everybody snapped to when the judge talked that they were scared witless of the old guy.

"Dalton Cullihue for the state, Your Honor." He picked up a file folder and flipped it open. "In the matter of Lee Sloane Edwards, the state alleges that the defendant, Lee Sloane Edwards, was arrested on the night of May the eighth of this year, ah, by, ah, Deputy David Woodie and charged with, ah, assault with a deadly weapon, resisting arrest, and violation of the Georgia Controlled Substances Act by virtue of possession of marijuana in an amount not exceeding one ounce."

"Thank you, Mr. Cullihue. Ms. Edwards, how do you plead?"

Walter stood up. "Your Honor, the defendant is prepared to waive reading at this time and go straight to trial."

"Excuse me?" The judge blinked. "A bench trial? Here and now?"

"Yes, Your Honor. I realize that it's unusual, but Ms. Edwards is convinced of her innocence in this matter. We've got all the necessary witnesses and all the necessary evidence present. Why not dispose of the matter right this minute?"

The judge frowned. "These are serious charges, Mr. Childs. Worst-case scenario, this young lady could be looking at close to thirty years in the penitentiary if the state proves all elements in the case."

"We're well aware of that."

"It's out of the question," Dalton Cullihue said. "We've got to send the alleged marijuana cigarette up to the state crime lab. It'll be four months before we get the results back."

"Supposing Ms. Childs stipulates to the marijuana," Walter said.

The district attorney's eyes widened. "Stipulate! You're just gonna flat *admit* that Deputy Woodie recovered marijuana from her vehicle?"

"Say we did. Are you willing to try this case here and now?"

Dalton Cullihue glanced over at the sheriff. Something seemed to pass between them. He turned back, shrugged. "I guess so."

"Who you planning to put on the stand, Mr. Childs?" the judge said.

"Just Ms. Edwards," Walter said.

The judge shrugged. "It's your funeral, Ms. Edwards. You want to go to trial?"

"If Walter, uh, if Mr. Childs says so," Lee-Lee said.

"All right, then," Judge Calhoon said. "Mr. Cullihue, let's try this puppy. And if you're both agreeable we know what this is about, let's skip the opening statements."

Both attorneys nodded.

"Proceed, Mr. Cullihue."

The DA stood. "I call my first witness, Deputy David Woodie." After the judge swore him in, Cullihue continued. "Deputy Woodie, did you have occasion to make an arrest in the early hours of the morning today, May eighth of this year?"

"Yes, sir."

"Please describe the events as they unfolded."

"Yes, sir. At around one o'clock this morning, I was patrolling out around mile marker number sixty-five on Georgia Highway Seventeen when I came up on a blue Suzuki Tracker. The blue Suzuki was driving at approximately fifteen miles per hour below the posted speed, and over the course of approximately one minute, it crossed three times over the center line in a manner consistent with the presence of an impaired operator. I then utilized my flashers and siren, whereupon the vehicle pulled over." He spoke in the usual singsong voice employed by cops when they are testifying.

"I then approached the vehicle and asked the operator for her license and registration. The operator was belligerent and refused to get out of the car or surrender her license. She also slurred her words. At that point in time, I detected a strong odor of beverage alcohol on or about her person. I reached through the window and removed the keys."

The DA interrupted. "Can you identify the operator of the vehicle, Deputy?"

Deputy Woodie pointed at Lee-Lee. "Her."

"The witness has indicated the defendant," Cullihue said. "Please continue, Deputy."

"When I asked the defendant to exit the car, she refused and told me quote unquote 'Go screw yourself, you homely ass fat SOB,' and various other things of that nature. At that point, the defendant exited the vehicle and attempted to strike me with her shoe."

"Hold on, hold on," Judge Calhoon said. "The Court would like to clarify something. This shoe, is this the so-called deadly weapon on which the ADW charge rests?"

"Uh, well, Your Honor," the DA said, "it has a very pointy heel."

"So noted," Judge Calhoon said dryly. "You may continue, Deputy."

"After the defendant attacked me with the shoe, striking me several times on the arm and face, I was forced to subdue her."

"Could you hold up your arm, Deputy?"

The deputy held up his arm, showing off several welts. "This here one is from the shoe, too," he said, turning his head and showing a gash on his face.

"For the record, the defendant has indicated several abrasions on the face and arms," Judge Calhoon said.

"So anyway," the deputy continued, "I cuffed the defendant and then asked her if she would give me permission to search her car. She replied, quote, 'You can do any damn thing you want, you big ape-ass jerk,' unquote. I then observed what appeared to be a marijuana cigarette on the seat of the car. I secured the cigarette and performed a field narcotics test for the presence of THC, the active ingredient present in marijuana."

"And did you receive a result from that test?"

"It come out positive. At that point, I placed the defendant under arrest and transported her to the jail."

"Thank you, Deputy. I believe that'll be all."

"Mr. Childs?"

Walter stood, buttoned his coat. "Hello, Deputy. I'm Walter Childs, with the firm of Harris, Dunwoody and Cobb in Atlanta, representing Ms. Edwards. I have just a couple of questions for you."

"Yes, sir."

"Hit you with a deadly shoe, huh?"

"Yes, sir, she did."

"I heard different."

"Different from what?"

"I heard she kicked you in the crotch."

The deputy flushed.

"For the record, I'd like to note the witness just blushed," Walter said. "Experienced officer like you? I'm surprised you let her get to the family jewels like that."

"I didn't."

Walter waved his hand, smiled easily. "So why was another deputy required to complete the arrest? It wasn't because you were lying on the ground, holding your goodies?"

"No, sir. Deputy Jennings just happened to have replied to my radio call for backup. I was, uh, securing the evidence while he placed her in handcuffs."

"The radio call. Was that before or after the defendant attempted to take your life with her shoe?"

Even the judge couldn't suppress a smile.

"Strike that," Walter said. "Did you ask the defendant her occupation?"

"No, sir, I did not."

"It might interest you to know she's a filmmaker."

The deputy shrugged. "All due respect, I don't care if she was an astronaut. She hit me with her shoe and she had drugs on her."

"Right, right. You testified that you observed a marijuana cigarette on the seat. You notice anything else on the seat there?"

The deputy frowned. "There was, yeah, some other stuff on the seat."

" 'Some other stuff.' " Walter nodded, gave the witness a serious face. "Like what?"

"A video-type thing? Some microphones?"

"Are you a trained videographer, Deputy?"

"No, sir."

"Any background as a recording engineer?"

"No, sir."

"So would you have been able to tell by observation whether any of that equipment was turned on?"

The deputy blinked, then rubbed his hands on his thighs. "Uh . . . I'm not sure."

Walter smiled. "Thank you, Deputy, that'll be all."

There was an uneasy silence. After a minute, District Attorney Cullihue stood and said, "The state rests."

"Mr. Childs?"

"I just have one witness," Walter said. "The defense calls Sunny Childs."

"Hold up now! Objection," Dalton Cullihue said. "You just now said you had only one witness and that was the defendant herself."

"I'm calling Ms. Childs as a rebuttal witness," Walter said. "The deputy alleged certain things on the stand that Ms. Childs is in a unique position to prove as untrue."

"Like what?" the judge said.

"I know I've been burning through the indulgence of this Court at a rapid rate, but I promise that her testimony will answer your questions better than I ever could, and it won't take more than fifteen minutes."

The judge licked his lip a couple times. "Why not. Proceed."

After I was sworn in, Walter turned to me and said, "Ms. Childs, what's your profession?"

"I'm a private investigator. I'm a partner in a firm called Peachtree Investigations in Atlanta."

"You have any specialized training?"

"Sure, I take seminars and courses on a regular basis to keep my skills up."

"Such as?"

"Well, last week I took a class in homicide investigation over in Birmingham, Alabama, that was held by the Jefferson County Sheriff's Department. I've taken photography courses, courses in forensic accounting, courses in surveillance, all kinds of things."

"Videography?"

"As a matter of fact, I took the FBI forensic-videography course at Quantico."

"Really? I thought only law-enforcement people took courses there."

"I have an inside connection," I said.

"So you're familiar with video equipment. How it operates, things of that nature."

"I am."

"Sitting next to your leg there," he said, "you've got a couple of metal cases."

"I do."

"What's in them?"

"Video equipment."

"Where did you get that equipment?"

"Out of the defendant's car."

"Have you examined their contents?"

"I have. There's a Sony HDR-FX1 hi-def video camera, a boom condenser microphone, a Sony monitor, a digital audiorecorder, various plugs and cables, spare batteries, things of that nature."

"Uh-huh. Are they in operating condition?"

"They sure are."

"You've checked?"

"I have. I've played back the camera on the monitor and re-viewed the last footage recorded on the machine."

"Okay, so let me ask you a hypothetical question. Drawing on your expertise as a forensic videographer, if this camera had been turned on last night when the arrest was made, would it have been capable of recording the events of that evening?"

"Absolutely."

"Thank you."

Walter looked at the ceiling for a long time. The fan turned lazily. "One last indulgence, Your Honor," he said finally. "What I believe we have here is a little dispute between an arresting officer and defendant. One can imagine a scenario in which a young woman was pulled over. Maybe she was fiddling with her video equipment, crossed over the center line a couple times out of inattention. A deputy observes this and pulls her over, honestly believing she's intoxicated. Maybe he's a little aggressive. Maybe she's a little mouthy. Things escalate needlessly. Whatever. Point is, once things get started, maybe this officer unwisely decides he's gonna get this girl no matter whether she's intoxicated or not, just because she's—pardon my language, Your Honor—because she's pissing him off. Hypothetically, this officer might, under the circumstances, go off half-cocked and decide to plant evidence gathered during some other arrest and use it to bolster a case against the operator of the vehicle."

"I object, Your Honor," Cullihue said. "He's making a speech. Based on evidence that the state has had no opportunity to review."

"Precisely," Walter said with a bland smile. "I have not introduced any evidence whatsoever. What I'm pointing out is the following." Walter turned to the sheriff. "If we were to play this tape on the record, right here in open court, and demonstrate clearly and unimpeachably that evidence had been planted by Deputy Woodie—Sheriff Powell, would you not be obliged to arrest Deputy Woodie? And Mr. Cullihue, would you not be obliged to prosecute him?"

The sheriff and the DA looked at my brother, stone-faced.

"In which case," Walter continued, "isn't it true that Deputy Woodie would very likely lose his pension, his career, and possibly even his freedom? All over a little misunderstanding in the course of a simple traffic stop?"

The judge's eyes glittered. No one moved.

"Doesn't that seem like it would be blowing this whole matter out of proportion?" Walter said. "Hm? Hypothetically speaking?"

The room was silent for a long time.

Finally, the district attorney stood. "Ah, Your Honor, could I take about five minutes to confer with my witness?"

•

The DA came back about two minutes later and said, "Your Honor, the state has decided to dismiss this matter without prejudice."

The judge glared at him, then turned to the deputy. "Son, it looks like you dodged one today. I hope you're prepared to send Mr. Childs a Christmas ham every year for the rest of your life, because you dadgum sure owe him. He could have ruined your life. Case dismissed."

•

After it was over and we were walking out to Walter's car, Lee-Lee said, "Man, this place sucks. You were right, Sunny. I should never have come here."

Walter and I looked at each other.

"That deputy knew my name," Lee-Lee said. "Not the name on my driver's license. Not what he would have gotten if he pulled it up on his computer. He called me Lee-Lee. He was warning me to leave this county."

Neither of us spoke.

"Somebody around here doesn't want this film made. Somebody around here is hiding something."

I sighed loudly. Not because she wasn't right–she was–but because I knew I was about to get sucked into the Great Lee-Lee Drama Vortex.

"This guy's innocent!" Lee-Lee said. "Somebody doesn't want me to find out. I mean, I'm not being paranoid here, am I?"

"No," Walter said softly. "Not if everything happened the way you said it did."

"Then we've gotta do something!"

Walter smiled. "I believe I just *did* something. Unfortunately, tomorrow I've got a big trial in federal court." He climbed into the front seat of his car. "Have fun, kids."

He drove away.

I took out my phone, made a call to my boss, Gunnar Brushwood. "Hi, it's Sunny," I said. "You're gonna have to get somebody to fill in for me on the Reynolds case."

"Sunny, do I need to remind you that Reynolds is the biggest client we've had in three years?" Gunnar said. "What in the world's going on?"

"Just the usual," I said. "Man falsely imprisoned for a murder he didn't commit, and I've got six days to save him before he fries."

"Oh," Gunnar said. "Well. That."

Then he hung up.

FOUR

We were standing on the curb when the DA, Dalton Cullihue, approached us with a big smile on his face, shook my hand vigorously. He was one of those guys who grabs your elbow with their left hand while they're shaking with the right and then seems to forget how to let go.

"There wasn't a thing on that videotape, was there?" he said.

"He admitted to you that he planted the dope, didn't he?" I replied.

Cullihue smiled thinly. "You're not answering my question."

"And I bet you're not gonna answer mine, either."

Cullihue laughed and finally let go of my hand. "Well," he said, "so y'all heading back to Atlanta, I guess?"

I looked around the town square. It looked like a lot of other little county seats in downstate Georgia. A row of low redbrick commercial buildings lining the main drag, Confederate soldier on a limestone pillar in front of an aging courthouse with a scabrous-looking gold neoclassical dome. Other than the new Sheriff's Department building, there wasn't anything in sight that had been built within fifty years. A few people wandered up and down the sidewalks—most of them old or poorly dressed, or both, moving in aimless slow motion. It was the kind of town where you came from, not the kind you went to.

"You know, Mr. Cullihue, I'm thinking I'd like to get away from the hustle and bustle," I said. "This place just seems so relaxing."

Cullihue smiled broadly. "It is, isn't it? It's a real treasure. A real jewel. A place like this has to be protected."

"Oh?" I said. "From what?"

He pointed his finger at me, winked. "You're *quick*," he said. "Just a figure of speech, though. I worked in Atlanta after I got out of law school, but I just never felt comfortable up there. Came back down here after a couple years and, by golly, it was like an old shoe. People speak on the street. You walk into a restaurant, they know who you are. We like it that way."

"That cuts both ways, doesn't it?" I said.

"I suppose it can be like living in a fishbowl here. Everybody knows your business, that kind of thing."

While we were talking, Lee-Lee had pulled out her camera and was walking around filming us.

"So you really gonna make a movie about that Weedlow boy?" Cullihue said to her.

"Yep," she said.

"I don't suppose you'd mind turning that off a second."

"Why?"

"Makes me nervous. Always hated having my picture taken. Strange quality in a politician, huh?" He laughed. "Seriously, though. You want to make a movie about Weedlow, you ought to find out the details of what he did, huh?"

"Are you offering to show us the case file?" I said.

He looked at me innocently. "It's a public record. Why would I mind?"

"I don't know," I said. "So far, y'all haven't exactly rolled out the welcome mat to Lee-Lee."

"That fellow David Woodie, he's a problem officer in my view. This is not the first time he's gotten a little . . . overzealous? Is that the word? But don't let one man give you the wrong idea about this town."

The DA's office was in a building behind the Sheriff's Department. As we trooped over, Cullihue gave us a canned speech about the town. "The town was established in 1818 by Colonel

William Flournoy. The territory had just been opened up to white settlement at the time, and the colonel bought virtually all of what is now Flournoy County. At the time, he was the largest single landowner in the state. During the cotton boom of the early nineteenth century, the town grew like a weed. Colonel Flournoy went bankrupt after the Civil War, and then, of course, you had falling cotton prices, and by the earlier twentieth century, the boll weevil hit. You might say the town hit its high-water mark about a century ago. In fact, if it wasn't for kaolin, I don't know if there'd be much left in Flournoy County anymore."

"Kaolin?" I said. "Who's that?"

Cullihue looked at me like I'd just told him I didn't know what an automobile was. "Kaolin. It's a *what*, not a *who*. Kaolin is a kind of clay that's mined here in Flournoy County."

"Clay, huh?" I said. "Doesn't seem like there'd be much money in dirt."

He laughed. "Kaolin's an amazing material. There are only a handful of sources for it in the world. Australia, China . . . and middle Georgia. Some of the best deposits in the world are right here in Flournoy County."

"What do they make out of it?" I said. "Pottery?"

"No, it's primarily an industrial additive. They use it in toothpaste, coated papers, paints, all manner of things."

We reached the office. Like the Sheriff's Department, it was a new building. And like the Sheriff's Department, it had what seemed to be an unusual amount of security for such a small town. He led us through a locked door with a camera over it and into a conference room that could have come from an old Atlanta law firm—soft leather chairs, long mahogany table, hunting prints on the walls.

"Please," he said, gesturing for us to sit.

Then he called out the doorway to someone we couldn't see: "Miss Anderson, could you be a doll, bring me that file on the Weedlow boy. And three cups of coffee while you're at it."

A minute or two later, a woman wearing a dress with large

magnolia flowers printed on it wheeled in a cart. On the cart were two cardboard boxes.

"That's a big file," I said.

"Most of that is appellate material," he said. "These death-penalty appeals generate an endless stream of paper. The interesting stuff is in the first box. You'll find a transcript of the trial, all the paper exhibits, plus the entire investigation file."

"Before we get started," I said, "I don't suppose you could give me a thumbnail sketch of the case."

"Sure. Happy to." Big smile.

Cullihue's smile dimmed as Lee-Lee took out her camera.

"Nah nah nah, hon," he said. "I'm talking to you as a courtesy, help you get your story straight. But I'm not prepared at this time to give an on-camera interview."

"At some later time, though, of course," Lee-Lee said.

Cullihue studied her for a moment. "We'll see."

"Did you prosecute the case?" I said.

He nodded. "I did." He leaned across the table, reached into the box, pulled out a couple of files, opened one, slapped a photograph on the table. "You want to do a movie about ugliness and the human capacity for evil, well, here it is. This right here's your whole story."

Lee-Lee and I looked at the photograph. It was a three-by-five print like you'd get from the photo department at Wal-Mart. The photo showed the inside of some kind of industrial building, a metal shed, harshly illuminated by the camera flash. Hanging in the middle of the room were two women. Their heads were covered with black plastic, which dangled in long points below them like the hats of Santa's elves. It was among the most horrible things I'd ever seen. Human beings reduced to meat.

"Whoa!" Lee-Lee said. She pointed her finger at the picture. "What's that?"

"That would be her entrails," Dalton Cullihue said. "They were both slit open from the pubic bone to the sternum. This is exactly as they were found by employees of the company at about seven A.M. on Monday, July twenty-four, 2000."

"What company?"

"DCI Mining. That's the company that operates the kaolin mines here, as well as a major processing facility. The land was a fairly old site that was just about mined out, so there wasn't a big crew there typically. The two bodies were found by the shift boss, a man by the name of Roger Wilbanks. Twenty-seven-year employee of DCI, spotless record, no arrests, no complaints, deacon down at First Baptist, never a suspect. The Flournoy County Sheriff's Department responded to the scene, secured the area, and began the investigation."

"Hold on," I said. "Flournoy County is how big?"

"Twenty thousand people or so."

"And how big is the Sheriff's Department?"

"Nine sworn officers, four or five civilians."

"At what point did they call in the assistance of the Georgia Bureau of Investigation?"

Cullihue cleared his throat. "Ah, the investigation was primarily conducted by the sheriff herself. Assisted by Deputy Woodie."

I let my eyes widen. "You are joking."

"Now, now, hold the phone. I know what you're thinking. Typically in a small jurisdiction like this, we call in the GBI on major cases. They got more experience, deeper bench, et cetera. But Sheriff Powell, she used to be a homicide investigator over in Macon. She's not just some politician with a badge."

"Okay," I said dubiously.

"Sheriff Powell found a pile of tools sitting on a card table over on the side of the room. Several of them had bloodstains on them. There was a screwdriver that matched puncture wounds on the bodies; there was a box cutter that was covered with blood; there were a couple of tools—hammers and whatnot—that we believed were used to, ah, sexually penetrate the victims."

I put my head in my hands for a moment. The whole thing

made me feel kind of queasy—and maybe a little sad about the future of humankind. "Oh man," I said.

"What's up with their feet?" Lee-Lee asked. "How come they're so white? Is that like some kind of weird ritual thing?"

"Lividity?" I said. "The combination of the ropes around their feet and the draining of blood might have caused them to turn white."

"Actually, no," the DA said. "It's kaolin. We believe that they were both walked through the kaolin pit barefoot. That caused their feet to get covered with clay. Among the interesting things about kaolin is that it has what's known as a high photo-reflectivity index. Which is a fancy way of saying it reflects light real good. That's what accounts for how white their feet are." He put another photo in front of us, a close-up of the curiously white feet.

"Where'd the case go from there?"

"They lined up all the employees of the place, said, 'Whose tools are these?' Nobody would admit to owning them. Then the sheriff noticed one of the hammers used in the crime had a pair of initials scratched in the handle. D.W. This kid Weedlow, his first name is Germind, but he goes by Dale. D.W., Dale Weedlow. So the sheriff took Weedlow downtown, says, 'How come your initials are scratched in here?' 'Well, okay, yeah, I admit they're my tools. But I didn't do nothing.' Now everybody around here knew this kid Weedlow. He'd been in trouble since he was knee-high to a gopher. Shoplifting, possession, breaking and entering, some petty stuff. So the sheriff interrogated him for a while, and ultimately he gave up the goods."

"He recanted later, though," Lee-Lee said.

Cullihue rolled his eyes. "Criminals are impulsive. Heat of the moment, it seems to make sense, confessing. But then a day or two later, they're sitting there in jail looking at life without parole, and they start thinking, *Hey, maybe I can beat this thing.* So they get to trial and they make up some big bunch of nonsense about how the cops deprived them of food and water, hit them with phone books, stuck their head in a toilet, whatever."

"Is that what he said?" I said.

"It's in the trial transcript," he said, digging out a thick type-script. He thumbed through it for a while. "Let's see. Here we go. This is direct testimony. His lawyer's a gentleman by the name of Ervin Kindred. We call him 'Kindred Spirits' around here." He winked at me. That was two winks at me in one day, which was way past quota, in my opinion.

Cullihue started reading from the transcript.

•

Kindred: Are you saying your alleged confession was coerced?

Weedlow: Yes, sir.

Kindred: Tell me about that.

Weedlow: Well, I just kept setting there, telling them I ain't had nothing to do with them two girls getting killed, and after a while they started to shout at me and call me a liar and what all, but I was just like, "Nah, y'all, I ain't did it." And they're getting madder and madder, and finally that big old deputy, this David Woodie character, he comes toting this dadgum Atlanta phone book into the room. Thing weighs about ten pounds. And I'm like, "Who you fixing to call?" And he's like, "You." And then he just warps me a big old lick upside the head.

Kindred: How hard did he hit you?

Weedlow: Knocked me slap out the chair, sir.

Kindred: And then what happened?

Weedlow: He played this little game. Set me up in the chair, knock me off, set me up, knock me off. Man, I still can't hear right in my left ear. But by God, I just kept telling him, "Man, I ain't did it."

Kindred: And yet at a certain point, you did confess.

Weedlow: Yes, sir. What it was, they drug me in the bathroom, wrapped this here towel around my face, then started dunking me in the toilet. The towel would get all wet to where you couldn't breathe, even after they'd pulled my head out the toilet. So I started blacking out. Man, I tell you, getting hit–I could deal with that. But this was like getting drowned. Over and over and over. I couldn't deal with it. So finally I was like, "Okay. Okay. I'll do it."

Kindred: You'll do what?

Weedlow: Huh?

Kindred: You testified that you said, "Okay. Okay. I'll do it." Okay, you'll do what?

Weedlow: Okay, I'll say I done it. So the sheriff, she comes in and says here's what you done, right? And she goes through it and tells me everything, what I supposedly done to these girls. And I said, "Okay, whatever." And she gives me a piece of paper and crayon and says, "Write it up."

Kindred: A crayon?

Weedlow: So I wouldn't stab nobody with it.

Kindred: I see. And that confession is what has been marked as State's Exhibit Seven.

Weedlow: Whatever the number was. Yes, sir, that one right there. State's Seven.

•

The district attorney stopped reading.

"Can I see the confession?"

He pulled out a sheaf of paper covered with scrawled words in red crayon. "Here it is."

Lee-Lee picked it up and said, "Not exactly strong on penmanship or spelling, huh?"

"Not exactly, no."

She started reading. " 'I went to the Dairy Queen on the bypass. It was two girls in a car. I knew them. It was Terri Ross and Brittany Woodie.' "

"Whoa!" I said. "Are you telling me that one of the victims was related to one of the investigating officers?"

"Now don't get your panties in a wad," Cullihue said, smiling. "I know up in Atlanta everything's all arm's length and what all, but down here everybody's related to everybody else. Half the white folks in this country are named Woodie. I'm sure they're shirttail kin—but it's not like she was his sister or something."

"Okay," I said. "Keep reading, Lee-Lee."

"Let's see. Okay. 'It was Terri Ross and Brittany Woodie. I decided I wanted them for my sexual gratification. I told them I could get weed and we could party. They got in my car. We drove out to the DCI mine on Old Cotton Mill Road. I didn't have weed. So they told me they wanted to get out of the car. I struck Brittany. Terri was screaming. I struck Terri with a screwdriver. I tied them up and violated them with a hammer. And a screwdriver. Anal and in the vagina.'" Lee-Lee looked up. "I'm not even gonna tell you how he spelled that." She looked back down, started reading again. "'They was dead. I put them on a rope and a chain and hanged them up and cut they guts out. To see what it looked like inside. All this is true to what happened.' It's got his signature underneath."

"That's it?" I said.

"Seems kinda sketchy," Lee-Lee said.

"What do you expect? This kid was not a literary genius," Dalton Cullihue said.

"Where's the autopsy?" I said.

Cullihue got a funny expression on his face for a moment. Then he seemed to recover. "Tell you what," he said, clapping his hands together. "I probably ought to get back to the salt mines. Let me suggest the following. I could get Miss Anderson to run you off copies of the whole trial, all the exhibits, whatnot, we could courier them up to Atlanta, and you could go over them at your leisure. How's that grab you?"

I looked at Lee-Lee.

"Atlanta?" I said. "Who said anything about Atlanta?"

"Yeah, we were kinda thinking about hanging around," Lee-Lee said. "Soak up all the friendly down-home atmosphere and everything."

Cullihue cocked his head. "Is that right?"

"Uh-huh," I said.

"Hope y'all won't get too bored. Not much nightlife around here."

"We'll manage," I said.

"Hey, speaking of which," he said. "There's gonna be a little get-together over at Mr. Justice's home tonight. It's the annual Blue-Gray Barbecue sponsored by the Rotary Club and the Chamber of Commerce. Since I happen to be the president of the Rotary Club, I think I could finagle you an invite."

"Who's Mr. Justice?" I said.

"You want to tell this boy's story in a movie, you need to see what impact a thing like he did has on a close-knit little community like ours. I'll introduce you to everybody."

"Yeah . . ." I said.

"Everybody wears Civil War outfits for the Blue-Gray barbecue, the whole nine yards. You'll have a heck of a time, I guarantee!"

"I'm short on hoop skirts," I said.

"Oh, don't worry about that. Come as you are. It'll be a time."

"Yeah, Sunny, it'll be a time," Lee-Lee said, kicking me under the table.

"Well, in that case," I said.

The district attorney of Flournoy County stood up. "Good. So that's settled. There's usually a fee for duplication, ten cents a page. But I think we can waive that for you." He winked at me again, then called out the door. "Miss Anderson! Come gather up these exhibits, get them copied for these nice young ladies."

And then he was gone.

"Who did he say this Mr. Justice guy was?" Lee-Lee said.

"He didn't."

FIVE

"Did you notice something funny?" I said to Lee-Lee. "How Cul-lihue changed the subject all of a sudden when I mentioned the autopsy?"

We had driven around for a while, finally found a hotel on the two-lane road just outside of town. It was a single story U-shaped structure that probably hadn't been nice when it was built, and had only gotten worse with age. The proprietor, a Mr. Patel—who was surely the cheeriest Gujarati on the planet—insisted on walking our bags over to the room and pointing out the many features of what he kept referring to as our "suite."

"Soap! Shampoo! Water glass!" he said. "Television! No HBO, unfortunately."

"Okay," I said. "Terrific. Thanks." I pulled out a dollar, trying to get rid of him.

"No no no!" he said, holding up his hands like I was about to shoot him. "Strictly gratis. A service of the establishment." He began pointing again. "Picture window! Lovely view of the swim-ming pool. Ice bucket!"

"Where's the ice machine?"

"Ah! Yes! Broken, unfortunately."

"Coke machine?"

He sighed loudly. "Yes, that, too, I am afraid, is undergoing re-pairs."

"How do you get to the pool?" Lee-Lee said.

"Oh, yes! Certainly. You may be interested to note that, unfortunately, the pump has developed a small leakage. A great deal of algae formed in the water and I was forced to drain it. For the protection of our guests, you see."

"Aw man!" Lee-Lee said.

"I couldn't agree more." Mr. Patel smiled broadly. "But one must be philosophical about these things."

"I was gonna lay out, work on my tan," Lee-Lee said.

"Lucky for you, the sun is, of course, functioning quite up to specification. Feel free to sunbathe on the veranda."

Finally, the cheery Mr. Patel went away.

"I'm gonna go lay out," Lee-Lee said.

I squinted at her. "Excuse me, Lee-Lee," I said, "but are you nuts? If I wanted to work on my tan, I could have stayed in Atlanta. This kid's gonna fry in six days."

"God!" Lee-Lee said. "You are so anal."

"Anal? You're the one who's making the film here. I can go back to Atlanta if sunbathing is higher on the agenda than–"

"Okay, *okay*. God. Whatever. I get it." She flopped on the bed. "What was it you were saying about the autopsy?"

Before I could answer, there was a knock on the door.

"We're never going to get rid of this guy, are we?" I said. But when I opened the door, it wasn't Mr. Patel. Instead, it was a young blond-haired man in an ill-fitting blue suit. He had traces of acne on his face and neck, and wore a cookie-duster mustache.

"Yes?" I said.

"Mr. Cullihue asked me to bring over these files for you, Ms. Childs."

"That was quick," I said. "How did you know we were here?"

The young man looked puzzled. "Ma'am?"

"I didn't tell Mr. Cullihue where we were staying. How did you know we were here?"

"You said you were staying at a motel, ma'am. There's only one motel in Flournoy County."

"Ah, of course."

After the young man left, I opened the box and spread the

photocopies out on the bed. There was a thick police file, murky copies of all the crime-scene photos, and a big stack of trial transcripts.

As I was sorting through the pile, I said, "So, when have you scheduled your interview with Weedlow?"

Silence.

"What?" I said. "You haven't got that set up yet?"

"Uh. I was kind of just thinking of going over to the prison and . . ."

"Oh for God sake, Lee-Lee," I said. "You can't just show up at a maximum-security prison and expect to waltz onto death row."

Lee-Lee blinked. "Yeah, hm. Maybe I should call them, huh?"

"Maybe you should." I sighed loudly. "You know what? Never mind. Let me do it."

Lee-Lee gave me a simpering look. "How come you always treat me like a baby?" she said.

"I wonder," I said.

I called my fiancé at the office.

"Special Agent Cherry," he said.

"Hey, Barrington, it's me. You know anybody down at the state pen in Jackson?"

"I've met the warden a few times. Jim Ricket? Jim Picket? Something like that."

I filled him in on what Lee-Lee was trying to do. "Let me make a couple calls," he said. While I waited for Barrington to call back, I continued looking through the trial materials.

"That's odd," I said.

"What's odd?" Lee-Lee said.

"Remember what I was saying about the autopsy?"

She blinked. "Uh . . ."

The phone rang. It was Barrington.

"Jim Pickets is his name," Barrington said.

"Who?"

"The warden at Jackson. You know how it is when they're

counting down for an execution, they get all squirrelly. But he's agreed to let you guys do an interview this afternoon."

"This afternoon?" I said. "We're a pretty stiff hike from Jackson."

"Then you better get moving. Your appointment's at one."

"Thanks a million," I said. "I love you."

"You, too."

I hung up.

"Better get your equipment, Lee-Lee."

"What for?"

"We're going to Jackson. Now."

•

Fifteen minutes later, we were in Lee-Lee's car, speeding toward the state penitentiary in a town called Jackson, located a little under an hour south of Atlanta. Lee-Lee always makes a point of driving at least twenty-five miles an hour above the speed limit. Normally, I complain about it. But today, we'd need her lead foot to get us to the interview on time.

"You were saying something," Lee-Lee said. "Before Barrington called? Something about the autopsy?"

"Yeah, remember how Cullihue changed the subject as soon as I mentioned the autopsy?"

"Yeah. Maybe we ought to have a look at the autopsy report." She slipped out of her seat belt, leaned back over the seat, her butt halfway up the headrest, steering the car with one bare black-toenailed foot while trying to scrabble around in the boxful of exhibits in the backseat. The speedometer was edging toward a hundred.

I considered the possibility of letting this crazy driving performance go on for a while, strictly in the interests of science, to see how long it would take for her to crash and kill us both. But then I decided, nah, maybe my commitment to Higher Knowledge wasn't all that big.

"That's the thing, Lee-Lee," I said. We were starting to drift into the oncoming lane. I put my hand on the steering wheel and guided us back to our lane. "It's not here. There's no autopsy report."

Finally, she sat back down, continued driving. "Huh," she said. "Isn't that a little odd?"

"A *little?*"

SIX

"A gun!" Lee-Lee said. "Dude! Can I hold it?"

We were at the warden's office, checking in.

"I've got a weapon to check," I said to the corrections officer who was admitting us to the warden's office. I turned to Lee-Lee. "And, no, you can't hold it. You'd probably shoot this nice guy, and then you'd be sitting there next to Dale Weedlow for the rest of your life."

I handed my .38 to the CO, who took it without comment.

"How come you're carrying a gun?" Lee-Lee said.

"This case I'm working on," I said. "I had a couple death threats. Nothing to worry about."

"Death threats! Oh, that is *so* cool!"

The CO handed us a couple of badges that said VISITOR on them and then said, "This way, ladies."

•

Eventually, the warden came out and led us down a path to the death-row facility. "A hundred and twenty-seven men in the death-row facility," he said. "All death-row inmates are housed separate from general population over there." He gestured at a large fence. "The actual executions are conducted at H-Six, which is over here." He pointed at another building.

We went through several more gates and into the death-row building itself. Once inside, we were separated from the prisoners by the bars of the cells as well as by a chain-link fence that was situated about fifteen feet from the actual cells. A television was blaring, and the inmates all stood up, crowded to the bars, stared at us. Well, stared at Lee-Lee, actually. I don't believe I've mentioned it, but Lee-Lee is one of the most absurdly beautiful people I've ever known. There were no catcalls or wolf whistles. Lee-Lee seemed to have stunned the inmates into silence.

"This is him," the warden said when we arrived at a cell toward the end of the row. "Weedlow! Hey! Your visitors are here."

Dale Weedlow looked up at us. Like the others, he stared. He had a wooden crochet hook in his hand, was crocheting something out of yarn. Hanging over the bed behind him was a large motorcycle made entirely from crocheted yarn, complete with engine, exhaust pipe, brake handles, and a headlamp. It must have taken months and months of work. Weedlow set down the crochet hook quickly, making an obvious attempt to hide it in his blankets. I guess he was afraid we might think it was a sissy kind of hobby.

"Can't go any further," the warden said. "You'll have to set up your camera out here, shoot through the fence. I'll give you an hour, okay? You need anything, CO Jepsum right there will help you out."

The warden pointed out a nearby corrections officer, then turned and walked away.

"Hi there," Lee-Lee said through the fence. "I'm Lee Edwards. The filmmaker? We exchanged some letters?"

Dale Weedlow blinked a couple of times. "Day-um!" he said finally. "I was expecting some middle-aged lady or something."

"I like your motorcycle," Lee-Lee said.

"It's a Harley '53 panhead," he said.

"Look, we don't have much time," I said. "Lee-Lee's gonna set up the equipment and then we'll start shooting, okay? My name's Sunny Childs. I'm Lee-Lee's cousin and I'm a private investigator."

"A private investigator." He looked at me with a flat, unreadable gaze. "What you investigating, ma'am?"

"Right now? You."

Dale Weedlow was about five six or seven and couldn't have weighed more than 130 pounds. "That right?" he said. "You gonna prove I'm all innocent and everything, save me from the needle?" He sounded cocky, ready to fight.

"Depends on what kind of impression you make," I said, giving him hard eyes.

"I like the other lady better," he said. "How 'bout her doing the talking instead of you."

Lee-Lee finished setting up. "I'm rolling," she said.

I stood back and crossed my arms.

"So, could you state your name?" Lee-Lee said.

"My name is Germind Dale Weedlow." He pronounced his first name *Jermaine*. "I go by Dale." He smirked. "But you can call me Daddy if you want."

I reached over, hit the stop button on the camera. "Okay, convict," I said. "We came here because there's a distant, distant possibility that you didn't do what they say you did. Now we can help you or not. You want to give us attitude, hey, we can pack up and let you fry next week."

"I ain't frying," he said sullenly. "Everybody convicted after May one, 2000, gets the needle."

"Glad you clarified that." I switched the camera back on.

Lee-Lee said, "Dale, what crime were you convicted of?"

"I was convicted of two counts of malice murder, sexual assault, rape, and kidnapping. Which these is all things I did not do."

"Did you know the victims?"

"Sure. Them and me both lived our whole lifes in Pettigrew, which is the county seat of Flournoy County. Little crummy old town, don't got more than a couple thousand people in it. Everybody knows everybody over there. Everybody's all up in your business, twenty-four/seven."

"The victims. Were they friends of yours?"

"Friends? Nah. They was both older–twenty-four, twenty-five year old. At the time of this here crime I was falsely convicted of, I was nineteen."

"But you knew them."

"To speak to."

"You like them?"

He shrugged. "Not much."

"Why not?"

"Hell, I don't like much of nobody. Wasn't nothing personal."

"What were you doing the weekend of July twenty-second and twenty-third, 2000?"

"Setting around the house smoking weed and playing video games."

"Anybody with you?" I said.

Dale Weedlow gave me a long gaze. "You starting to sound like that sumbitch Cullihue, that there DA over in Flournoy County."

"We're just trying to get the story straight."

"Look, my mom was around some of the time. Mostly dead drunk. Her colored boyfriend, Tremaine Davis, who's now in the joint his own self, was there for a while. Which he was stealing my weed and getting drunk, too, so he wasn't no use as a witness on my behalf, neither. Plus which, I went out and walked around in the woods, did a lot of stuff by myself, so there's no way really I could prove I didn't do what they said."

"In the woods?" I said.

"See! There you go again, taking that tone!"

"What did you do in the woods?" I said.

"They ain't *nothing* to do in that town. *Nothing.*" He practically spit the words out. "Godamighty, I wish I'd of been born someplace else. Bangladesh'd been better. Nah, all it was, I used to go wander around out in the woods looking for stuff."

"Stuff? What stuff?"

He looked at the ground for a minute, like we'd caught him picking his nose or something. "Just . . . stuff. The only thing I ever liked in school, back in sixth grade, we had to go out and find different types of leaves. Press them, dry them out, write down the name in a book. I don't know why, but I liked that." He smiled wistfully, stared off into distance. "Man, I miss trees. I don't know if I miss people, but I miss trees." His face fell. "Well. Anyway, so I started collecting stuff. Leaves mostly. Eventually, I'd collected leaves from every tree in the county."

"How about that," Lee-Lee said.

Dale Weedlow's eyes narrowed. "You making fun of me?"

"Huh-uh. I had to do that same thing in sixth grade. I still remember it."

Weedlow studied her for a minute, then said, "After I'd run out of trees, I started in on weeds. Which is harder. Eventually, I near on to run out of weeds, too, though, so I started in on bugs."

"No kidding," I said.

"Found me a beetle one time that supposedly don't even live in North America. Sent it up to this man at the University of Georgia. He wrote back and thanked me, said he'd put my name in a book for what I done." He stared down the length of the row of cells for a while. "Didn't never see that book, though. He was probably just bullshitting me anyway."

"What was his name?"

"Dr. Arthell B. Garrison, Ph.D. Said in that letter if I ever wanted to study entomology at the University of Georgia, he'd be glad to help me out." He smiled thinly. "Me! Can you imagine that? Me in college? Man, I barely made it through eighth grade. Anyway, I got bored with bugs after a while. Started in on geology." He struck a pose, like he was trying to impress us. "That's where the money is, man."

"What do you mean?"

"You come all the way over here to hear this boring stuff? Don't you want to hear how I gutted them ladies, raped them with a screwdriver, and all that. That's what they usually want to know about."

"Did you?" I said.

"Did I what?"

"Gut those women?"

"No."

"Then tell us about geology."

He glared at me for a minute, then said, "You want me to bore you to death, okay. I might as well take somebody with me when I go." He let out a short barking laugh. "Here's what it is. The state of Georgia, you basically got the coastal plain, which is sandy soil and sedimentary rock. Formed when the oceans was real high back in the Cretaceous period. Up north, you got the tag-end of the Appalachian mountain range, which is all igneous rock. That kind of settles down into the Piedmont, which is red clay soil over all kind of different rock—igneous, mostly. Now right smack in the middle, you got what they call the fall line. That's where the Piedmont drops off into the coastal plain. It's called the fall line because it kind of jumps down and you get waterfalls on all the rivers. Anyway, Flournoy County is dead in the middle of the fall line. What happens, all this erosion where the coastal plain hits the rocky substrate of the Piedmont, it wears away all these rocks, exposes all kind of interesting geological stuff. I mean, interesting if you like that type of thing...." He trailed off.

"Earlier you said geology is where the money is."

"Yeah. What it is, there's this clay that you can find all along the fall line in Georgia. It's called—"

"Kaolin."

His eyebrows went up. "So you know what I'm talking about."

"I know it has a high index of reflectivity," I said. "I know they use it to make toothpaste. Now you know everything I know on the subject of kaolin."

"Well, that's more than all these idiots around here," he said, looking down the row of cells. "Swear to God, these morons around here, they'll talk your ear off, but all they talk about is food, pussy, and Jesus. Pardon my French. It'll about drive you crazy."

"You were saying about kaolin . . ."

"Kaolin is a sedimentary deposit of rock that was worn away and deposited back in the Cretaceous. Then sharks' teeth and shells and other calcareous substances were laid overtop of that sediment. With water and compression working on them over time, combining the rock sediment and the calcified..." He coughed. "Hell, y'all don't care about that. Bottom line, all these geological processes combined to create kaolin. And kaolin's worth money. It's scattered around all out there along the fall line of Georgia, on over into Alabama. Now Flournoy County ain't nothing much but woods, see. There's places in Flournoy County ain't nobody been to in thirty, forty, fifty years. So if you find you some land that had kaolin on it, man, you could get rich. So I'd just go out in the woods and hunt around. Figured if I kept it up, someday I'd find me a nice big vein, make me a mint."

"How much land did you own?"

He looked at me like I was crazy. "Me? Own land? What I look like to you?"

"Then what good would it do to find kaolin out in the woods if you didn't own the land?"

He stroked his face thoughtfully. "Well, see, it's like this here. There's only one company that mines the land in Flournoy County. That's DCI. They don't own no land. They just own leases. See, if you got a piece of property that's got kaolin on it, you can sell off a mineral lease. That gives whoever you sell the lease to a right to drive up on your property, bulldoze a big old hole in your yard, rip out all the kaolin they can find, and then sell it. Out of that, they'll give you what they call royalties. It's like a percentage of what they find."

"So you figured that you'd find a vein of this stuff," I said, "go to the owner, buy the leases for cheap, and then what."

"Call up DCI and give them a lease on a lease."

"A lease on a lease. You can do that?"

"Sure. Subleasing. People do it all the time."

"But you never found anything."

He looked at me for a long time, some kind of vague, bitter amusement building in his eyes. "You know what I found the weekend them girls got killed? I found the mother lode."

"You're kidding me."

He laughed humorlessly. "I kid you not, man. They was a landslide on a piece of property owned by a timber company about two, three miles from my house. Where the topsoil come off, it showed up a nice big old vein of top-grade white. I spent two solid days in them damn woods drilling holes." He shook his head in wonderment. "That vein run over a thousand linear foot, anywhere from twenty to sixty foot wide. If it run back slantwise, the way they usually do? I wouldn't be surprised it was four, five million cubic yards sitting in there."

"What's a cubic yard of kaolin worth?" I said.

"Runs about ninety dollars a ton. There's about a couple, three cubic yards to the ton."

My eyes widened. "You're saying . . ."

He nodded. "Yep. A hundred million dollars' worth of east Georgia High Gloss sitting under that hill."

"You tell the sheriff about this? You take them out there, show them the holes, anything that might have proved you were there?"

Dale Weedlow took out a stick of chewing gum, put it in his mouth. "How dumb you think I am? Give away a hundred million dollars?"

"It's not exactly doing you a lot of good right now, is it?"

Weedlow chewed the gum for a while. "I knew I ain't killed them ladies," he said. "This is America, man. I couldn't believe I'd get convicted of something I ain't did. So I kept my mouth shut about what I seen out there."

"Let's talk about that," Lee-Lee said. She had been fidgeting around while Weedlow talked geology. "Why do you think they convicted you?"

Weedlow laughed. "Looking back? I didn't have a chance. There wasn't nothing they *couldn't* have convicted me of."

"Why, though?"

"Okay, first, it was my tools that got used to kill them girls. That was my bad luck. I worked at that mine for DCI, cleaning up, fixing stuff, mowing the grass, whatever. So I had tools. Whoever it was, they could have took any tools they wanted. There was six, seven of us working there. All of us had tools laying around. Happened they took mine. So that's where it started. After that, it just snowballed. That sheriff, she had it in for me. I mean, realistically, I was a nuisance-type guy. I'd been arrested for shoplifting, selling a little weed, stuff like that. I be honest, I don't know when to shut my mouth. Every time I'd get popped, I'd cuss and get all lippy with the deputies, whatnot. No wonder they didn't like me.

"Then here comes this Deputy Woodie. He's first cousins of the second gal that got killed. Brittany Woodie. They was real close. People use to joke they was a little *too* close . . . if you know what I mean."

"Dalton Cullihue said they were just shirttail kin," I said. "He said half the people in Flournoy County are named Woodie."

"Wouldn't be the first time he lied," Dale said. "Cullihue knows good and well they're first cousins. Anyway, like I was saying, David Woodie's the number-two guy on the investigation. He decides I've did it. So when I won't confess, he beats the crap out of me. Uses a phone book so it won't leave no marks. When I still won't say I done it, he basically drowns me. Just keeps drowning me and drowning me. Finally, I can't take it no more. So the sheriff comes in and she gives me all the details, how the crime went down. I mean, she didn't dictate it or nothing, but she's like, 'You took off their clothes in the car, right? You made them walk naked through the mud, right? You hung them up in the shed by their feet, right? Where'd you get the trash bags you put over their faces?' Like that. By the time she's done, I got a nice clear picture how the whole killing went down. So they give me a crayon and some paper and I wrote it up just like she told it to me."

"But if you weren't there, wouldn't there have been at least a couple inconsistencies?"

"A *couple*? Man, I've seen the transcript of the trial. There's more inconsistencies than you can shake a stick at."

"Why didn't your lawyer bring this out at trial?" I said skeptically.

"You mean besides the fact he's a broke-down alcoholic who's totally in the pocket of the district attorney, who's totally in the pocket of the superior court judge, who's totally in the pocket of Earl Justice?"

"Wait a minute. Who's Earl Justice?"

"He owns DCI. Which means he basically owns the whole county."

"You're making it sound like it was one big conspiracy," I said.

"Look, Terri Ross was Earl Justice's right-hand man. Can a lady be a right-hand man? Well, you get what I'm saying. They worked together and they was close. Real close. I'm not saying they were having an affair or nothing, but they sure got on awful good. I got no doubt it freaked him out when she got killed. So all he had to do was put down the word–'Squash this little turd, Dale Weedlow'–and, boom, it was a done thing."

"Hmm," Lee-Lee said.

"You don't believe me? Look at that autopsy report. That's the whole key to it."

"The autopsy report?" I said. "What's so special about the autopsy report?"

Before Weedlow could answer, I heard a voice behind us. "Sorry, ladies." It was the warden. "I'm afraid your hour's up."

"Just a couple more minutes," Lee-Lee said.

"No, ma'am. Don't work that way in the penitentiary, I'm sorry to say. One hour means one hour."

"But–"

"The autopsy report is gone," I said to Weedlow.

His face went white. "What?"

"Ma'am," the warden said. "Ma'am, you need to turn that camera off, get moving."

Lee-Lee turned the camera off, started putting away the equipment. All I could hear was the whirring of fans–there was no air-conditioning on death row–and the hubbub of prisoners holding conversations in shouted voices. They had to yell because they couldn't leave their cells.

"You really think it's possible?" Weedlow said as Lee-Lee snapped the camera case shut.

"Possible for what?" I said.

"All this time I been praying somebody like y'all would come here," the prisoner said. "Somebody who could see that it wasn't me that done it." He slumped back on his bed. "Now I'm afraid it might be too late."

"Let's go, ladies," the warden said again.

"I ain't a bad person!" Dale Weedlow yelled as we were hustled away by the big corrections officer, his voice lost among the death-row conversations. "Find that autopsy report! You find it! You'll see!"

He was still yelling as we worked our way down the chain-link fence. But his words were lost in the noise.

SEVEN

Lee-Lee and I arrived at 7:30 for the Blue-Gray Barbecue at Earl Justice's house. Though, I have to say, the word *house* just doesn't quite hack it to describe the place. Château? Manse? Palace? It was more along those lines. It was on the crest of a hill, with about ten acres of manicured lawn in front, a horse pasture off to the left, an immense stone barn off in the back.

A row of cars was pulling into a crescent-shaped drive. White men in butternut uniforms got out, assisted their white wives out of their cars, and then handed the keys to black men in nineteenth-century livery.

I couldn't have felt more out of place as I climbed out of the car in my usual black turtleneck and black slacks. Well, that's not right. Lee-Lee—now *she* was out of place. The dyed black hair, the heavy black eyeliner, the nose ring, the black fingernail polish, the Marilyn Manson tattoo, the slinky red dress. Everybody on the veranda pretty much stopped and gawked at her.

A man detached himself from the knot of *Gone With the Wind*–looking gawkers and came toward us. He was probably in his late fifties, an inch or two above six feet. His thick white hair was swept straight back from his forehead and was a good deal longer than you'd have expected to see on a middle Georgia businessman. His eyes were a pale, sparkling blue. He wore the uniform of a Confederate general, including a cavalry hat with a yellow feather and a long curved sword. "Y'all must be Sunny and

Lee-Lee!" he said. "I'm Earl Justice. Welcome to the Blue-Gray Barbecue!"

I returned his firm handshake and looked around. "I'm seeing a lot more gray than blue, I must admit, Mr. Justice," I said.

"Earl! It's Earl," he said. He had one of those boozy old southern accents, the kind they used to hand out at Duke and Vanderbilt and Sewanee. Then he grinned. "And, yeah, you not gonna see a great, *great* deal of blue uniforms at this party." He turned from me to Lee-Lee. He made no attempt to shake her hand or to disguise a long, slow look up and down her figure. He spread his hands as though to encompass her entire form. "My, my! All this and a brilliant filmmaker, too. I don't know if our little town will be able to withstand such an onslaught of talent and glamour. The ladies around here will be saying catty things about you for years!"

I have seen men with feral charm in my day, but not many to top Earl Justice. He was like a movie star, practically bludgeoning you with charisma. He took Lee-Lee by the arm, walked her toward the door, and the crowd parted like tiny boats before some giant ocean liner. I trailed behind, ignored by all.

One of the many liveried black men opened the massive front door and we entered. I was surprised to see that the house was relatively modern inside, with walls crowded by good pieces of modern art. I saw a Chagall, a Kokoschka, and a Mondrian before we'd even passed the coat-check room. (Yes, he had a coat-check room in his house.) Another footman or butler approached us and Earl Justice snagged Lee-Lee a flute of champagne. I grabbed a scotch on the rocks.

Justice showed us the house. He had perfected the art, like many clever and powerful men, of being wittily self-deprecating and self-aggrandizing at the same time—a kind of sham modesty, which was amusing despite its obvious transparence. Finally, he lodged us in a large room, the walls of which were covered not in art but in the heads of dead animals. There was quite a collection of firearms in a glass-fronted cabinet on the wall.

"Please," he said. "Sit."

We sat. Earl Justice settled in across from Lee-Lee, took off his hat, and then looked into her eyes for a while. "One of the trials of living in this town is the paucity of interesting specimens of humanity," he said. "You can't imagine how pleased I am to have two visitors of such *interesting* qualifications."

Under the charm offensive, Lee-Lee had been reduced to a giggling freshman at sorority rush by now. "Oh now, Earl, don't be silly," she said.

"So beautiful, so young, and yet so accomplished!" Earl Justice looked into her eyes without seeming even to blink. "I am in awe of filmmakers. Really. I am."

I felt like saying, Look, I'll just step outside and you can go right ahead and start taking your clothes off. But before I got the chance, the laser beam of his charm suddenly shifted in my direction. "And you! You solved that big case with the country singer a few years back, didn't you? What was her name?" He snapped his fingers. "Georgia Burnett?" Then he reeled off about four or five other investigations I'd been involved in—none of which had been particularly newsworthy, but which had saved various insurance companies a great deal of money. "Fabulous work! Remarkable!"

The hairs went up on the back of my neck. It was information that he could only have gotten by paying someone to investigate me. He knew that I knew this. It was a message.

He turned back to Lee-Lee. "So. This documentary you're making. Tell me all about it."

Before I could punch her or shut her up, Lee-Lee was babbling away about how she had stumbled across the case, how she was interested in man's capacity for evil, all this sophomoric film-school hooey. "But now that we're here," she said finally, "and I've started looking into the case in more detail, I'm really not sure that—"

I interrupted. "Now, Lee-Lee, you're gonna bore poor Earl to death." I stood. "Earl, I know you need to get back to your guests."

Earl never took his eyes off Lee-Lee's face. "You were saying, hon?"

"Seriously, Lee-Lee," I said. "You've barely started the movie. You hardly know anything at this point. It ruins the mystery if you go around telling everybody what the movie's about before you've even finished it."

I was completely ignored. Lee-Lee blabbed everything. About how she'd been pulled over and arrested the night before. About how there really wasn't any tape in the camera showing Deputy Woodie tossing the pot into her car. About how the DA hadn't given us the autopsy. About our visit to death row.

When she finally shut up, Earl Justice nodded soberly. "Mm!" he said. "You have an enormous gift for narrative." He continued to nod. "But I expect you know that."

Lee-Lee gave him the sorority-girl giggle. It confirmed everything I knew about her—that underneath all the boho jewelry and tattoos, she was just another clueless southern cutie. I love her to death, don't get me wrong. But the way I figured it, she had no more business being a documentary filmmaker than I had being a trapeze artist.

"One thing I have learned, though," Justice continued, "is that in all stories, there are two sides. Wait here." He picked up his cavalry hat, stroked the feather meditatively, then walked out of the room.

As soon as the door had closed, I put my hands around Lee-Lee's neck and pretended to choke her.

"What!" she said.

"Are you out of your mind? He's the most powerful guy in this town. All he has to do is snap his fingers and your little movie project is history."

Lee-Lee blinked. "He wouldn't do that. You saw him. He's a really nice guy!"

"Nice guy? Tell that to Mr. Moose over there." I pointed to a huge morose-looking head hanging on the wall. "Lee-Lee, he had an extremely close relationship with one of the victims! You know how emotionally invested relatives and friends of victims get in cases like this? Not a chance in hell you'll convince this guy that Dale Weedlow is innocent."

Lee-Lee looked around vaguely. The glittering glass eyes of all the animals that Earl Justice had killed stared back at her. "Oh," she said. "I hadn't thought of that."

The door opened and a woman walked in. She wore a hoop skirt and her hair was done up in ringlets that must have kept her three hours at the hairdresser.

Earl led her over to the couch, sat her down. "Lee-Lee, Sunny, this is Mrs. Lucille Ross. She's Terri Ross's mother. Ms. Ross, this is Lee-Lee Edwards and Sunny Childs. They're making the film about Terri's murder."

The woman looked resentfully at us. "Is it true?" she said. "Y'all coming around here saying Dale Weedlow didn't do this?"

Lee-Lee withered, sank into her chair.

"Look," I said. "We're just examining the facts. The film isn't made. All we're doing is—"

"Facts!" Her face had gone hard and white. "You want to know facts? Sit there and listen, I'll tell you *facts*."

"Yes, ma'am," I said. "That's why we're here."

"You might even want to film this, Lee-Lee," Earl Justice said mildly. "Hm?"

"Don't you dare," Mrs. Ross said.

"Now, Lucille . . ." Earl Justice put his hand on her bare shoulder.

"Get your hand off me!" the victim's mother snapped.

Justice smiled thinly.

"Dale Weedlow claimed in court that he barely knew my daughter," Lucille Ross said. "Is that what he said to y'all, too?"

Lee-Lee nodded.

"I bet he didn't tell you that two weeks before he killed her, she'd had to call the sheriff to send a car over because he was sneaking around her house. I bet he skipped over that. I bet he skipped over the part about how he made rude sexual remarks to her when he came by the office to pick up his paycheck the week before, didn't he? I bet he kind of forgot to mention how after she told him to stop talking like that and embarrassed him in front of his friends, that he later told one of his little pothead buddies how she needed her attitude adjusted with a stiff piece of steel. Am I shocking you? I hope so. I been shocked enough that I don't shock much anymore." She stared defiantly at us. "And that last one didn't even make it into the trial. That only came out later."

"I know you're angry, Lucille," Earl Justice said. "We all are. But how about you just tell them about Terri. What a good girl she was. How full of promise."

Lucille Ross's face slowly softened. Finally she said, "My daughter Terri had the sweetest disposition. You'd get the impression meeting her that she was all milk and cream. But she was tough as nails, too."

"Don't know where she got that from," Earl Justice said.

Lucille Ross laughed, very briefly. "I'm proud of her in a million ways. She went to college on a full scholarship. Could have stayed up there in Atlanta, got a good job and all. But she didn't like it up there. She was just a small-town girl, I guess. Went to church every Sunday and Wednesday. Liked telling the truth. Liked looking people in the eye on the street. She was just a straight arrow. A straight arrow from the minute she left the bow. When she put her mind to something, it stayed put. And smart? My *goodness!* She started working for Mr. Justice the summer after she got back in town. Started out doing secretarial work. But by the time she died—which was only a few years after she started working for Mr. Justice—she was in charge of all kind of legal work, leases, contracts. She used to talk to me about all this financial stuff—whew! Went right over my head."

Earl Justice nodded. "It's customary when someone dies to spread around all kind of pleasing eyewash about their character. But in this case, it's true. I believe that if Terri had stayed at DCI, she'd have ended up running the company. She was that good, that smart, that solid, that dependable. I trusted her with every aspect of my business. *Every* aspect. And as people around her will be quick to tell you, that is not something that I do lightly."

We sat quietly.

Earl Justice looked around the room. "I suppose I do need to get back to my duties as host. But I thought it was important y'all had a chance to meet Terri's mama. I watch crime shows on TV now and then. It's easy to be cavalier about tragedy when it's far away from you. But when it comes to you right up close, you start to see how every time somebody dies, it leaves a hole in the world that can't ever be plugged." He put one hand to his eye as though to stop a tear. And I sensed this was not him being a ham, but a sincere gesture. "I was crazy about that girl. Hell, everybody in this town was. You want to make a movie about what happened, Miss Edwards, you better do honor to that girl's memory. Before you do anything else."

"Yes, sir," Lee-Lee said.

•

We went out and found the barbecue in the back, cooking on big grills made from oil drums that had been cut in half down the middle. There was more black guys running the grills, all the white folks eating the pig.

I looked up and saw Dalton Cullihue coming toward me, a plateful of barbecue in his hand. He held up a forkful of it at me. "Don't it just melt in your mouth?" he said.

"Yes, it does," I said. "What's the secret?"

Cullihue pointed at an aged black man behind the grill. "Right there. His name's Love Pinkston. If that boy had opened a restaurant in some big city, he'd be a millionaire by now." He motioned to the old man. "Love! How you doing today, sir?"

The old man bowed. "Fine, Mr. Cullihue. Fine. And you?"

"Fair to middling. Fair to middling. Every year I say it and every year it's true, but by golly I believe you've topped yourself again. This year is the apex, Love. I don't believe you'll ever beat this pig."

"Raised it myself, sir," Love Pinkston said. "It's a purebred Duroc sow. These here factory farms can't breed them. Too feisty.

You put a thousand Durocs in a barn, they'll kill each other by nightfall. But they no substitute, sir. No substitute."

"That's what you ought to make a film about," Cullihue said to me. "Factory hog farms. They're barbaric. They got one of those farms over in Hancock County, just next door to us, ten thousand head of hogs in three barns, each one about the size of a football field. You know they cut the tails off all the hogs? Otherwise, they'll chew them right off each other! You can smell it four, five miles away. Barbaric."

"That's right, Mr. Cullihue," the cook said.

Cullihue turned back to the cook. "This lady's making a movie about Dale Weedlow. Can you believe that?"

"A movie about Dale Weedlow!" the cook said. "Well if that don't beat everything. Excuse me, I need to tend to the other grill."

As the cook moved away, Cullihue said, "Typical colored. Long as you're standing there, he smiles at you like you're his best friend. Turn your back for half a second, he starts making trouble."

"Oh?"

"That old spear chucker's been suing DCI for close to ten years. Why Mr. Justice keeps hiring him, I can't fathom."

"It's probably the barbecue," I said.

Cullihue took a forkful of pork, shoved it in his mouth, rolled his eyes in pleasure. "You're right. It *is* the barbecue."

"What's Mr. Pinkston suing DCI for?"

"Nothing," he said disgustedly. "I been a lawyer—what?—twenty-odd years and I've never seen a colored man file a lawsuit that amounted to a hill of beans."

"Speaking of the law, I'm glad I caught you," I said. "I appreciate your getting those transcripts over to me so quickly. But there's something missing."

He raised one eyebrow, looking around the big yard as though suddenly interested in the crowd. All the people looked like extras from a Civil War epic. "Oh?"

"The autopsy report."

Cullihue made a pretense of spotting someone in the crowd. "Daryl Sinclair!" He poked his fork in the air. "How the hell are you, boy? I been needing to get with you for weeks." He turned to me. "Scuse me, hon, I need to scoot. Just call my office in the morning; we'll get you all fixed up."

I finished my barbecue, tossed my empty plate in the trash.

"Your cheek," a voice next to me said.

"Excuse me?"

I turned and the cook, Love Pinkston, was holding something out to me, a paper napkin. "Your cheek, ma'am," he said, touching the side of his face. "You got a little sauce on your cheek."

"Oh."

I took the paper, wiped my cheek. When I looked at the paper, it had come away clean. "Did I get it?" I said.

But the old man had gone back to the grill and didn't seem to hear me. I wiped again. Nothing. I frowned, wadded up the napkin. But as I was about to throw it away, I noticed something written on the back side. I unfolded the napkin, turned it over.

Written in black ink was:

404-555-5000
LAW OFFICES OF
EMMET DIGGSBY, JR.

When I looked up from the paper napkin, I saw the old man walking slowly across the yard. I followed him around the corner of the house. But when I got there, he was gone.

On the other side of the yard, I saw Lee-Lee talking to Earl Justice again. She laughed and threw her hair back, her mouth wide open.

To no one in particular, I said, "I don't know about this."

EIGHT

"We got it all wrong, dude," Lee-Lee said. "There really is an American heartland, you know? Where people tell the truth and believe in God and salute the flag..."

It was a few minutes past nine the next morning and we were eating at the meat-and-three café in downtown Pettigrew.

"I'm not quite following you," I said.

"Here's this little guy in the middle of this idyllic little town, he's like a cancer. You know? Sitting around playing Xbox and smoking dope and listening to heavy metal on his Korean stereo, watching *Cops* on the cable TV. It's like he's the embodiment of soulless modernity in the middle of this fragile, beautiful thing, this amazing little town. You know what I mean?"

"Are we talking about the same idyllic community where you just got framed for possession and assault?"

"I mean, sure, okay, there's a bad cop here who plants dope in the occasional out-of-towner's car. But what's he really trying to do? He's trying to sterilize the wound, keep out the rot."

"Uh-huh."

"What this film really needs to be about—it's gonna be about the war in this country between people who have beliefs and values versus the people who subscribe to some kind of destructive, soulless modern ideology."

"Who put all this malarkey in your head?" I said. "Earl Justice?"

"No! Hey! God!" Lee-Lee glared at me. "Why are you such a cynical person?"

"Cynical? Me? I'm not the one with the tattoo of Marilyn Manson on my shoulder," I said.

She looked down at her shoulder. "A youthful error," she said. "I've been meaning to have that removed for like a year."

I drained my coffee. Typical Lee-Lee. One minute, she believed something with every fiber of her being; ten minutes later, she was arguing its opposite as though her life were at stake. And never a shred of irony, never the slightest self-reflection, never any recognition of how ridiculous it made her seem. Her mind changed like the tide, completely and without reservation. Another few minutes and she'd forget her entire speech about the soullessness of modern culture. "Come on," I said. "Let's go."

"Where?"

"Back to Atlanta."

She looked puzzled. "We can't do that. I need to shoot some video of the town. Get the old Confederate cemetery and the courthouse; then there's this *totally* cute little white frame Church of God out on Route One Seventeen. . . ."

I stood. "Let's go."

"This is *my* film, dude!" she said.

"Come on. Time's a-wastin'. We need to pick up a copy of that autopsy before we go."

"Why are you stressing about this autopsy?" she said. "It's like all I hear out of you. Autopsy, autopsy, autopsy. The guy stuck a screwdriver in those poor girls and then cut their guts out. What more do you need to know?"

•

I was not shocked to find out that nobody at the Flournoy County DA's office knew where the autopsy report was. "Mr. Cullihue's in trial right now," his secretary said. "I'm sure when Mr. Cullihue gets back, he'll be able to find it."

"Sure," I said.

It took us about two hours to get back to Atlanta, park downtown, and walk to the office of Emmet Diggsby, Jr., attorney-at-law. He was in an office building south of the federal courthouse that was filled with the offices of lawyers who–judging by the general drabness and disrepair of the place–didn't seem to be doing all that well for themselves.

We walked into an office on the sixth floor, found a slightly chubby black guy with dreadlocks sitting at a long table, pecking on a computer keyboard. He looked startled when we walked in.

"I'm looking for Mr. Diggsby," I said.

"That's me."

"Emmet Diggsby?"

He nodded.

I introduced Lee-Lee and myself and said that I was trying to find out if he had any information about Dale Weedlow.

He frowned. "Who?"

"Dale Weedlow. He was convicted of killing a young lady by the name of Terri Ross about six years ago. He's scheduled to get the needle in five days."

At the mention of Terri Ross, Diggsby's face hardened. "I'm sorry, but as a matter of policy, I don't speak to private investigators."

"Oh, I'm not really working for anybody. My cousin Lee-Lee here is making a movie about Dale Weedlow and–"

"I'm going to have to ask you to leave, ma'am."

"But–"

"Now!" He picked up the phone. "I'm dialing nine-one-one. You don't leave, I'll have the cops throw you out."

"Love Pinkston recommended I talk to you."

Diggsby's face took on a complicated expression. There was affection in his eyes, but also a certain wistful bitterness. Finally, he set the phone down and said, "How is Mr. Pinkston?"

"Still making some fine barbecue."

"Don't even *tell* me that." Diggsby shook his head sadly. "I'm on that diet where you eat seaweed and protein shakes."

Diggsby pointed to a couple of ratty chairs. "Look, I don't imagine I can help you. But I guess it wouldn't hurt to talk."

Lee-Lee switched on her camera.

Diggsby said, "Thing is, I don't know anything about this Dale Weedlow. Not really."

"Then just tell us what you do know."

"Like I say, probably nothing. But I guess I'd need to kind of back up a little and explain how I got involved with that godforsaken Flournoy County. How much do you know about the kaolin business?"

I held up my hand, index finger and thumb about half an inch apart.

"Okay, well. I'll start from the beginning. In the late nineties, I was a naïve young kid straight out of law school. I started my own firm. One of the first cases I took on was Mr. Pinkston's. He owns a little farm down in Flournoy County. Somewhere along the way, he sold off mineral leases on his property to a mining company by the name of DCI. They paid him something like two thousand dollars cash, then had him sign a contract spelling out the terms of any further royalty payments he'd receive. The leases allowed them to mine any location on his property, build any sort of access roads they deemed necessary, basically create any kind of havoc they chose. And in return, they would pay a royalty to Mr. Pinkston of five percent on any minerals discovered—exclusive of development costs, certain overhead items, certain processing and transportation costs, blah blah blah blah.

"Well, come to find out, there's a big old vein of this kaolin stuff right in the middle of his largest field. They tear down a stretch of timber, start driving giant earthmovers and bulldozers, et cetera, through his yard, throw up a chain-link fence around a large piece of his property, and begin peeling off what they call 'the overburden.' That's a fancy name for all the dirt that's on top of the vein of kaolin. In so doing, they messed up all his fields, so he couldn't plant but about half the crops he'd planted the previous year. And after doing all that, tearing out what we ultimately estimated to be eight hundred thousand cubic yards of dirt from his field, they put a padlock on the fence and drove off, leaving a giant hole in the ground. In return for this, he received checks over the course of several years totaling less than fifty thousand dollars. Which is barely as much money as he would have made farming the land."

I was still trying to see how this connected to Dale Weedlow. But I figured he'd get there eventually. "Okay," I said.

"The raw stuff coming out of the ground, if it's high-grade ore, is above ninety percent pure. So if they took eight hundred thousand cubic yards of dirt, subtracting out the overburden, there was bound to have been a good one hundred thousand cubic yards of kaolin. You ever priced kaolin?"

"What did Dale Weedlow say?" I said to Lee-Lee. "Like ninety dollars a ton?"

Diggsby smiled—a little bitterly, it seemed like. "Well. Yeah. He would say that. If you asked somebody in the Accounts Payable Department at DCI, however, they'd tell you raw kaolin is worth a few cents a ton."

"I don't get it."

"The kaolin industry likes to make a big deal about the fact that kaolin is not what you call a dig-it-and-ship-it mineral. Coal, for instance, you just dig the stuff up and it's ready to go. Kaolin, on the other hand, has to be processed. Therefore, the price per ton of the raw clay is determined by the market. And the market is set by the processors. You go to a processor, tell them you have X amount of clay, and they'll say, 'Fine, we'll pay you X dollars per ton.'"

"Okay."

"Only it doesn't work like that. All kaolin miners are also processors." Diggsby squinted at me. "Am I boring you?"

"No, no," I said. "I'm just trying to connect a lot of dots in my head. I'm trying to see what this has to do with the movie Lee-Lee here is making."

"Here's the point. Dig a ton of coal out of the ground, you can sell it directly to the international market. Not kaolin. See, when the processor and the miner are the same guy, he can set any price he feels like. He can say, 'Well, yeah, the price per ton of this raw material is ten cents.' Meanwhile, he's selling the processed material for a hundred dollars a ton."

"That's kind of a big spread."

"No kidding."

"So a company can find a deposit on land owned by some poor shmoe, pay them peanuts—because it's more than they had before—and then walk off with all the profits."

"That was the contention of Mr. Pinkston's lawsuit." Diggsby smiled bitterly again. "But proving that this is an unfair transaction? Not so easy."

"So what happened to the lawsuit?"

"Oh, we certified as a class action pretty quickly, but then it sort of hit the shoals. Seven years later, it's still sputtering along. These companies have probably invested two to three million in the case by now. They hire experts, they depose witnesses, they file motions, they file requests for admission—endless amounts of paper. It's a war of attrition. I roped a few other lawyers into coming on board with the case way back when. It looked good for a while. But now?" He shrugged.

"So where's the connection to Dale Weedlow?"

"About a year into the case, I got a call from a young woman. She said she had proof that DCI had been screwing their leaseholders. I asked her what the substance of her proof was, and she said that DCI had established a series of offshore corporations that acted as buyers of the raw clay coming out of their mines These shell companies bought the ore, then 'resold' it to DCI. This allowed them to claim that they were offering 'market price' to the leaseholders, when, in fact, it was totally bogus. She said she had proof that there was double bookkeeping going on. DCI would record a sale from the mine at some low price, then a buy from this offshore company at a higher price. Somehow, this allowed them generate a bogus tax loss and to pay a fire-sale price to the people who leased them their land. Killed two birds with one stone. Then the offshore money would be repatriated through phony invoicing and whatnot. Finally, she told me, 'I'll meet you next week and give you proof.'"

My eyebrows went up. "Wow. What happened?"

"She never showed. She had never told me her name, by the way. But later on—I mean at least a year later—I found out that this young woman Terri Ross had been killed the night before I was supposed to meet her. And apparently she was sort of a special assistant to this man Earl Justice, who owns DCI. I figured it had to be her. But by then, Dale Weedlow was in prison. I figured, Okay, maybe it's just an unfortunate coincidence."

"Do you really believe that?"

Diggsby cleared his throat, looked out the grimy window. "This case sucked my lifeblood out. I spent everything I had on it for the first few years. Which wasn't much. But by the time that I found out about Weedlow, I was on the verge of bankruptcy. And I was nowhere near proving my case." He stared for a while. "Tell you the truth, I sat around for a whole weekend with a picture of that young lady in my lap. Got it out of the newspaper. Sat there drinking beer and asking myself if I had the nerve to go the next yard in this case."

"And?"

"You ever see that movie with John Travolta where he plays this lawyer who sues a chemical company on behalf of some people who may or may not have gotten diseases related to chemicals dumped by this company up in Massachusetts? Well, this lawyer pretty much goes crazy, spends all the money he has, bankrupts his partners, ruins his marriage, all this stuff—but in the end, he wins, gets this huge pile of money. See, for ever guy like that, there're a thousand guys like me who take on some obscure little class action and then get ground into the dirt by companies and lawyers with resources you just wouldn't believe. Well, I realized that if I went down the path of trying to find out what had happened to that girl . . ." He shook his head. "I have a son. I have a wife. I have a little house over in DeKalb County that I own. It's not a big, shiny, inspiring, made-for-TV-movie kind of life. But it's okay. If I'd gone down that road, odds are I'd have lost everything. I'd have wrecked everything I touched. And all my sad little clients down in Flournoy County? They'd still be poor as dirt."

"And in your heart?" Lee-Lee said.

He looked up, frowned. We had almost forgotten she was there.

"In your heart!" Lee-Lee said. "Why do you think she died?"

Diggsby shook his head. "I can't go there. I can't."

"You think Terri Ross got killed because of your lawsuit," Lee-Lee said.

"The world's a mess. That's what I think." Diggsby took a long breath. "You mind turning off that camera?"

Lee-Lee killed the light on the camera, hit the off button.

I stood. "Thank you for your help," I said.

He shrugged. "Y'all seem like nice people. Your lives will be a lot easier if you'd just do a little movie on the many salutary effects of the kaolin industry on middle Georgia. They'll probably give you a medal down there."

As I stood to go, I said, "If we found proof that DCI was shafting the people who owned land where they were mining—"

"That was six years ago. If Terri Ross had those documents back then, they're gone by now."

•

On the way back to Flournoy County, my phone rang. A collect call from Jackson penitentiary. It was Dale Weedlow.

"Miss Childs?"

"How you doing, Dale?"

"I just called to say . . ." I could hear him breathing. "I been in prison a long time now. Sometimes you forget how to act."

"Okay."

"I just wanted to say I was sorry if I'd said anything to offend y'all."

"Okay."

"I swear to God I didn't do this thing."

"I believe you."

"Please," he said. "I'm so scared. Nobody believes me. I don't want to die in this place." He started crying.

"We're trying to find the truth," I said.

"Please..." he said, his voice cracking. "Please! Don't let me die!"

"I'm doing everything I can," I said. Then I hung up.

"Who was that?" Lee-Lee said.

"That was the cancer of modernism that's destroying the traditional values of Flournoy County. He was hoping we would keep him from getting poisoned to death five days from now."

She sat silently for a while; then she put her head in her hands. "I'm so confused," she said. "What's the story? What are we doing here?"

"I don't know about you," I said, "but I'm just trying to find the truth. Without that, there is no story."

She looked at me for a minute. "Why do you do that?" she said finally.

"Do what?"

"Talk to me with that tone of voice."

"Okay, so I get impatient with people who try to make simple things complicated. Find the truth. What's so hard about that?"

"Well, I'm just glad life is so easy for you."

I had to laugh. "Easy! Who said anything about easy?"

"Plus, you always have to have the last word."

"No I don't."

"Yes you do."

"No I don't."

"You do!"

"No I don't."

She made a face at me, like, *See!*

NINE

We drove back to Flournoy County, pulled up in front of the office of Ervin Kindred, attorney-at-law. It was a beautifully proportioned neoclassical Victorian with a large portico and tall Corinthian columns. As we walked up the steps to the front door, though, the picture deteriorated a little. The white paint was peeling here and there and you could see signs of dry rot in the woodwork around the door and windows.

A bell tinkled when we walked in. We found ourselves in a silent, slightly musty foyer with a grand staircase leading up to the second floor. There was piece chain across the stairwell with a sign on it that said DANGEROUS STAIRS—DO NOT USE!

"Hello?" I said.

There was no answer. "Whoa," Lee-Lee said. "Kind of creepy."

We walked deeper into the building. I looked into a room and a woman of a certain age glanced up from a cheap office desk. I could see a pair of very thick, very white ankles peeking out under the desk. "Oh, sorry, dear!" she said. "I wasn't sure if I heard the bell or not."

We walked in and introduced ourselves. The woman at the desk told us she was Aimee Wallace and that she was Mr. Kindred's secretary. She then spelled her name and said that it was pronounced *em-AY,* in the French manner, because her grandmother on her mother's side was from Louisiana. She also said that she had heard all about us and our exciting project and that everybody in the town was terribly, *terribly* interested in our work, and just *so* fascinated, and me a real private *investigator,* and Lee-Lee such a glamorous and *unusual* young woman. She went on in this vein for a while.

I finally managed to interrupt and ask her if Mr. Kindred was in.

Her face composed itself. "Mr. Kindred is indisposed," she said.

I looked at Lee-Lee. Lee-Lee looked at me. I remembered what the district attorney had said Ervin Kindred's nickname was. Kindred Spirits. I had wondered at the time what that was all about. "Indisposed?" Lee-Lee said to me. "You know the last time I heard that? Your mama used to say that about her third husband—what was his name?"

"Roy Leesum the Third," I said.

"Yeah, him. She always used to say he was indisposed."

"Meaning he was drunk," I said.

"Well, my goodness!" Aimee Walker said. "I hope you're not implying something by that!"

"Oh my gracious, no," I said. "Lee-Lee never implies anything. But we really do need to talk to Mr. Kindred soon."

"Maybe tomorrow," Aimee Walker said. "He has a very tender constitution."

A voice came out from the door behind her. "Aw for Christ sake, Amy. Just let 'em in. If you don't, they'll just be back buggin' me tomorrow."

"He's really not well," Aimee—or was it Amy?—said.

"We'll just be a minute. You have been *so* sweet, Ms. Wallace," Lee-Lee said, brushing past the desk and through the door. I followed her while Aimee Wallace clucked and fussed.

"Sit down, sit down," a voice said. The voice was deep and rich, and testified to many years of cigarette smoking. The room was almost completely dark. Only one shaft of light came through the blinds, leaving a thin bright stripe hanging in the air across the room. I could make out a desk, several chairs, and a man-sized lump on the other side of the room. "I apologize for the dimness, but I'm recovering from the Blue-Gray affair last night. Afraid I tied on one too many." The voice was coming from the lump. As my eyes adjusted, I was able to make out a man lying on a leather couch.

"Can I offer y'all a drink? I'm enjoying a Bloody Mary at this moment—strictly for medicinal purposes, of course."

"Thanks, no."

"Y'all are, of course, wasting y'all's time. I am unable to comment on a case that is still under appeal."

The shaft of light hit the wall on the far side of the room, lighting up a large diploma. "Harvard Law," I said. "Boy, not many Harvard men around here, I bet."

"Ah, the flattery approach," he said. "I'm afraid I'm not quite drunk enough to respond to that yet, young lady. My recommendation would be bullying. That's the customary approach in Flournoy County anyway."

"Sir," I said. "You seem to find this a lot more amusing than I do. Someone's life is at stake."

"The appeal to my better nature! That hadn't even occurred to me. It's been so long since anyone even *tried* that."

"Turn the camera on, Lee-Lee," I said.

She did as I told her. The harsh camera light flooded the room, revealing a tall, haggard-looking man huddled under a blanket. He was in his fifties, and had probably been very handsome once. But—as they say—the years had not been kind to him. He put a hand over his eyes. "Jesus God!" he said.

"Sit up!" I snapped.

He sat up unsteadily, one hand still covering his eyes. He was clean-shaven, but he had missed a patch of white hair high on one cheek.

"Dale Weedlow says you were drunk during the trial."

"I wouldn't remember," Kindred said.

"Is that an attempt at humor?"

Kindred didn't answer.

"Weedlow says you botched his trial."

"That, I'm sure you're aware, is the standard appellate strategy of virtually every man on death row." He paused. "Sadly—given the pitiful amount of money allotted by the state of Georgia for the defense of criminal suspects–the claim is often an accurate one."

"You think you botched the trial?"

"I could hardly be expected to say so on tape, young lady," he said, finally taking his hand away from his eyes. His skin was blotchy and his blue eyes were red-rimmed.

"But in retrospect. Might there have been some holes in the case that you could have been more vigilant about exploiting?"

"Every trial in history is subject to a certain degree of Monday-morning quarterbacking."

"Walk us through the case," I said.

The lawyer ran his hands through his hair, then yelled, "Amy, get us some coffee, would you?" He sighed. "Poor Amy. Poor sad Amy."

"What could you have done better?"

"Let's wait on the coffee," he said. And with that, he sat and stared at the wall, running his hands slowly up and down his thighs until Amy or Aimee came back with three cups of tepid but strong coffee. Kindred drained his coffee, then took a long pull on his Bloody Mary.

"You were saying," I said.

Kindred stood unsteadily, put on his suit coat, and smoothed down his tie. It was a nice suit and a silk rep tie. He sat up straight. If you didn't look too carefully, he could have come off as entirely respectable. "The following is my statement for your film." He cleared his throat. "I make it a policy of mine to assume neither guilt nor innocence on the part of my clients. I simply defend them. Germind Dale Weedlow was charged with malice murder and various lesser charges. I defended him. Notwithstanding his somewhat disagreeable personality and his extensive criminal record both as an adult and as a minor, I defended him with no less energy than I would any other client. The case against him consisted primarily of a great deal of forensic evidence and a signed confession by Mr. Weedlow. He disavowed the confession in trial. But the fact that it corresponded in great detail to the actual circumstances of the murder made the case a difficult one to defend. Furthermore, there was corroborative testimony from a gentleman by the name of Randall Travis Miller, the fiancé of one of the victims, placing Mr. Weedlow at the Dairy Queen on the night of the murder. In his alleged confession, Mr. Weedlow allegedly admitted to having picked up the two victims there. While I felt professional disappointment with the verdict, I cannot say I was surprised by the outcome. Thus endeth my statement. Now please, in the name of holy charity, turn that dadgum light off."

"Keep rolling, Lee-Lee," I said. Then I turned back to Kindred. "What about the autopsy?"

"I have completed my statement."

"Do you have a copy of the autopsy? I'd like to review it with you."

"Young lady, I have completed my statement."

"You *do* have a copy of the autopsy."

The lawyer's hand had begun to develop a tremor. "Ladies, we are done talking. I'd ask you, please, to leave."

"I've read the transcript," I said. "You didn't even cross-examine the forensic pathologist. You stipulated to the whole thing."

"Leave now!" Kindred's voice had gotten high and tremulous. "I'm warning you."

"Was there pressure on you from Earl Justice?"

"Get out!"

"A little bit of that customary bullying you were talking about?"

Suddenly, Kindred reached into the drawer of his desk, pulled out an ancient Colt revolver with ivory grips that had gone yellow with age. He pointed it at my face. "Young lady, don't make me . . ."

The gun trembled in his hands. "I bet that old thing won't even shoot," I said. "Put it away. Let's be civilized here."

The gun went off with a terrific bang. I could hear the bullet pass my ear with an eerie snap. It was obvious he wasn't actually trying to shoot me. But still. My heart immediately started going about two hundred beats a minute. "Okay, you know what," I said. "I think maybe we will go after all."

We stood very, very quickly and left him standing there in the dark, waving his old pistol.

As we got into the outer office, Aimee Wallace was looking at us with fury in her eyes. "Look what you made him do!" she shouted. "He's not a well man! You are terrible, terrible people."

"You know," I said, "if you had a copy of that autopsy report, I promise we'd never come back and disturb you."

"He burned that report a long time ago!" she said. And then her eyes widened as she realized she had said something she shouldn't.

"He burned it?" I said. "Are you serious?"

She just kept staring at me.

"Why would he do that?"

She didn't answer. Instead, her face went slack and slowly drained of color. Then she slumped forward in her chair.

"What's up with *her*?" Lee-Lee said.

I pointed to a small round indentation—almost like a dimple—on Aimee Wallace's left shoulder.

"She's going into shock."

Lee-Lee frowned, looked curiously at the indentation. She couldn't quite figure out what it was.

"I believe he shot her, Lee-Lee," I said.

TEN

We spent several hours giving statements at the Sheriff's Department regarding the accidental shooting of Aimee Wallace. When we were done, I asked Sheriff Powell if I could examine the evidence from Dale Weedlow's trial. She said that wouldn't be possible. The district attorney, Dalton Cullihue, was standing on the other side of the room, talking to one of the EMTs who had treated Aimee Wallace for the gunshot wound. "Dalton," I called to him, "can I look at the trial evidence?"

He looked uncomfortable.

"Don't make me start making phone calls," I said.

He sighed. "Let her in the evidence locker, Renice," he said to the sheriff. "Just put somebody in there with her, make sure nothing gets tampered with."

The sheriff scowled.

"By the way," I said to the district attorney. "I'm not gonna forget about the autopsy report. How about you cough that up, too."

"You still after me about that?" he said. "I thought somebody had sent that over."

"No, actually not."

"Boy!" His eyebrows went up. "I'll be durn. I'll have to check on that."

"That would be nice."

"What's going to happen to Ervin Kindred?" Lee-Lee chimed in.

"It was an accident," Cullihue said. "We'll probably fine him for discharging inside the city limits or something."

"He was trying to shoot me!" I said.

"Aw, now don't be getting all melodramatic. Ervin said his hand was shaking and the gun went off by accident. I believe him."

I rolled my eyes, then turned to the sheriff. "Where's the evidence lockup?"

•

The evidence room was situated in the back of the building, where it doubled as a broom closet. "You use this as a broom closet!" I said. "You ever heard of chain of custody?"

"The room's locked and the janitor's under strict instructions not to touch nothing," the sheriff said. "We don't have any problems with it." She pointed at a gray metal shelf along the back. "The evidence for Weedlow's trial is all in that box on the bottom shelf. Don't be messing with anything else. You can set it on that table, but you can't open the evidence bags and you can't take it out of the room. Clear?"

"Sure."

"And Deputy Woodie's gonna be keeping an eye on you." She indicated the big deputy who had been responsible for framing Lee-Lee.

"Great," I said. "Could you frisk me now, Sheriff? I'd like you to verify that I'm not carrying large quantities of drugs into this room."

"I guess that's the type of thing that passes for humor up in Atlanta, huh?" the sheriff said. Then she left me.

Deputy Woodie stood by the door, watching me with an amused expression on his face as I pulled the cardboard box labelled WEEDLOW off the bottom shelf on the other side of the room.

I opened the box. On top was a log sheet listing everything in the box. Beneath that was a jumble of bags, each sealed with a red label–numbered and signed by Sheriff Powell. The ones that had been used in trial each had a second label, this one blue, with the trial exhibit number written in black ink. Some were plastic Baggies; others were brown paper. The brown paper ones contained tools and bloodstained clothes. The Baggies contained fiber evidence and other small items.

I wrote down a list of all the exhibits on a legal pad, then started going through the box.

I wasn't really sure what I was looking for. I just went through the log, pulled out each bag in turn, verified that it was what the log listed. Then I looked at each item. There wasn't anything that seemed especially noteworthy about any of the items. Since I couldn't open the bags, I had no way of examining the contents of the paper bags–other than to squeeze them. As best I could tell, all the paper bags contained what the log said they did. After I examined an item, I ticked it off my list, taking notes as I went.

When I was done, I checked my list. There was one piece of evidence that I hadn't checked off. Judging by the trial exhibit numbers–which were perfectly consecutive–it hadn't been used in the trial. I checked the log again. I couldn't find evidence control number 0021-43. 0021 was the case number; 43 was the item number. There was no description on the log, just the number 43. I hunted through the box again. It was definitely missing.

"You got a missing piece of evidence here," I said.

Deputy Woodie fished around in his pocket, threw a quarter on the table in front of me.

"What's this?" I said.

"It's a quarter. Call someone who cares."

"Lost evidence is a very serious thing, Deputy."

"Is it really?" he said, giving me a mock-sincere look. Then he sat down on a folding chair on the other side of the table, put his feet up on the table. He was wearing snakeskin boots. "I got news for you, hon, this ain't Atlanta. Sometimes things get lost. We don't permit ourselves to get all worked up over it."

I just looked at him.

"Shoot, Ms. Childs, sometimes even *people* come up lost in this county." He smiled at me. "Be a shame if you was to be one of them."

"If you're trying to scare me," I said, "it's not working."

"I'm just making a observation, hon," he said. "Take it for what it's worth." He took out an extremely large folding knife, started cleaning his nails.

"I'm done here." I reloaded the box, put it back on the shelf. "I'd advise you people to unlose item number forty-three."

"Or what?"

"Or I'll be making more calls to the governor."

"If you're trying to scare me," he said, still working on his nails, "it's not working."

ELEVEN

"Quite the day of excitement, ladies, yes?" It was Mr. Patel, the owner of the hotel. He had brought Lee-Lee and me a small quantity of ice cubes wrapped in a paper towel. They had obviously come from his own freezer. Apparently the hotel ice maker was still broken.

"Is there anything that happens in this town that everybody doesn't know about within five minutes?" I said.

Mr. Patel looked thoughtful. "No, I would say not. I understand Miss Wallace's injury is not serious?"

"They said she's going to be okay," Lee-Lee said. "The bullet didn't hit any bones or major arteries."

"And the famous autopsy report? Have you located it yet?"

I shook my head in amazement.

"Are you saying that everybody in this entire town knows we're looking for the autopsy report?" Lee-Lee said.

"Oh yes. As I say, very little escapes notice." He dropped the ice cubes into the ice bucket with a flourish. "Complimentary!"

I looked into the ice bucket. Four or five ice cubes lay in a little puddle at the bottom. "Thank you," I said. "You really shouldn't have."

"My recommendation, ladies," Mr. Patel said, "would be to speak with Mrs. Charles Woodie, the mother of Brittany Woodie. I like to think of Brittany as the forgotten victim in this tragic matter. Terri Ross was, of course, quite the stunning young beauty and scholar. Not to mention upcoming person of business. So her friend Brittany remains, to this day, in a bit of a shadow. Brittany's mother remains embittered about the whole affair."

"How so?" I said.

"Why don't you ask her yourself? I shall have my son Sunil motor you over. He operates the taxicab service here and knows exactly where she lives."

"We have cars," I said.

"Nonsense!" He picked up the plastic tongs and dropped the few meager pieces of ice in a pair of glasses. "Relax. Enjoy yourselves. I shall return momentarily with a Coca-Cola. Then you shall go with my son!"

•

Sunil Patel was a bored-looking young man with an earring and hair that was moussed up into little points, each of which had been dyed blond. He wore a very large gold watch on the hairy wrist that dangled like a dead animal from the window of the cab. He made no move to help us get into the aging minivan.

"Back door's broke," he drawled. "You gotta come in the front door, crawl over into the back." His accent was indistinguishable from that of any middle Georgia redneck. We got in and he started driving. "Y'all probably can't wait to get out of this miserable town, huh?" he said.

"It's been interesting so far," I said.

"Yeah, I'll bet." He snorted. "Me, I'm saving money. Couple more months driving this cab, boy, I'm outta here for good."

"Oh yeah?"

"Buying a doughnut shop over in Milledgeville," he said. "Maybe invest in a hotel, too."

"That's nice."

"I'm joking," he said. "Every Gujarati in America owns a frickin' hotel or a frickin' doughnut shop. You get ten Gujaratis together and all they talk about is how to squeeze the last nickel out of some fleabag motel. That and how they're gonna marry off their sons to nice Gujarati girls." He parodied his father's accent: " 'It will be sensational marriage, my son. Her father owns two very prosperous Dunkin' Donuts in Greenville, Mississippi.' Screw that, man. Nah, see, I'm a singer. I'm moving up to Nashville. Definitely next month. Or at least by early fall. Get myself a contract with one of the publishers up there, write country songs. After that, I'll try to get a record contract."

"No kidding," I said.

"Sunil Patel–country legend. Got a ring to it, huh?" You couldn't quite tell if he was joking or not. He pulled up in front of a small brick house just outside the Pettigrew city limits.

"This is it," he said. As we were about to get out, he said, "Ask her about RT Miller."

"He was Brittany's boyfriend, right?" I said. "The one who said Dale was at the Dairy Queen that night?"

Sunil looked at me like I was some kind of idiot.

"What," I said.

Sunil Patel's brow furrowed. "Didn't you know?"

"Know what?"

"How long you been here?" He sounded disgusted. "I thought you were s'pose to be like some kind of ace investigator."

"Just say what you're trying to say."

"Pshh!" he said. "Man, everybody in town knows it was RT Miller that killed them two girls."

•

The door to the house opened before we had a chance to ring the bell. I had been a little apprehensive because, in my experience, the families of victims tend to get angry at people who want to investigate once a trial is over. But as it turned out, my worry was wasted.

"I was wondering when y'all would finally get here," the woman who opened the door said brightly. She was wearing heavy makeup and a fashionable blouse that showed a little more cleavage than a fifty-odd-year-old woman needed to be showing. Her hair had obviously been tinted and cut very recently. "I'm Tonya Woodie. Come in, come in, come in!"

She led us into the house and pointed to the far side of the room. "Now I thought maybe y'all could shoot toward that chair over there. I've put Brittany's picture up behind the chair. You can set up your camera right here. I'll get y'all a glass of tea."

She came back with two glasses of iced tea, fussed over us a little bit and then sat down in the chair, just so, her back straight, bosoms out.

"Do I look all right?" she said, smiling.

"You look fabulous," Lee-Lee said. "I *love* that haircut."

"I went to Macon," she said. "When I heard y'all was making this movie, I knew I had to look my best." She cleared her throat. "Well? Y'all ready?"

Lee-Lee turned on the light and started shooting.

Without waiting for a question, she carefully placed both her hands flat on her left knee and began. "My name is Mrs. Charles Woodie," she said. "I have been a widow since my daughter was nine years old. I sell automobiles at Renfrow Buick Pontiac over in Murphy, where I have been the number-one salesperson for over a decade. My daughter, Brittany, was murdered six years ago at the age of twenty-four." She smiled brightly.

"You sound like you've thought a lot about what you want to say," Lee-Lee said. "Why don't you just talk, and then we'll ask questions when you're done."

"Good." She took a breath. "I was, of course, very interested in the trial of Germind Dale Weedlow. I attended the trial in its entirety, including all pretrial motions, jury selection, and sentencing. I have come to the conclusion that the trial was a miscarriage of justice. I base this on the following four issues.

"Issue number one. It is a well-known fact in this town that Deputy David Woodie has used what they call coercive techniques to obtain confessions from suspects. Deputy Woodie is my husband's nephew and I have heard him brag at family occasions how he done this. I heard him say with his own mouth that he has put towels around people's faces and shoved them in a toilet. Which is exactly what Germind Dale Weedlow claimed was the way that he forced this here so-called confession." She smiled again, as though she had just explained all the great features on the new Buick Regal.

"Issue number two. Germind Dale Weedlow is about as big around as a pencil. How, may I ask, is a little bitty fellow like that gonna force two grown women in a car? He never said nothing about using a gun to do it, and there was never no weapon found to indicate he had.

"Issue number three. At the time of her murder, my daughter had just broke up with her boyfriend, Randall Travis Miller—he goes by the nickname 'RT.' Now, RT had beat my daughter unconscious on three separate occasions, which I knew about. The night before the murder, he had come around her house with a shotgun, saying how he was going to kill her. RT is a large, mean, intimidating type person. Could he force a couple gals into an automobile, him and his shotgun? Boy, you better believe it."

And suddenly, she was not smiling anymore. The mask had come off. Hatred and anguish and loss were radiating out of her like a wave of heat.

"That sumbitch is walking around this town every day with a big old grin on his face, knowing he killed her, knowing he got away with it. He's a smart boy. Smart enough to have drug them girls out to where Dale Weedlow worked. Smart enough to have done what he did with Dale's tools. Smart enough and evil enough to have done all that sick stuff." Her teeth were gritted. "I see him on the street every day. Him smiling at me—'How you doing, Ms. Woodie?'—knowing what he done and what he got away with? My God, it takes every ounce of strength I got not to shoot him dead on the sidewalk."

She sat there, eyes brimming with tears but not quite ever spilling over. She took two long, slow breaths. "But I will not let him have the pleasure. He'll have to answer to God one day. And I believe, if there's any good in the universe, that the Lord will let me stand beside Him as He casts that little man down into the lake of eternal fire."

She cleared her throat and smiled her steely smile. "Okay, point number four. Mr. RT Miller testified in court that he had seen Germind Dale Weedlow at the Dairy Queen the night they was killed. But you can ask any of–what?–ten or twelve people in this town who he has personally spoke to and said that he never seen any such thing."

Then she stopped talking and sat looking fixedly at the camera, a bright open-lipped smile on her face.

"So," I said. "Do you have names of people who heard this?"

"I've prepared a notebook for you," she said. "It includes a full list of names."

"You have a theory about how it happened?"

"I do, as a matter of fact. I believe that Terri Ross went over to Brittany's apartment. There's a time line that I've taken the liberty to prepare, which will indicate when she left her own home. I believe that Mr. RT Miller arrived shortly after that, intending to murder my daughter. He then busted into the house and found that Terri was there. Or maybe she walked in on him getting set to kill her. Whatever. Point is, he thinks, *Uh-oh! I'm fixing to get found out.* So he gets them both in the car, takes them out and kills them. I believe he had intended to frame Dale Weedlow from the get-go. Terri just happened to get in the way."

I looked at Lee-Lee. "Can you think of anything else?" I said.

"Mrs. Woodie," Lee-Lee said, "do you happen to know where we could get hold of the autopsy report?"

Brittany Woodie's mother smiled. "Of course, honey. I have a copy right over there in my files."

TWELVE

When we got back to the hotel, my cell phone rang. It was Dalton Cullihue. "Boy, Sunny," he said, "we're having a heck of a time finding that autopsy report. We got this new gal doing the filing in here and, I tell you what, we've had no end of trouble with her."

"Really?" I said.

"Really."

"Well, hey, don't worry about it," I said. "I'm sure it'll turn up eventually."

There was a brief pause. "Well, all right, then," he said. We hung up. I bet he thought he'd really put one over on me.

•

I lay on the bed that evening and read through the autopsy report that Brittany Woodie's mother had given me. It was signed by a guy named Dr. Troy Thallberg.

"That's odd," I said after I'd spent a little time with it.

"Lemme see," Lee-Lee said.

"Hold on," I said. "I'm still trying to make sense of it."

"Did you take classes in condescension, Sunny? I mean, this is *my* movie. How come I don't get to read the autopsy report first?"

"How many autopsy reports have you read in your life?" I said. "Would you even know what to look for?"

Lee-Lee waggled her black-painted fingernails in the air. "What*ever*."

"Usually, these small jurisdictions send bodies up to the Georgia Bureau of Investigation's lab in Decatur for autopsies. Only the counties around Atlanta have their own medical examiners."

"So?"

"So normally the report would be on GBI letterhead and it would be signed Dr. So-and-So, Forensic Pathologist, Georgia Bureau of Investigation."

Lee-Lee dived onto the bed next to me, stared at the report for a minute. "This one just has his signature."

"That's what I'm noticing. He must be a freelancer."

"Is that allowed?"

I shrugged. "Beats me."

"So what's it say?"

"It says both of them died from exsanguination."

"Huh?"

"Exsanguination. Meaning they bled to dead."

"Stop the presses."

"Yeah," I said, "but there's something odd here." I pulled out the folder containing the trial exhibits and said, "Check out this photograph."

Lee-Lee squinted at it. It was the photo that showed the two women hanging from the ceiling of the shed. "It's hard to make out much detail in these photocopies of the pictures."

"Yeah, but look. Even given the quality of the copies, what do you see that's different between the two?"

She shrugged. "This one has a tattoo."

"Okay, yeah, that would be Brittany. But that's not what I'm getting at."

"What's all this black stuff on the floor?"

"Now you're asking the right question. The black stuff is blood. Look. Under Terri's body, there's a big blob of blood. But under Brittany's?"

"Hardly any."

"What does that mean to you?"

Lee-Lee frowned. "Are you saying..."

"The heart's no longer pumping, so you don't bleed much after you're dead."

"Which means she wasn't killed while she was hanging there."

"Whereas Terri was."

"Okay . . . so what does that mean?"

"I don't know. But I think we need to ask Dr. Thallberg."

"What did he say in the trial?"

"Looks like he basically said that they both received similar wounds and that they both died the same way." I flipped to his testimony in the trial transcript. "Quote: 'Cullihue: "Dr. Thallberg, what was the cause of Miss Ross's death in simple terms?" Dr. Thallberg: "She bled to death from multiple wounds." Cullihue: "And Miss Woodie?" Dr. Thallberg: "The same."'"

"So he doesn't specify exactly which wound or anything?"

I shook my head. "Nope."

"Are they usually that vague?"

"This guy testified for a total of about five pages. That's maybe fifteen minutes of testimony. I've never heard of a murder trial where the ME didn't take at least an hour."

"That seems strange."

"We need to talk to old Doc Thallberg." I looked through the transcript. "Says here he lives in Atlanta."

Lee-Lee picked up her cell phone, called information. "Yeah, I'm trying to get the number for a Dr. Troy Thallberg. What? No listing? Can you check all of Georgia? Nothing at all?" She hung up. "That's weird. I hope the guy hasn't died or something."

I plugged my laptop into the wall, logged on to the Internet, ran a search.

"Troy Thallberg, plastic surgeon in Detroit; Troy Thallberg, internist in Maine; Troy Thallberg, proctologist in Florida . . ."

Lee-Lee came and looked. "What about that one?" she said, tapping her finger on the screen. "It's a news article."

"Forensic pathologist loses licence?" I said, reading the abstract. "Oh, this is too good."

THIRTEEN

The phone rang in our room, waking me up. The digital clock next to the bed said 12:29 A.M.

I picked up the phone. "What?"

"Y'all the ones making that movie?" A woman's voice.

"Who am I speaking to?"

"I need to talk to you." The woman's words were slightly slurred, like she'd been drinking. "Meet me at Parker's. Now."

"What's Parker's?"

"Out on Highway Seventeen, right before the county line. It's a nightclub."

"Who am I speaking to?" I said again.

But the line had gone dead.

"Lee-Lee," I said, clipping on my gun. "Get your camera."

"How about I get the gun and you lug the camera," she said.

"Nice try."

•

The woman on the phone had called it a "nightclub." That was an awfully generous use of the term. It was a shack. There were no signs to tell you it was Parker's—just a row of Harleys lined up out front and a red neon Schlitz light in the window of the slapped-together wooden structure. But since it was the only structure at the county line, it had to be the right place.

We pulled into the gravel lot and parked. A large fat man in a black leather vest lay facedown near the door in a puddle of something I didn't really want to spend a lot of time identifying.

"You think he's dead?" Lee-Lee said.

"Don't know," I said. I could see he was breathing–probably just drunk–but it was more fun to leave Lee-Lee in doubt.

"Refresh my memory. Why are we here again?" Lee-Lee said nervously.

Lee-Lee is not exactly the soul of caution, so when even *she* gets apprehensive around a place, you'd better believe you have reason to worry. "Don't exactly know."

"Maybe we ought to stay in the parking lot," she said. "Let whoever it is find *us.*"

"I'm sure there's just a bunch of good old boys in here who like driving hogs and pretending they're bad boys," I said. "Nothing to worry about."

"I still say we ought to wait in the car."

"How bad could it be?" I got out of the car, stepped over the fat drunk, walked toward the door. Lee-Lee grabbed the video camera and followed me. Lynyrd Skynyrd was playing on the stereo as we walked in. Loud. There were three guys at the bar. One of them had a shaved head and a swastika tattooed just above his neck. The next guy had jailhouse tats crawling up his entire arm. The third wore a black T-shirt that said MOTORHEAD on it.

"Then again," Lee-Lee said.

The three men looked around and stared at us. So did the guy at the pool table with the foot-long bowie knife strapped to his leg. So did the bartender with the missing eye. Let's just say it was not a comfortable moment. These were not good old boys. These were criminals.

For about half a second, I considered walking out. But I could see that these people were predators. If we retreated, they'd follow us right into the parking lot. It would take thirty seconds to get back to the car, start the car, get out. Plenty of time for something really bad to happen.

"Whatever you do," I said to Lee-Lee, "don't look nervous."

Then I strolled slowly across the room toward the jukebox, taking my time, trying to look like I wasn't the least bit worried about anything. I could feel everyone in the room looking at us. I smiled at the guy with the swastika on his neck. When I reached the jukebox, I reached around back, unplugged it.

"Hi, folks," I said loudly. "Somebody just called me on the phone. She sounded drunk and stupid. Any of y'all seen somebody like that here tonight?"

"What the–" It was the guy with the swastika. He was staring at me with cold black eyes.

In for a penny, in for a pound. I figured the best defense is a good offense. "I asked you a question, son," I said. There were no women in the bar. Whoever had called, she wasn't here now. "Somebody called me. Who was it? Was it one of your skanks?" I looked around, meeting everyone's eyes. "Yours? Huh? Yours?"

I'd caught them off guard, but I could see they were rallying. The guy with the swastika stood up. "Baby, you in the wrong place."

"You ever hear that song by Dr. John?" I said. "'I was in the right place, but it must have been the wrong time'? Maybe it's the wrong time for *you* to be in here." I had my hand under the tail of my shirt, cradling the butt of my Smith & Wesson.

"I don't understand a word you just said," the swastika guy said. He snapped his fingers at the guy with the bowie knife. "Grab the girl with the nose ring. Bust up her camera while you at it."

A thought flashed briefly through my head: *You should have listened to Lee-Lee and stayed out there in the parking lot.* But it was too late for that kind of thinking, so I brushed it aside.

I pulled my .38, aimed it at the bald guy with the swastika on his head. "If your boy touches her, son," I said, "I'm gonna start tacking holes in your chest."

Nobody moved.

"I asked a question. Who called me?"

"I don't even know who you are," Swastika said.

"Anybody?" I said. "Anybody? Who called me?"

I could see the bartender's hand creeping toward the bar. "Uh-uh!" I yelled at him. He froze.

Swastika, however, edged toward me. He had one hand draped loosely at his side.

"Drop the shank, asshole," I yelled at him.

"You just called me a dirty name," he said. "That hurts my feelings." Everybody laughed.

"Drop it."

He didn't drop whatever he had in his hand. But he had stopped moving–for the time being.

"Start taping, Lee-Lee," I said.

"Huh?"

"Now. Start taping."

She swung the camera up a little uncertainly and then the bright light went on. I walked swiftly over to her. My plan, such as it was, was to distract them, move quickly to the door, and leave. "What's your name, convict?" I said to the guy with the bowie knife. "Huh?"

He looked at me sullenly.

I walked toward the bar. "How about you?" I said to the guy with the black T-shirt. "What's your name? You like making phone calls?"

He winced at the light.

I was careful to stay out of lunging distance from Swastika. He had struck me from the beginning as the leader here, the most dangerous man in the room.

"Swastika," I said. "You? You like making phone calls, wasting my time?"

I could see him calculating times and distances, how quickly he'd be able to get to my gun, overwhelm me with his size and speed.

I didn't give him the chance. I moved toward the door.

"You ladies have a nice day," I said.

Unfortunately, when we reached the door, it was blocked. By

someone very tall and broad. My first thought, was, *Oh well. I tried.*

It was David Woodie. The deputy who had arrested Lee-Lee.

"Well now lookie here!" he said brightly. He had a lump of Skoal under his lip. "Somebody called in a disturbance. Anything going on? Huh?"

Nobody spoke. They all looked at him with flat, empty expressions. Swastika casually dropped his shank. It stuck point-first in the wooden floor right behind his boot. "Nothing going on here, boss," the bartender said. "Y'all see anything?"

"Other than this here crazy lady with the pistol?" the guy with the bowie knife said.

"Hon, you need to put that weapon down," Deputy Woodie said.

"When I'm out in the parking lot," I said.

He smiled. "Have it your way," he said, making a decorous sweeping motion toward the door.

I nodded toward Lee-Lee, waited for her to leave, then followed her. The fat guy was still lying on his face in the parking lot. I holstered my pistol when I reached the car.

"Girls, I got to tell you," Deputy Woodie said mildly, "this just wasn't a smart place to be coming at this time of night. Lot of the fellows in there are a little rough around the edges."

"*You* called us, didn't you?" I said.

He looked at us with an expression of exaggerated innocence. "Do what?"

"What did you do? Get some drunk you picked up on a DWI to make the phone call? Let them off with a warning in return for doing you this favor? Something along those lines?"

"Why would I do that?"

"You were hoping we'd come out here, get the hell beat out of us—or worse—and then you'd walk in and 'save' us. After which, you'd politely suggest that Flournoy County just probably wasn't a healthy place for us to be."

"You have got one fertile imagination," he said. "While you're on the subject, though, the county line's right over there. You could be back in Atlanta in, what, a couple hours? Nothing like being home in your own bed to promote that general sense of well-being that we all crave."

"You're probably not as dumb as you look," I said. "But still. You don't strike me as leadership timber. No offense."

"None taken." He spit a wad of tobacco on the dirt. "You, on the other hand, are probably a good deal dumber than you look. Otherwise, you wouldn't be here."

"My point," I said, "is that I don't think you're calling the shots. Somebody told you to lure us out here. Who was it?"

"*Lure!*" He shook his head. "I swear on a stack of Bibles, I don't know what you're talking about." I couldn't tell from his expression whether he was messing with me or not.

"We got a call from a woman. She said she knew something about Dale Weedlow."

"Hey, all I know, we got a nine-one-one about somebody getting a butt whooping out at Parker's. Since that ain't the case, I'm leaving." He worked the wad of tobacco around with his tongue, then smiled, showing off a row of brown teeth. "Just remember what I told you about people getting lost around here."

"Right."

He climbed into his car, gave us a leisurely wave. "Y'all drive safe."

"You gonna do anything about that guy?" Lee-Lee said, pointing at the fat man lying on the ground.

"Nah, I got a bad back. Wouldn't want to strain nothing trying to move him." The deputy looked down at the fat man meditatively. "By golly, he's a big'un, ain't he." Woodie gunned the engine and fishtailed onto the road, showering the fat man with gravel.

"You think we should help him?" Lee-Lee said.

I gave her a look.

"What!" she said.

"You mind driving?" I said to Lee-Lee. My hands were shaking so hard, I didn't think I was going be able to get the key in the ignition.

She hopped in and off we drove. "Sunny," she said. "You *rock*!"

I looked at my shaking hands and wondered what I was doing there.

•

When we got back to the motel, there was a piece of paper thumbtacked to the door. Scrawled in black felt-tip marker was a message: IT COULD HAVE BEEN A LOT WORSE. NEXT TIME IT WILL BE.

Lee-Lee stared at it for a long time. "Maybe we ought to go," she said finally.

I didn't answer. I just ripped the message off the door, opened the room, threw the wad of paper in the trash.

"Sunny, I'm scared! I don't know if I can take much more of this."

"Lee-Lee," I said, "you started this."

"It must be great always being the strong one," she said sarcastically. She glared at me for a minute, then went in the bathroom and slammed the door. I could hear her crying.

"You think I wouldn't rather be lying in my own bed?" I whispered.

But I don't guess she heard me.

FOURTEEN

I lay in bed for a few hours, flopping around without sleeping. Finally I got up, plugged in the laptop, went in the bathroom, and sat on the toilet while I searched the Internet for more information about the pathologist who had done the autopsies. Eventually, I found that Dr. Troy Thallberg now lived in Tuscaloosa, Alabama, a two-hour drive from Flournoy County. I went back to bed around five o'clock and finally slept for a little while.

•

In the morning, after getting no answer to our repeated calls to Dr. Thallberg, I figured we'd better drive over.

When we got to the address listed in the phone book, all we found was a run-down strip mall. Most of the stores were empty. The only functioning businesses were a check-cashing store with lots of dog-eared Spanish signs in the window and a martial-arts school.

We got out of the car and walked up and down, looking into the empty spaces and checking the address numbers over the doors.

"There's the address," I said when we got to the end of the row. "Two ninety-one Hubert Street." When I went up to the door, I found a gold sign lettered on the glass: TROY KWON DO—WORLD'S MOST EFFECTIVE MARTIAL ART.

"*Troy* Kwon Do?" Lee-Lee said. "Isn't it supposed to be *Tae* Kwon Do?"

"I bet that's our boy, Troy Thallberg."

That's when I noticed a tiny hand-lettered sign next to the door. It read:

CUT-RATE AUTOPSY SERVICES, INC.
RECEIVING DELIVERIES
AT <u>REAR DOOR ONLY</u> !!!!!!

I knocked on the door. Nobody answered.

"Look," I said. "The martial-arts school has a different telephone number from the one I've been calling. Lemme try that one." I pulled out the phone, dialed. After a minute, a pugnacious voice answered. "Troy Kwon Do, world's most effective martial art, Grand Master Troy speaking, how can I help you?"

"Dr. Thallberg?" I said. "Dr. Troy Thallberg?"

"Who is this?" the voice demanded.

"My name is Sunny Childs. I'm involved in a documentary film project about the Dale Weedlow case and–"

There was a click and the phone call was over.

"He hung up on me," I said.

Then I heard a door slam, followed by the sound of running feet. "He's boogying out the back door!" Lee-Lee said.

We ran around behind the building, but it was too late. The alley behind the strip mall was empty. I heard a car door slam and a screech of wheels. We turned and ran back to the parking lot just in time to see an old T-top Camaro with a scoop on the hood peeling out onto the road.

"Let's go!" Lee-Lee said.

We jumped in the car and Lee-Lee roared out of the parking lot, a big grin on her face. In seconds, the needle was on ninety. We could see the Camaro way off in the distance.

"Don't you think you're going a little fast?" I said.

"Hey, you want to catch him, don't you?"

The Camaro turned right onto another road and Lee-Lee followed, tires screaming. "Lee-Lee, you're gonna kill us!" I shouted.

"Remember what I wanted to be before I decided to be a documentary filmmaker?"

"A naval architect?"

"No, before that."

My knuckles were white from holding on to the door handle. "A painter?"

"After that."

I shrugged.

"A NASCAR driver? Remember? How I took all those driving lessons out at the track?"

She jammed on the brakes, nearly rear-ending a pickup truck in front of us. Then she flung us into the oncoming lane, barely avoiding a head-on collision with a school bus.

"Troy Kwon Do, my ass," she yelled as we fishtailed back into our lane. "Your kung fu is garbage, Dr. Thallberg!"

And she *was* gaining on the guy. We were only about a quarter of a mile behind Troy Thallberg's car and gaining fast.

Thallberg hung another right.

Which is when I heard the siren. I turned and there were blue lights in our rearview mirror.

"Aw man!" Lee-Lee said. "Why does this always happen to me?"

"I can't imagine," I said.

•

"Eighty-five bucks!" Lee-Lee said, waving the ticket in the air. "Man, that *so* sucks."

"Well, you were going sixty-three miles an hour over the speed limit," I said. "I'd say you got off easy."

"That cop was a total dick."

"Yeah," I said. "Let's go eat."

We stopped and had breakfast, then drove by the Troy Kwon Do school. There was no Camaro in the parking lot. "I got an idea," I said. I called the number for the school.

The phone rang twice, then a message said, "Congratulations, you've reached the hombu dojo of Troy Kwon Do International, the world's most effective martial-arts system. Please leave a message. If you can't wait to get started turning yourself into a lean, mean fighting machine, call me on my cell at three-two-four-five-five-five-one-two-two-eight. Ooooosssss!"

I dialed the number for Thallberg's cell and then handed my phone to Lee-Lee. "Tell him you want a private lesson. This afternoon."

The good thing about Lee-Lee is that she isn't fazed by much of anything. She took my cue and ran with it. "Hi," she said. "Grand Master Troy? Yeah, my name is Lee. My boyfriend has been beating me up and I'm like really . . . I'm just . . . I'm ready to stop taking it, you know what I mean? Uh-huh. Uh-huh. Wow! You were the world champion! Wow! This sounds like *so* what I'm looking for. Really? So, like . . . would it be possible to have a private lesson? Yeah? Actually, now would be great. Oh. And can I bring a friend?"

She hung up the phone, finished eating her hamburger.

"He said he was the world champion of cage fighting or something," she said.

"Him and every other Tae Kwon Do teacher in America."

"You think he's *lying?*" she said.

•

Ten minutes later, we were sitting on our haunches in the shabby little dojo, listening to Troy Thallberg drone on about how great his martial-arts system was and how if we signed a three-year contract for ninety-five dollars a month, we could be guaranteed a black belt. In my view, any martial-arts instructor who promises a black belt to somebody in return for a given amount of money should be taken out behind the barn and horsewhipped. But that's just me. I had not bothered to tell Thallberg that I had spent the past fifteen years of my life training in the martial arts, and that I taught a women's self-defense class back in Atlanta. But then, he hadn't asked.

"Yeah, that sounds cool," I said when I finally managed to

break into his monologue, "but could you kinda show us some stuff first? Give us the flavor before we start signing things?"

Troy Thallberg was about my age, mid-thirties, with a shaved head. His excessively large muscles and creepy-looking brow ridges told me that he'd gone a little heavy on the steroids over the years. He wore a camouflage-colored karate uniform. His belt was red-and-white-striped. Hanging on the wall was a bunch of certificates that he had awarded himself, the newest-looking one saying that he was a ninth-degree black belt. In the karate system I study, ninth- and tenth-degree belts are reserved for people in their sixties and seventies who have made major contributions to the martial arts over the course of their entire lives. This was not one of those guys.

Thallberg showed me his teeth. "Ah, you're from Missouri, huh? The Show Me State, huh? Huh?" He motioned to Lee-Lee. "Stand up."

She stood.

"Okay, Lee, your friend here likes asking questions instead of listening to sensei. Let's see how that works for you." He put Lee-Lee in a headlock. "Okay, Missouri, so now I got your friend Lee here in a control maneuver. You're from the Show Me State, so show me what you're gonna do about it."

"Well," I said, "I'd hate to hurt you or anything. . . ."

Lee-Lee's face had gotten red and I could see that Troy was squeezing her way too tight.

"Oop! Hup! Nope!" Troy Thallberg squeezed a little harder. "No talking, sweetheart. You're from the Show Me State, so show me. I got your friend in a headlock, so show me how you're gonna help her out."

I walked across the room to a rack of weapons, pulled out a jo—a four-foot-long oak staff—then I walked back to where they were standing.

"Sweetheart," he said, "that's a very dangerous weapon. You need to put that back. But you better hurry, because while you're being a wise guy, I'm choking your friend out." He gave a hard yank on Lee-Lee's neck. She gasped.

I figured the guy was a grand master of the world's most effective martial-arts system, there wouldn't be any harm in my trying to hit him with the jo. I whipped it around, aiming for his head. Dr. Troy Thallberg's eyes widened slightly—just before the loud cracking sound.

.

By the time Troy Thallberg came to, Lee-Lee and I had dragged him into the back room. There was a stainless-steel sink in the corner, a tile floor with a drain in the center, and a stainless-steel gurney in the middle of the room. A rubber hose ran from the faucet up to a hook on the ceiling, from which it hung down over the gurney.

"So," I said. "Cut-Rate Autopsy Service? That really inspires confidence."

Troy Thallberg sat up slowly, holding his head. "What happened?"

"I hit you in the head with a stick," I said.

He looked around, still dazed. I dropped a news article on his lap, the one about how he'd lost his medical licence. He stared at it for a while.

"First off," he said finally. "This is totally not accurate. I did not *lose* my medical license. It was suspended. Temporarily. That's in the past. At this time, I happen to be fully licensed to practice medicine in the state of Alabama."

"What happened back in Atlanta?"

He shrugged. "Look, I was slamming the 'roids a little heavy back then. This pencil-necked sales guy at the mall refused to take some merchandise back and my temper got a little out of hand. There was a little, uh, pushing and shoving. Unfortunately, Macy's had some kind of dumb zero-tolerance violence policy or whatever and they pressed charges. It was all totally bogus, but still I ended up having to plead to assault. That's a felony. You get convicted of a felony, the state licensing board gives you an automatic one-year suspension of license."

"And when did that happen?"

He stared at me for a minute. Then something came over his face, like he suddenly remembered what had just happened. "Hey! You just hit me in the head."

"That's what I told you about a minute ago."

"You're that PI that's been bugging me, aren't you?" He lumbered to his feet. "Get the hell out of my dojo."

"I thought this was an autopsy room."

"Whatever. Get the hell out."

I didn't move. "Tell me about the autopsy. Terri Ross and Brittany Woodie."

He picked up a push broom that was propped against the wall, unscrewed the handle, waved it at me. "Out. Now."

"Or what?"

"You caught me by surprise, babe. That ain't gonna happen again."

"Go ahead," I said. "Hit me. Then you'll lose your license for good."

"I'll tell them you hit me first." He pointed at the welt on the side of his head. "I've got the bruise to prove it."

"And the cops will believe you. A grand master of the world's most effective martial art getting hit upside the head by a skinny little woman." I shrugged. "Hey, you're welcome to try, but I don't know if I'd stake *my* entire future on a bet like that."

Troy Thallberg glared at me. Finally, he threw the broom handle across the room. "Whatever. Stay here all day. But I'm not talking to you."

"Does the city of Tuscaloosa require some kind of special license so that you can cut up bodies in the back of your Tae Kwon Do school? And is your landlord aware of what you're doing here? I could make some calls and find out."

Dr. Thallberg's face sagged.

"Half an hour," I said. "We'll be out of your life for good. All you have to do is talk to us."

He sighed. "All right, all right, all right."

"On-camera," Lee-Lee said.

Thallberg took three long, deep breaths. "Fifteen minutes. But that's it."

•

"Here's how it works," Dr. Thallberg said. While Lee-Lee was setting up her camera, he had gone back into the autopsy room and changed into a suit coat and a button-down shirt. He still had the camouflage karate pants on, though. It was quite a look. "All the Atlanta jurisdictions have their own medical examiners. But everybody else in the state uses the GBI. The way it works, the GBI bills them on a per-autopsy basis. No negotiation. It's just, boom, here's the bill."

He hooked a finger into the collar of his shirt, loosened his tie a little. It still looked very tight on his huge veiny neck. "Some of these little counties, they can barely afford to keep the lights on in the sheriff's department. A homicide prosecution can cost you upward of half a million dollars. These little burgs'll go bankrupt. So they cut costs where they can. I underbid the GBI. It's that simple." He smiled thinly. "Low overhead, that's my secret."

"You're a trained forensic pathologist?" I said.

He cleared his throat. "The AMA states that neither residency training nor board certification in a medical specialty are an absolute prerequisite for practicing in that specialty."

"So you never had a residency in forensic pathology?"

"Uh . . . I did, yeah, uh, *begin* my residency in forensic pathology."

"But you didn't finish."

"I switched to obstetrics and gynecology."

"So why aren't you still practicing as an OB-GYN?"

He hooked his finger under his collar again. "It was basically an insurance thing," he said.

"Humor me and flesh that out a little," I said.

"Well, I was involved in a . . ." He licked his lips, picked up a water bottle next to his leg, took a long pull. "Atlanta is a very litigious area. I had the bad fortune to be on the wrong end of several lawsuits involving, you know, brain-damaged babies and stuff. Totally not my fault, needless to say. But you know how insurance companies are. They're craven jerks. Ultimately, because of just like a small handful of totally groundless lawsuits, I was unable to get obstetrical insurance. So I'm like, *Well, maybe I'll try this forensic pathology thing.* Turned out to be a great gig. No overhead, no receptionists, no medical techs, no nurses. It was going along real good until—"

"Your dispute at the mall."

"Yeah."

"All right. So. Dale Weedlow."

"I get a call from the sheriff of Flournoy County. She's like, 'We're in a budget crunch—blah blah blah—can you cut us a deal—two autopsies, one special price, that type of thing?' I said, okay. So the bodies show up and I open the bags and I'm like, *Oh Jeez!* Guts coming out and flies and everything. I mean, you get used to this stuff and all, but—" He cleared his throat.

"Bottom line here is, you cut corners on the autopsy."

"Hey! Look!" Troy Thallberg's face hardened. "I take my work very seriously."

"Still. They have a suspect in custody. They have a confession. You have guts hanging out, flies all over, they chiseled you down on the price . . . So you figure, *Hey, let's not knock ourselves out. This one's a no-brainer.* Right? That a fair assessment?"

"I conducted a routine and thorough examination according to standard protocols."

"Uh-huh."

"I con*ducted* a rou*tine* and *thorough* examin*a*tion according to—"

"Yeah, you just said that. Were there any differences in the two reports? Did you find significant differences in time of death or cause of death between Brittany Woodie and Terri Ross?"

"Let me see the report." I handed him the autopsy report. He leafed through it. "Basically, no. Both died roughly thirty-six to forty-eight hours before they were found. Both were stabbed repeatedly and then slit from the pubic bone to the sternum."

"The cause of death?"

"I concluded that the stabbings killed them."

"The stabbings alone? Or the stabbing and gutting combined?"

"Sort of a combination."

"Specifically, how was it done?"

"Basically, he hung them up and tortured them to death. What exact stroke of the knife killed them—or the screwdriver or whatever?—you couldn't pinpoint it. It was cumulative. They bled out."

I handed him the photograph I'd showed Lee-Lee the night before. "Did they give you these photos?"

"It's been a while—but that's standard practice. I'm sure I would have seen them."

"So you looked at this one?"

He shrugged. "It was six years ago. Plus, this is not a big help." He held the smudgy black photocopy up so it was visible to the camera.

"Look on the floor there," I said. "What's that?"

He squinted. "It appears to be a puddle of blood."

"One puddle of blood? Or two?"

His face drained of color. "No, that's—wait . . ."

"There's a large puddle of blood under Miss Ross. But under Brittany?"

"That can't be."

"Tell me about postmortem bleeding."

Troy Thallberg continued to stare at the photo. "There was blood all over them! It was almost impossible to . . ."

"Isn't it true that once a person is dead, the body doesn't bleed in the same kind of quantities as it does while the heart is still beating?"

Thallberg shook his head but didn't answer.

"Brittany was killed somewhere else, wasn't she?" I said. "Then she was hung up there, stabbed, violated, cut open so that it would look like she and Terri were killed the same way, by some crazed sex killer. But that wasn't how it went down, was it?"

Thallberg sat, still as a stone.

"You autopsied Terri first. She had obviously bled all over. You got done. It was getting late; you were tired, you were irritated that you had to do all this work for so little money—whatever. So you fudged the second report. Didn't you?"

Thallberg stood. "We're done here."

"You didn't autopsy Brittany at all, did you? You don't have the first clue what killed that girl. Or where she died."

He pointed his finger at me. "That kid confessed! It doesn't matter."

"It does and you know it. And when we find out what really happened—"

Thallberg turned abruptly and walked back into the back room. The lock clicked shut.

"It's gonna come out!" I yelled.

Lee-Lee looked at me and shrugged. I shrugged back.

Lee-Lee aimed the camera at the door, then walked over to the door and started pounding. "Dr. Thallberg? Dr. Thallberg? Do you have any idea what really killed Brittany Woodie? Dr. Thallberg?"

There was a short sharp bang.

Lee-Lee looked around at me, eyes wide. "What was that?"

I didn't say. But it was obviously a gunshot.

"Dr. Thallberg!" She pounded on the door some more.

I went over and switched the camera off. I had a sick feeling in my gut.

"I don't think he's coming out," I said.

FIFTEEN

We were tied up for the rest of the day in Alabama, getting things sorted out with Troy Thallberg's suicide. It turned out he had a history of personal problems that went way beyond the ones we'd found out about. Drug problems, rehab, steroid abuse, sexual-harassment allegations from female martial-arts students, a brief hospitalization for psychological problems, and a string of police citations for belligerence and odd behavior in Tuscaloosa. No one seemed shocked that he'd killed himself.

By the time we got back to Pettigrew, it was well past dark. I drove straight to Tonya Woodie's house. She was just driving up herself, in a sparkling-clean late-model Buick. We got out of the car.

"How you doing, Mrs. Woodie?" I said.

She smiled her bright, fierce smile. "I sold two Park Avenues and a used TransSport with a three-year after-market warranty," she said. "I didn't think about my daughter more than five times. It was a good day."

I told her what we had found out that day about the falsified autopsy.

"What should I do?" she said.

"I think she should be exhumed and reautopsied," I said. "But I guarantee you, people will fight you on it."

Her jaw hardened. "We'll see about that." She pulled out her phone. "Lemme talk to Mr. Justice." She waited awhile, then said, "Earl? It's Tonya Woodie. I need my little girl dug up and autopsied.... Don't you give me that. Don't you dare. You know as well as I do that you can make it happen. I want her body coming out of the ground first thing tomorrow, and don't you give me a lick of shit about it."

Then she hung up and smiled.

"Oh, I'm feeling good now." She lighted a cigarette, started pacing up and down next to her car, seeming not to notice our presence. "Feeling good now."

SIXTEEN

"We've only got three days till the execution," Lee-Lee said as we drove back to the motel. "We really need to find something fast."

"We need to know more about this trial." I frowned. "You know what? I've got an idea." I turned the car around and headed for Milledgeville, the nearest town of any size. The hospital in Milledgeville was where Ervin Kindred's secretary, Aimee Wallace, had been sent after the accidental shooting in his office.

•

I bought a bouquet of daylilies in the little flower shop near the front door of the hospital, then took the elevator to the second floor. We found Aimee Wallace sitting in her room, reading her Bible while *Entertainment Tonight* played silently on the TV over her bed.

"Brought you something," I said.

Aimee Wallace closed her Bible, keeping her finger stuck in the middle of it to mark her place. "Well, that's very sweet of y'all," she said, without a trace of warmth. I could hardly blame her for not being eager to see us.

"We just wanted to apologize for all the trouble we made," Lee-Lee said. "We feel terrible about what happened."

I put the flowers next to her bed. I was surprised to see there weren't any other flowers in the room at all. It suggested to me that she didn't have many friends. "How are you feeling?"

"I'll be fine," she said. There was a brief, awkward silence. "I don't want you to think that Mr. Kindred meant to pull that trigger."

"Oh, sure," I said. Anything to be obliging.

"It's just his hands shake sometimes."

"I know what you mean," Lee-Lee said. "One time when I was in college, me and some friends were drinking Jägermeister and–"

I gave her a look and she shut up.

"He's a brilliant man, you know," Aimee Wallace said. "Everybody knows he's the best lawyer in this part of the state." She sniffed. "Or he used to be anyway." She had unrequited love practically stamped on her face. I had sensed it even when we were in the office. But now I was sure, she was madly in love with poor old Ervin Kindred.

I sat on the edge of her bed. "You've done everything you could to help him, haven't you?" I said.

She took a deep breath, stared out the window. "I have prayed and prayed and prayed and prayed. I've thrown out his liquor. I've washed his clothes. I've begged him to stop. I've written his children. I've just tried so hard."

I patted her hand.

"He wasn't always like this," she said. "Back in high school, all the girls had a crush on him. He and Earl Justice were in the same class, you know. Earl was the quarterback of the football team and Ervin was a receiver. They went to the state play-off that year. Don't remember if they won or not. Ervin got that scholarship to Harvard, and it was like the most glamorous thing. Half the town went down to the train station to see him off. That was when they still had a train running through town.

"He came back and got married, started practicing law with his father. Then he got married. He married Earl Justice's sister, you know. Rose. Most beautiful girl ever lived in this town. And they were so happy. You could see it on their faces. Made all of us jealous just to be in the room with them." She smiled wistfully, with just the smallest hint of bitterness around her eyes.

"Rose got the diagnosis, oh, must have been when their boys

were in elementary school. Took her five years to die. Brain cancer. Toward the end, she couldn't talk, couldn't feed herself, couldn't walk. Oh, it was just the most awful thing. Ervin suffered so. Ervin was never the same after that. He'd always liked a drink–but not in a bad way. But after his wife died, people used to say, 'Oh, he's sitting around at home drinking by himself.' I thought it was just malicious gossip. Because you never saw any sign of it during the day. If anything, he was a better lawyer after his wife passed away. I think the work distracted him from everything that hurt him inside. He stayed strong till the boys graduated high school. But after that . . ."

She shook her head sadly.

"After that, he stopped trying."

We sat for a while. I was hoping I could get things moving toward the trial, but I wasn't sure just how to do it. It's a delicate thing. I was afraid if I pushed, she'd freeze up. She was no dummy. If there was anything wrong with that trial–and I believed there was, and I believed she knew it–she also knew that we had the potential to make the man she loved look like a fool. Or worse. I was trying to figure how to get her there, when I looked over and saw Lee-Lee crying, tears just rolling down her face.

"Oh, honey," Aimee Wallace said. "It's okay. You don't need to be like that."

"Sometimes the world just seems so damn *sad*," Lee-Lee said.

Aimee Wallace nodded.

"It's like you're rolling along and everything's fine. And then suddenly–" Lee-Lee snapped her fingers. "Suddenly it all goes wrong."

Aimee Wallace nodded again.

Lee-Lee pawed at her face, smearing her mascara all over the place. "Sometimes I just hate this world."

Aimee Wallace blinked. She had a funny expression on her face, like nobody'd ever said a thing like that to her before, like it was something she'd been thinking for a long time, a sentiment that she had hidden away, unwilling even to admit to herself. "Yes," she said softly. "Sometimes I do, too."

Lee-Lee turned and looked her in the eye, an intent expression coming across her face. "What happened in that trial, Miss Wallace?"

Aimee Wallace turned away.

"I mean—something happened. Didn't it?"

"I believe it was the last straw," Aimee Wallace said. "Even then, you'd never have known about Ervin's . . . problem. He might take a drink or two late in the afternoon. He might look a little ragged around the edges in the morning. But it never affected his work. Never. Not until that trial."

She opened her Bible, glanced at it, closed it again.

"Ervin was court-appointed. That was not the usual thing. Most court-appointed work goes to a fellow over in Milledgeville. But after Dale Weedlow got arrested, we got a call from Judge Calhoon. He just called up and said, 'Ervin, you're it.' Ervin didn't have to ask what he meant. He just hung up and said, 'Amy, I got a bad feeling about this.' He calls me Amy, you know. Always has, even though my name's Aimee.

"Anyway, he went over and met with that Weedlow boy, and when he came back, he said, 'They're gonna railroad this kid, Amy.' And I said, 'He didn't do it?' And he said, 'I don't know. Maybe he did.' So he started talking to witnesses. He started looking at the evidence. For a few days, he got real excited. He was talking about how this whole case was gonna fall apart. It was almost like the old Ervin was back." She closed her eyes. "He even brought me flowers one day!" She smiled. "But then . . ." Suddenly, her face took on a closed look and she stopped talking.

"Then what?" I said.

She shook her head sharply. "What's wrong with me? Why am I talking to you?"

I couldn't quite think what to say.

But Lee-Lee still had that intent look on her face. "You know why!" she snapped.

Aimee Wallace looked at her for a long time; then she nodded vaguely. "There was one witness that we couldn't get to talk to us–RT Miller, Brittany's boyfriend. A terrible person. He was fixing to testify that Dale was at the Dairy Queen the night of the murder. So one day Ervin puts on his coat and says, 'Well, I'm just gonna have to go talk to RT Miller myself.' And he went out there, talked to RT Miller, and when he came back, he had a big old bruise on his face. But he was kind of grinning. He said, 'RT Miller may have just kicked this old man's butt. But he gave up something.' I said, 'What did he tell you?' And Ervin said, 'It wasn't *what* he said. It was what he *didn't* say.' And I said, 'I don't understand.'

"Ervin just smiled at me. Like he was keeping some kind of secret from me. 'Just you wait.' He winked at me. 'Just you wait, Amy,' he said. 'When he gets on the stand, I'm gonna break that nasty little SOB like a matchstick. Him and that fool that did the so-called autopsy.' Then he kind of danced around the room. I hadn't seen him like that in years. It just lit up my heart!"

"What went wrong?" I said.

Aimee Wallace looked out the window. "One day, Earl Justice came by the office. Earl and Ervin had been friends all their lives, but over the years they'd drifted apart. Especially after Rose died, Earl's wife kind of failed to include him in their circle. So it was a little unusual, him visiting the office. Anyway, they went into Ervin's office and closed the door. Then there was a lot of shouting."

"What did they say?"

Aimee Wallace's face went blank. "I couldn't say."

"You can't? Or you won't?"

"There are things I can't say. Things I will never say."

"But . . ."

The room was silent for a long time. Finally, Aimee Wallace said, "Earl left and Ervin shut his door and stayed in there all afternoon. When it was time to leave, I found him lying on the floor. He'd been drinking vodka straight out of the bottle all afternoon."

"And then?"

She shrugged. "You know the rest."

"Tell us," I said. "Please. An innocent man's life is at stake here."

"You can read the transcript for yourself."

"Come on," I said. "You can do better than that."

"The defense stipulated to the autopsy."

"*Mr. Kindred* stipulated to the autopsy."

"Ervin was not himself," she said primly.

"What was wrong with stipulating to the autopsy?" Lee-Lee said.

"That autopsy was a joke. Read the two reports. Except for the location of the wounds on the two girls' torsos, they're the same thing. Word for word. You don't stipulate to a key element of the prosecution. On his worst days, Ervin knew that."

"You're saying Earl leaned on him somehow and he threw the case."

Aimee Wallace clenched her jaw. "I'm saying that Earl Justice must have done something terrible to Ervin. Because Ervin is a good man. Ervin would never throw a case."

"But he did that time, didn't he?"

Aimee Wallace didn't speak.

"Why would Earl Justice have an interest in this case?"

"Earl Justice is a man who never let his marriage vows stand between him and any woman he was interested in. . . ."

"What do you mean?"

"I don't think it was a coincidence that it was the day after Ervin spoke to RT Miller that Earl came over."

"What are you saying?"

"I don't guess anybody ever gave him a DNA test or anything. But it's pretty generally acknowledged around town that RT Miller looks an awful lot like Mr. Justice."

"You're saying RT Miller is Earl's *son?*" Lee-Lee said.

No answer.

"Miss Wallace," I said. "Are you saying that Mr. Kindred found evidence that might have showed it was RT Miller who was guilty? And not Dale?"

Aimee Wallace took a deep breath and then opened her Bible. "I've said too much already," she said. "And if y'all ever ask me these questions again, I don't care what the circumstances, I'll never speak a word."

Lee-Lee said, "But Miss Wallace we need this on tape."

"We're talking about malpractice, young lady," Aimee Wallace said calmly. "If any of this came out, they'd disbar him. Mr. Kindred has nothing left but his work. If he were disbarred, he would drink himself to death inside of six months. I will not have that on my conscience."

"But—"

"Thank you for the lovely flowers." Aimee Wallace didn't look up. "I'd like to get back to my Scripture now."

SEVENTEEN

They dug up the body first thing the next morning. I had to make a lot of phone calls—to my brother Walter, to Barrington, to everybody I knew in the GBI—trying to get the autopsy moved to the top of GBI's list. It took a while, but by the time Brittany's casket came clear of the ground, I had secured a commitment from the GBI medical examiner that Brittany Woodie would go to the top of the queue. The autopsy, they said, would be done by nightfall.

I stood with Brittany's mother at the edge of the cemetery, watching the backhoe as it loaded the casket onto the back of a flatbed truck. Lee-Lee was shooting the scene from a tripod near the grave site.

"This may not help us at all, Tonya," I said. "The autopsy might not show a thing."

Brittany's mother took a pull on her cigarette and said, "Better'n a poke in the eye." She pointed her cigarette at the casket. "Six years, look how good it held up. That there casket cost nine thousand six hundred forty dollars. I bought it at cost. Steel-lined box, pressure-treated wood, gold-plated bronze fittings. Pays to buy quality. That's what I tell my customers." She blew out a long trail of smoke. "Pays to buy quality."

•

"So," I said to Lee-Lee, "you up for talking to this RT Miller guy?"

"No time like the present," she said.

I called the hotel. "Mr. Patel."

"Sunny Childs! Where were you yesterday? We were quite literally insane with worry!"

"In Alabama. So, look, do you know where RT Miller works? We need to talk to him."

"Mr. RT Miller! Oh, he's a very bad fellow, I must tell you."

"Where does he work?"

"At DCI, of course. He operates some sort of huge machinery. Past tense, actually. Sadly, the mining industry is going through quite a slump at this moment. I have heard that Mr. RT Miller was laid off recently."

"So where does he live?"

"I will send Sunil. You must have a man with you when you confront this beast, Mr. RT Miller."

"We'll be fine."

"No, no. Absolutely out of the question. I'll send him over to the cemetery right this very minute. Chop-chop, as they say."

"How did you know we were—" I didn't bother to finish my question. "Never mind, everybody knows everything about everybody."

"See! You are learning!"

•

Sunil Patel arrived at the cemetery about half an hour later. Which didn't seem very chop-chop to me, given that nothing in the town was more than a two-minute drive from anything else. He had Toby Keith blasting on the stereo, and a guitar sitting in the passenger seat, with a seat belt wrapped lovingly around it.

"What up, y'all?" he said.

"We're going to see RT Miller."

"Man, y'all are crazy," he said. "That boy'd just as soon kill you as look at you."

"Your dad says you're going to protect us," Lee-Lee said.

Sunil turned, looked her up and down wistfully, then said, "Sweet thing, I'm a lover, not a fighter."

As we drove, Sunil sang along with Toby Keith. He had it down perfect—every redneck dipthong and hiccup, every nasal vowel. He was actually pretty good.

"I'll wait out here," he said when we pulled up in front of a mobile home a few miles outside of town. "If you need anything . . . call nine-one-one." He laughed loudly.

"Thanks," I said. "You're a prince."

We climbed out, walked down the cracked concrete path, and up to the door. I banged hard with my fist.

"It's open, for God sake! You don't got to break down the door."

We walked in, found a tall man sitting on the couch in his undershorts and undershirt, drinking beer and watching a female bodybuilding contest on an extremely large TV. He looked up at us for a minute, his gaze lingering for a while on Lee-Lee's chest, then looked back at the television. RT Miller was handsome in a corn-fed redneck sort of way. Kind of like Toby Keith, come to think of it.

"What y'all think?" he said, gesturing at the TV. "These gals all rug-munchers or what?"

"Look, Mr. Miller," Lee-Lee said. "The reason we're here—"

"I know why you're here. Grab a beer and sit down. But if you point that camera at me, so help me God, I'll crack it in half." He showed no trace of emotion whatsoever as he said this.

"So, Mr. Miller, you know that everybody in this town thinks it was you that killed those two girls, not Dale Weedlow," I said.

He smirked briefly. "Call me RT," he said. "Everybody else does."

"You want to answer the question?"

"I wasn't aware there was one."

"*Are* you aware," I said, "that people think you killed Terri and Brittany?"

"You been talking to that Brittany's mother, ain't you?"

"We've talked to a lot of people."

Miller looked out the window, eyed Sunil's taxi. "What's happened to this country?" he said. "I try to be tolerant, but these sand niggers turn my stomach." He stood, picked up a baseball bat that was leaning against the wall, and strolled down the walk toward Sunil's minivan. Sunil was sitting on the back bumper, playing guitar.

"Uh-oh," Lee-Lee said.

"Gimme that!" Miller said, yanking the guitar out of Sunil's hand. He tossed the guitar up in the air like a baseball, took a nice lazy swing at it that smashed the sound box to matchsticks. "Now get off my damn street, boy, or the next one's gonna be upside your head."

Sunil stared at him, shocked, then jumped back in the van and sped away.

Miller walked back into the house, smiling pleasantly. He set the bat down next to his legs, clapped his hands together. "Everybody in this country just took responsibility like that, we wouldn't be having all these terrorism problems, would we?" He ran one finger idly around the knob on the end of the bat. "Now, what was it y'all was asking me?"

"Did you kill those girls?" Lee-Lee said.

"Which girls?" Miller pretended to be puzzled.

"Terri Ross and Brittany Woodie."

He snorted. "I heard they was raped with a screwdriver. Now I ask you, what kind of sissy would do a thing like that when they got ten inches of manhood to work with?" He held the bat up between his legs, laughed. He set the bat back down, ran his finger around the tip again. I noticed he had a crude jailhouse tattoo on the back of his hand.

"What did you do time for?" I said.

"The first time?" He smiled briefly. "Or the second time?"

"Either."

"First time was simple assault. Hit this fool with a baseball bat. The bar where it happened? They found one of his teeth drove half a inch into the wall."

"And the second time?"

"That'd be rape." He smiled. "Sorry to disappoint, hon, but it was only statutory. I ain't never forced myself on nobody. I consider that to be unsportmanlike."

"Usually statutory rape ends up as a plea from some nastier charge."

"Not when it's the judge's daughter." He cackled. "You should have seen that old bird's face. Give me a big speech about the sanctity of a girl's maidenhead. I swear to God, his exact words. If he'd of knowed how many men his little virginal daughter had been banging, he'd of throwed a rod, I tell you what. I was just the unlucky one to get caught."

"Can you account for your whereabouts on the night of the murder?"

"I was playing cards with some buddies of mine. It's all on record. I only went out once, and that was for about twenty minutes. Went down to the Dairy Queen to get a burger."

"Who were you playing cards with?"

"I just said. Some friends."

"Names."

"I don't have to give you no names. It's on record."

"Where?"

"In some police file, I'm sure."

"Earl Justice hired you, knowing half the people in town suspected you of killing one of his employees?"

"One? They was both his employees. Brittany worked in the same office Terri did."

I looked at Lee-Lee. Lee-Lee looked at me. We'd obviously had the same thought. What if it was Brittany—rather than Terri Ross—who had contacted the lawyer in Atlanta?

"You ever hear Brittany talk about a lawsuit? Maybe some papers she found that proved DCI was—"

"That ain't how I know Earl Justice don't believe I killed them girls."

"What do you mean?"

"You just not asking the right questions."

"What *are* the right questions?"

He stared at the TV, ignoring me as he watched a scary-looking woman posing in a red-white-and-blue bikini.

"What *are* the right questions, RT?" I said.

"Boy, these here plasma-screen TVs are nice, huh?" he said. "You could practically lick the sweat off that gal's buns, couldn't you?"

I made a quick grab for the baseball bat, but he snatched it away. "Uh-uh, baby," he said. "Everybody in town's talking about what you done to that karate dude over in Alabama. You ain't touching *no* sticks in my house."

I looked at Lee-Lee. "Y'all just don't have *any* secrets in this town," she said.

"No, we do not," RT Miller said. "Tell you what, though, I might be willing to tell you what you want to know."

"What's the catch?"

"Y'all ask me a question. If Marilyn Manson here"—he pointed at the tattoo on Lee-Lee's shoulder—"if Marilyn takes off an article of clothing, I'll answer. We just keep going till she runs out of clothes."

"Forget it," I said.

"You're a little on the skinny side, but if you got any more to ask, I'd consider letting you take your clothes off, too."

I ignored him. "Before she died, did Brittany ever tell you about a bunch of papers that Terri had gotten from DCI? Papers that would have proved Earl Justice was screwing people out of kaolin royalties? Papers that would have cost Earl Justice a lot of money?"

"Maybe," RT Miller said. "That's my first answer. Hon, you can either take off your shirt or your pants; I don't care which."

"No, let's play a different game," I said. "Let's do it this way. How about every question you *don't* answer, I break something. Now, did she ever tell you about those papers or not?"

RT seemed vaguely amused. "Hon, you talking pretty big for a girl that don't even got a stick in her hand."

I did a side thrust kick into the plasma screen. It cracked in half, smoke coming out of the middle, circuits frying. "Who says I need a stick?" I said.

"Oh no," he said. "No, you didn't." He picked up his baseball bat, rared back to swing it at me.

Smooth move, Sunny, I was thinking.

"Don't even think about it, RT," a voice said.

We all turned around. There was Sunil standing in the doorway, pointing a mammoth pistol at RT Miller. It must have been a .44 Magnum. I mean huge.

"All right, boy," RT said, tossing the bat on the floor, "let's don't start writing checks we ain't prepared to cash."

"While he's pointing the gun at you," I said quickly, "I'll repeat my question. Did Brittany tell you about some papers that Terri got from DCI?"

RT looked at me for a long time. "I might have heard Brittany say something about having some papers."

"Let me be clear. Brittany had the papers? Or Terri?"

"Well, it wouldn't have been Terri Ross."

"Why not?"

"Terri Ross was Little Miss Loyalty," he said finally. "She and Earl Justice was tight, man. She wouldn't have sold him down the river like that."

"Would Brittany have?"

RT Miller put an aggrieved expression on his face. "Look, you come out here accusing me of stuff, you bust my TV. I ain't got nothing to do with none of this. This is wrong. I'm a workingman, just try to scrape by. I ain't talking to you no more."

"Why should I believe anything you say?"

"You asked earlier whether Earl suspected I had anything to do with Terri and Brittany getting killed? Shoot, if he had even a *suspicion* I'd killed Terri, I'd of been flat *done* in this county. Instead, he hired me. What's that tell you?"

"Huh," I said.

"He *knew*," RT said. "He *knew* I ain't did it."

"Maybe we should go, ladies," Sunil said. "While he's still calm."

It seemed like a valid point. We hustled out the door and down the street toward the minivan, which was parked about two hundred yards away.

"I'ma send you a *bill* for that TV!" RT Miller yelled after us from the door of his mobile home; then he threw down his bat, extended his left hand, and shot us a bird.

"Dog!" Sunil said when we reached the minivan. "I think I might have crapped my pants."

"I thought you hung us out to dry when you drove off," I said.

"Just a little strategic withdrawal, girls," Sunil said. "I parked around the corner and came back."

"You did good," Lee-Lee said, putting a hand on his shoulder. Then she kissed him on the cheek. Sunil looked at her like he'd just been kissed by an angel.

"Let's just go," I said.

EIGHTEEN

We drove up to Atlanta, took I-20 over to Decatur, a suburb of the city where the GBI had its headquarters complex. As we pulled into the parking lot, I saw Tonya Woodie standing out front of the GBI medical examiner's building, smoking a cigarette. She held up the butt toward us as we approached. "Figured I might need a little fortification before I went inside." Then she stubbed it out.

We were met in the lobby by Dr. Irene Moss, the chief medical examiner for the state. On all the TV shows, medical examiners are beautiful and fiery and witty. I can't say it's true of every ME . . . but very few of them are either beautiful or fiery or witty. They tend to be, well, kind of odd. Dr. Moss was no exception. She was tall, pale, humorless, awkward, just the slightest bit creepy.

"Come back to my office," she said. "We'll talk."

There was no chitchat. She just launched into her speech, like she was testifying in front of a jury. Her voice was loud and monotonous, her consonants strongly dentated.

"I completed the autopsy of Brittany Dawn Woodie today at three P.M. She had been embalmed and buried. You bought a very nice coffin, Mrs. Woodie."

"It pays to buy quality," Tonya Woodie said. "That's what I tell my customers."

"The body was in an excellent state of preservation, given the length of time she had been buried. There was general dessication and some necrosis of tissues in peripheral areas, but by and large, a remarkably well-kept body. Congratulations."

"Thank you," Mrs. Woodie said.

All of which seemed pretty weird to me. Congratulations, your daughter makes a nice mummy.

"Before beginning my autopsy, I reviewed the police file, including all photographs of the crime scene. I did not, however, review the report of Dr. Troy Thallberg until after completing my own autopsy."

As she spoke, Dr. Moss did not refer to any notes, apparently keeping a complete record of the autopsy in her head.

"I began my autopsy by conducting an external examination of the body. The subject weighed one hundred and eight pounds and was five feet two inches tall, both of which are less than the recorded numbers for the subject in life but are consistent with dessication and postmortem tissue shrinkage. I found that the subject had a large vertical incision from the pubic bone to the sternum, which had been crudely sutured. I found multiple stab wounds in the thorax. The entry wounds were torn rather than sliced, but minimal and ovoid. This makes them consistent with a rather dull implement, such as a screwdriver or similar tool, rather than with a knife—which would have left a thinner and neater wound—or with an ice pick—which would have left a smaller, circular wound.

"Investigation of the hands and arms noted no bruising, torn fingernails, or other evidence of defensive wounds. The age of the body makes this part of the examination particularly problematic, however, as the extremities were the least well preserved parts of the body. These observations, however, are consistent with the photographic evidence provided by the district attorney's office.

"I further noted evidence of blunt-force trauma to the skull, specifically four depressed cylindrical fractures of the cranium. One here, one here, one here, one here." She pointed to her own head: hairline, behind the ear, twice on the back of her head just above the neck. "Based upon the location and shape of the wounds, I would say that the first blow was to the front of the head and was struck by a right-handed person. The wounds were consistent with a stick or cylindrical piece of metal. This blow probably rendered her unconscious. At that time, she probably fell and was struck three more times from above, also by a right-handed person.

"I removed the top of the skull, taking care not to disturb evidence of fracturing. Bone fragments were noted in the brain at locations corresponding to three of the four blows to the head. This indicates that she was struck very hard with an extremely hard and heavy object."

I might have expected Tonya Woodie to break down or leave the room, but she just sat there motionless, hands folded on her knee, a fixed and queasy smile on her face.

"The brain was removed and weighed. It was found to weigh six hundred and thirty-two grams, a weight consistent with normal dessication. The entire brain was coated with dried blood, indicating extensive subdural bleeding. Further investigation revealed multiple hematomas corresponding to the blow sites.

"I then examined the body cavity. A small quantity of dried blood was noted in the body cavity. Organs were removed and weighed, with no remarkable findings. That in itself is remarkable. No wounds to the internal organs were noted. My conclusion, based upon this finding, is that the initial incision to the thorax was performed prior to the stabbings. The digestive organs, by and large, had fallen out of the body and were therefore not punctured.

"I then went back and reviewed the photographs provided by the Flournoy County district attorney. Based upon my review, I noted that there was not a significant amount of blood beneath the hanging body. I would also point to photographs of the body that revealed the presence of a whitish chalky substance. Presumably, this substance was washed off by the undertaker before embalming, as I did not find any trace of it during my examination.

"Finally, I examined the rectum and vagina. There were multiple abrasions in both, but no evidence of bleeding. This is critical, because it is the one area that I feel confident would not have been washed or otherwise interfered with by the undertaker.

"Another important point. Based upon my examination of the incision, I believe that the victim was cut from the pubic bone to the sternum. This would be a natural cut to a body that was hanging. Had the incision been made while the victim was lying down, it would have been more natural for the incision to have been made from the sternum to the pubic bone as the head interferes with one's cutting arm when going from pubic bone upwards.

"It is difficult to draw absolute conclusions. The body was cleaned and embalmed after the first autopsy. There may have been significant quantities of blood found in the peritoneal cavity. There may not have been. This is an important point. If there were, that meant she was alive when the incision to the thorax was made. If not, she was already dead by that time. However, as noted, the vaginal damage appears not to have caused bleeding.

"However, it is my medical opinion that the cause of death was most likely blunt-force trauma to the head. The wounds to the victim's head were substantial and fatal. Whether the stab wounds and the incision occurred immediately, it is not entirely possible to say. However . . . based upon the fact that the incision appears to have been made while the victim was hanging, and based upon the lack of blood on the floor and based upon the lack of blood in the vagina, I would judge that the victim had expired before she was ever hung up.

"In my conclusion, I will state that cause of death was blunt-force trauma. Type of death was homicide.

"Now, let me speak to the general nature of the crime. It is my belief that the victim was struck repeatedly in the head by a right-handed person. Furthermore, based on the lack of defensive wounds, I believe the victim knew the attacker. I believe the victim was hung up after she had died and was then stabbed, cut, and penetrated with tools. I believe she probably did not suffer at all."

A long, slow breath escaped from Tonya Woodie's lips. I put my hand on hers, squeezed. "Thank you, honey," she said.

"I have not had occasion to examine the other body, of course, but based upon the amount of blood present on the floor in the photograph, I believe she was probably killed in an altogether different way from Miss Woodie. It would seem that the logical conclusion is that someone was attempting to make their deaths seem similar—when, in fact, they were quite different. Perhaps even, in some respects, unrelated."

"Unrelated?"

"I'm not comfortable drawing too many more conclusions. What I am suggesting is that this crime scene was set up to look like something it wasn't. Someone was hiding something. Perhaps Miss Woodie was killed in an altercation; then Miss Ross arrived and the killer realized he would have to kill her, as well. He then set up this bizarre crime scene in an attempt to make it appear they had been killed by a sexual predator. Bottom line, I believe the 'torture' of Brittany Woodie was faked."

"Thank you, Doctor," Tonya Woodie said softly.

"I should also note that once I completed my work, I reviewed the autopsy report produced by Dr. Thallberg. It is quite clearly a fraudulent report. He conducted no examination whatsoever. I intend to report him to the AMA, to the state medical licensing board, and to the attorney general of the state of Georgia. I hope that not only will he be stripped of his license to practice medicine, but that he will be criminally prosecuted."

"No need," I said. "He killed himself yesterday."

"Good for him," the doctor said in her loud monotone. "That will save me at least twenty hours of tedious and distracting effort."

"How soon can we have a report?" I said.

"My assistant is printing it up as we speak." She stood abruptly.

"You'll have to wait in the lobby, though. I have to go to ballet practice now."

We walked out to the lobby, sat in silence.

"Ballet practice," Tonya Woodie said finally. "Wouldn't have seen that coming in a million years."

NINETEEN

The next morning, Lee-Lee said to me, "You know, we need to go out to the crime site, shoot some video."

"We better call Earl Justice," I said, "get permission to go on his land." I called DCI, asked how I'd go about getting permission to shoot at the pit where the crime had taken place. I got bounced around, finally reached Earl Justice himself.

He laughed. "I thought y'all would have been gone by now."

"Nope." I repeated my request for permission to film the crime scene.

"Hon, nothing personal, but ain't a snowball's chance in hell I'm gonna do that. Besides, I don't own that land. We mined there under lease."

"So who owns it, then?"

"I'm afraid I can't divulge that," he drawled. "You girls have a nice day." He hung up.

When I told Lee-Lee what Justice had said, she went, "Hey, supposedly it wasn't even a very active mine six years ago. I bet there's nobody there at all. Let's just sneak in."

•

It took us some winding around to find the property. The road it was on was not on any of the maps in my car. All we had to guide us were the trial transcripts and a hand-drawn map made by the Sheriff's Department, which said "Not to scale" at the bottom.

"You think that's it?" Lee-Lee said.

We were on the side of a rutted gravel road, unmarked, surrounded by a thick stand of planted pine. Looking through the trees, I could see a flash of something white—a rusting sign attached to a chain-link fence. "One way to find out," I said.

Lee-Lee grabbed the hi-def camera and we started hiking through the woods. The pine trees were planted in rows, so it was almost like walking in a cathedral. The pine needles on the ground absorbed all noise. There were no birds, no squirrels, no nothing. Planted pine forests are biological deserts. The decomposing needles turn the soil acidic and the unbroken cover high above discourages the growth of all bushes, weeds, and seedling. It was a little creepy.

After a couple of minutes, we reached the fence. It was about eight feet high, topped with razor wire. The sign on the fence read NO ADMITTANCE WITHOUT AUTHORIZATION. There was an identical sign posted about every hundred feet along the fence.

"Doesn't look much like a mine," Lee-Lee said.

On the other side of the fence was a broad meadow. "They must have filled in the hole," I said.

"Who's going over first?" Lee-Lee said.

"Lift me up," I said. Lee-Lee laced her fingers together. I pulled a Leatherman out of my purse. It was one of those multitools with a screwdriver and a saw and all that stuff. Included was a wire cutter. I clipped a few loops of razor wire, pulled them free from the top of the fence, and heaved them into the bushes, cutting the crap out of my hand in the process. Then I climbed over.

Lee-Lee handed me the camera, then climbed over, too. When she got down, she turned on the camera and panned slowly across the meadow.

"To see it today," she said in the stilted voice of a TV newscaster, "this peaceful site hardly seems to be the scene of a terrible crime. But six years ago, two depraved and grisly murders were—"

"I hope this is not going to be that kind of documentary," I said. "I hate that kind of thing."

Lee-Lee looked at me peevishly. "All you do is criticize. Can't you be the least bit supportive?"

"I'm here, aren't I?"

Lee-Lee frowned suddenly, cocked her head.

"What?" I said.

"Did you hear that?"

"Hear what?"

"I thought I heard a door slam."

We crouched motionless, scanning the big meadow. It must have been eight or ten acres in size. Nothing moved at all.

"Let's go," I said, pointing to the large metal building on the far side of the meadow. "That's where it happened."

We hiked across the meadow, tried the door. It wasn't even locked. I pushed the door open and we walked in. I flicked the light switch, but nothing came on. The power had been disconnected.

Lee-Lee turned on the camera and the light threw a feeble white glow across the room.

"Whoa!" Lee-Lee said. "The card table is still there."

She pointed. And sure enough, the table on which the murder weapons had lain was sitting there against the wall, exactly as it had been shown in the crime-scene photos.

Lee-Lee filmed as we walked toward it. The light was eerie, not quite making it to the far corners of the room. "Oooooo-oooo-ooooo!" Lee-Lee said, making a kid's spooky ghost noise.

We had reached the table, when the two of us froze.

BANG!

"I heard it that time," I said.

"What was that?"

"I don't know."

"Let's hurry," Lee-Lee said.

I looked at the table. There were no tools on it anymore. On the floor underneath it, though, were a number of boxes. I looked at them, then pulled the photocopies out of my purse, compared them to the crime-scene photos. The boxes had been there for six years. Untouched, apparently.

I pulled the first box out. It was empty.

I pulled the second one out. It, too, was empty. Lee-Lee swung the camera toward us. I was about to push the boxes back, but I caught a flash of something. I leaned over and grabbed it.

"What is it?" she said.

"A cuff link." I held it up in the light. It was gold, rectangular, with a small diamond set into the corner.

"You think it might be the killer's?"

"Strong possibility. It's not the sort of thing mine workers wear."

Lee-Lee zoomed in closer. "I don't much see RT Miller as the cuff-link type, do you?"

"No, I don't," I said.

"Any monograms or anything?" Lee-Lee said.

I shook my head.

BANG! This time it sounded like somebody had just kicked the side of the shed. Suddenly, I had a terrible thought that RT Miller might have tracked us out here.

"Uh-oh," I said, tucking the cuff link into my pocket. "We better get out of here. Fast."

We ran to the door and out into the meadow. We were too late. Standing in front of us was a man. But for a minute, I didn't see his face. All I saw was the gun. It was a shotgun, the barrel looking about a mile wide as it pointed toward my face.

TWENTY

"Oh," the man with the gun said. "You."

The man pointing the gun was black, elderly, dressed in a pair of overalls and a white shirt. It was Love Pinkston, the barbecue cook who had been suing Earl Justice all these years.

"What are *you* doing here?" I said.

"I own this property." He lowered the gun. "DCI leases it from me."

"So this is the property you sued Earl Justice over?"

He nodded. "Y'all talk to that lawyer up in Atlanta?"

"Yes."

"Then I expect y'all got questions for me. It's just about lunchtime. Come on over."

We walked slowly across the meadow. "I used to raise peas, corn, sorghum out here," he said. "Now I can't do nothing with it. DCI still pays me a couple dollars a year to maintain the lease. There was an automatic renewal clause in the lease, I got no control over it. Mr. Justice does it just to spite me, so I can't do nothing with it myself. As you can see, they ain't mining it no more. So it just lays here. Every penny they pay me goes straight to the property taxes."

"You think you'll win the lawsuit?"

He shook his head. "Nah. But a lawsuit takes on a life of its own. Everybody gets dug in; ain't nothing you can do about it."

We passed through a gate in the fence and down a little path that led to a small white frame house with a tractor parked next to it, and a barn and a hog pen out back. Several large brown hogs were moving around in the pen, jamming their noses in the mud.

"I'll be just a minute, ladies," Pinkston said.

We stood in the yard for a while; then Pinkston came back out with a tray. On the tray were three paper plates containing large piles of pulled pork, a stack of white bread on the side, and slaw, plus three glasses of iced tea. "Dig in," he said.

We stood in the yard while we ate. The barbecue was as good as ever–smoky, rich, with just enough kick in the sauce. The hogs in the pen snuffled nervously, maybe recognizing the smell of one of their kinfolk.

"So were you here when the murders took place?" I said.

"I must have been," he said. "I never heard nothing, though."

"How far is it from your house to that shed?"

"About a quarter mile. If the shed door was closed, they could have screamed all day long. I'd have never heard nothing."

"You ever speculate about what happened?"

"Speculate? No ma'am."

"Where do you think the killer parked? He must not have parked right by the shed, because he walked them through the mud."

"That's what he wanted you to think, at least."

I frowned at Mr. Pinkston, puzzled. "What do you mean?"

"He was parked right next to the shed. Wasn't no need to walk them through all that mud."

"What do you mean?" I said. "You *saw* the killer's car?"

"Sure," he said impassively. "The driveway to the mine ran right slap up by my house. Five years they ran that mine, there wasn't a minute of it I wasn't picking dust out my teeth, all them trucks and graders and loaders and tractors driving by."

"What did the car look like?"

"One of them fancy English automobiles. What you call them?"

"A Rolls? A Jaguar?"

He snapped his fingers. "Jaguar. That's it."

"Really?" Lee-Lee said. "There couldn't be many of those around here."

"Oh, no, ma'am. Not many a-tall."

"I assume you told the sheriff."

He kept chewing the sandwich. "No, ma'am."

"Why not?"

"I look like a fool to you?"

"Not really," I said.

"Only one Jaguar in town back then. Nice red Vanden Plas."

"You *know* who drove the car?"

"I ain't no fool. I might sue Mr. Justice. But, my goodness, I ain't gonna tell the high sheriff that it was Mr. Earl Justice's automobile drove up here that night. No telling what might happen to me."

"Good God!" I said. "Earl Justice's car was here the night those girls were killed?"

"Mm-hm," he said mildly.

"Your lawyer," I said, "told us that a young lady called him the week before Terri and Brittany were killed. The woman said she had documentation proving that people who were leasing land to DCI were being cheated."

"Yes, ma'am, he told me that, too."

I set my empty plate on the wheel of the tractor next to us. "Well, come on! It doesn't take a genius to connect the dots."

"No, ma'am." He took my plate, then Lee-Lee's, set them on the tray.

"Can we interview you?" Lee-Lee said, picking up her camera.

The old man looked impassively at her. "Let's wait on that just now, ma'am," he said, "see how things develop. Y'all have a blessed day."

He took the tray and hobbled back toward the house.

TWENTY-ONE

"Look at the report," I said.

After our lunch with Love Pinkston, we had gone to find Dalton Cullihue. We had finally managed to track him down at the Big Lake Hunt and Skeet Club, where he was shooting skeet with a couple of his friends.

"I'll look at the report presently, Sunny," he said. "Pull!" Two orange clay pigeons flew through the air. Cullihue hit the first, missed the second. "*Son* of a gun!"

"Time's a-wastin' here, Dalton," I said. "This report demonstrates clearly that this kid deserves a new trial. At a minimum."

"Defense stipulated to the autopsy. You can't go back and claim defect to something you stipulated to. That ain't gonna fly."

"No responsible attorney would stipulate to the autopsy."

"The autopsy wasn't an issue in the trial."

"It sure should have been."

"Look, Mr. Weedlow has already appealed, based on inadequate counsel, and his appeal was denied. It's a moot point. You can't appeal the same issue twice."

"But *you* could petition for a stay, say there's new evidence, that the prosecution's no longer comfortable with the verdict."

"Pull!" He fired again, this time nailed both clays. "Ha!" he said.

"I trust you'll at least read the report."

"Look, it's irrelevant. Dale Weedlow confessed. He tried to weasel out later. Now he's gonna die. A few blemishes in the autopsy will not change my mind."

"Blemishes! His whole so-called confession was based on a reconstruction of the crime, which was fed to him by the sheriff. His entire confession scenario is directly contradicted by this new autopsy report. Dale Weedlow said he hung them up while they were alive and then tortured them. This report says clearly that's not what happened."

"I'll look at the report," he said. "But unless you got another suspect—a solid suspect, not just somebody that people *think* might have done it—then don't waste your time looking for me to go running up to the governor with some kind of clemency appeal."

"There's a missing piece of evidence. Evidence control number oh oh two one-four three."

"These things happen. Was it used at trial?"

"No."

"Well, there you go. Probably wasn't even important."

"Or the Sheriff's Department hid it because it shot a hole in their case."

"Come on, we could sit here doing this all day, finding minor inconsistencies in Weedlow's trial. Give me a suspect. Give me evidence."

"You know," I said, "I have a witness who places a car at the scene of the crime that night. And it's not Dale Weedlow's."

"I suppose this alleged witness never bothered to tell this to the sheriff?"

"Well..."

"Uh-*huh*. And I bet this alleged witness also probably knows exactly and precisely whose car it was, based on—what, the plates, the distinctiveness of the automobile, something like that?"

"As a matter of fact, yes."

"Terrific. And who is this witness?"

"I can't say."

"Oh, I see." He smirked. "So whose car did this mystery witness see at the scene? Probably somebody he didn't like much, am I right? Happens all the time. People get in a custody battle, a business deal that goes wrong, whatever—and all of a sudden they're seeing all kinds of criminal behavior from the person they're in the dispute with. Every time a witness comes forward—especially after years have gone by—you got to ask, *What's their motive?*"

He was right about that much. Love Pinkston certainly had motive to dislike Earl Justice.

"Well, well, well!" a voice behind us said. I turned and there was Earl Justice, pulling a double-barreled English shotgun out of a walnut case. "Lee-Lee! Miss Childs—we meet again! I'd invite y'all to do some shootin' with us, but I'd be afraid to turn my back on you with a gun in your hand." He smiled broadly. "Hey, I'm just fooling."

"Well?" Dalton Cullihue said to me. "Whose car *did* your mystery witness see at the scene of the crime?"

"Never mind," I said. "I'll tell you later."

"I thought time was a-wastin' and all that," he said.

I turned and began walking toward the parking lot.

"Moody little critter, ain't she," Earl Justice said.

A rumble of laughter followed me as I walked away.

TWENTY-TWO

I called Walter in Atlanta and said, "Need some advice."

"Sure."

"You've got an in with the governor. I think it's a pretty sure bet this kid didn't kill those two girls. But we haven't figured out who did it yet. We're getting close to the deadline. How do we get a clemency appeal to the governor?"

"Normally, a clemency appeal would be handled by the attorney for the death-row inmate. I think the governor's chief of staff would be the guy who handles it within the governor's office. He's a guy named Arnold Arnold."

"Boy, give his mom and dad an *A* for originality."

"Better yet, he's actually Arnold Arnold *the Fourth*. Not a big family history of thinking outside the box. But anyway, I'll make some calls and find out what to do."

"Great."

"Meanwhile, you need to get in touch with this kid's appellate attorney."

"I'll do that."

•

The attorney handling the appeal turned out to be a lawyer from Atlanta–no surprise there–named Karen Spruel. Lee-Lee had traded phone messages with her a couple of times in her not very thorough research for the film, but they had never met. I called her office and her secretary said that she was actually on her way to Flournoy County, that she should be arriving any minute.

"Where's she staying?" I asked. Looking out the window of my hotel room as I talked, I saw a battered Honda pulling into the lot. A chunky, harried-looking woman was getting out. She had a hook where her left hand was supposed to be. "Hold on," I said. "Her left hand . . . is it, uh . . ."

"Yeah," the secretary said. "That's her."

•

I walked out of the room and called across the parking lot. "Karen Spruel?"

The harried-looking woman looked at me nervously. "Yes?"

I walked over and introduced myself. "Oh! God!" she said, clutching her chest comically. "You about gave me a heart attack. I get death threats every time one of these cases gets close to conclusion."

"'Conclusion,'" I said. "That's a mild word for a man getting killed."

She laughed brightly. "I've been practicing death-penalty law for fifteen years. If you take these cases too personally, you burn out fast. I always try to keep the big picture in mind."

"Bless your heart," I said. "I've never been real good at that."

"The death penalty is an assault on the American proletariat," she said. "One day, we'll all be free of this kind of oppression. In the meantime, I just keep fighting my little fight."

"'Proletariat,'" I said. "I haven't heard that word since I dropped out of the commune back in '68."

Apparently, she didn't get my joke. She gesticulated enthusiastically, waving her slightly scary-looking prosthesis uncomfortably close to my face. "Everywhere in America, there are little places like this, little places where the hopes and dreams of the poor and working class get squashed and ground down—or worse, bought off."

"I think your hook's caught in my shirt," I said.

"Oh! Sorry!" She untangled her hook from the hem of my T-shirt, leaving a small gash in the fabric. "I get a little carried away sometimes."

"Look, you want to come over after you get settled?" I said.

"Actually, I'm glad I found you. I assumed your boss would want to interview me for the film."

"My boss."

"Lee Edwards? You are working for her, aren't you?"

"Something like that," I said.

"Excellent," she said. "She seems like a very committed young woman."

"Uh-huh," I said.

•

I went back to the room to find Lee-Lee, but she had gone out by the nonfunctioning pool to sunbathe. Committed indeed. The lawyer came over to our room about five minutes later and said, "Well, you ready to tape my interview?"

I said, "Lee-Lee's gone out for a moment. But before I get her, I was kind of hoping to talk with you a little. We've uncovered some really important information."

"About what?" she said.

"It looks very much like Dale Weedlow might be innocent."

She looked at me curiously, then she began laughing brightly. "Oh, you had me going for a second there, Sunny!"

"No, seriously," I said. "I don't think Dale Weedlow killed those two women."

The lawyer sat on my bed and kind of bounced up and down a little. "Yeah," she said. "Innocence. Hm."

"What?" I said.

"Well, I don't mean to sound condescending or whatever, but the first few times you get involved in death-penalty cases, you tend to get distracted by the whole innocence thing."

"The innocence thing."

"It's like I was saying earlier. There are larger historical forces at work here. If you get too embroiled in the minor particulars, you sometimes get distracted."

I raised one eyebrow. "Minor particulars. Like whether he did it or not?"

She dismissed this trifling issue with a flick of her hand. "Yeah, well, they're all innocent, aren't they? In a way? Deprivation, abuse, broken families, poverty, oppression, unfulfilling work, low IQs—whatever. It's not like most murderers *chose* to be killers. They were forced into a box by historical circumstance."

I was starting to get frustrated. "That's what I'm saying. I don't think he *is* a killer."

She patted the bed with her hook. "Isn't this a great little hotel? It's kind of like a model for the world historical situation right now. A guy comes halfway across the world with the intention of becoming, you know, a bourgeois plutocrat, and meanwhile the Coke machine's broken, the pool's empty, and there's no ice."

"I have evidence," I said. "The autopsy was a fraud."

"I'm afraid that's probably not dispositive," she said.

"His lawyer was a drunk."

"True. But we already lost our appeal based on incompetent counsel."

"Brittany Woodie may have stolen a bunch of extremely incriminating documents from Earl Justice. They could have cost him millions in this lawsuit. None of this came out in the first trial."

"I hate to tell you, but the Supreme Court of Georgia really, really, really doesn't like new evidence. We've exhausted our appeals based on error in the first trial. No, at this point, unless you can think of an ingenious technical argument, then poor old Dale's pretty much screwed. You're not a lawyer, are you?"

"No, but we're turning up a lot of fresh evidence...."

"I think you should prepare yourself. Obviously, I'll file the standard clemency appeal. But odds are strong that poor old Dale's gonna die tomorrow." She smiled the sunny smile of a woman undistracted by minor particulars, then she stood and looked out the window at the pool. "Boy, it's a shame about that pool. I could sure use a swim right now."

●

After we finished filming an interminable interview with Karen Spuel and she finally left our hotel room, I said to Lee-Lee, "Boy, you hear cops complain about pinko defense lawyers all the time, but—wow—an honest-to-God *actual* Communist! I thought she'd never shut up about the proletariat and Trotsky and world historical forces and all that crap."

"Why do you have to be so critical?" Lee-Lee said. "She seemed very committed."

"Yeah," I said. "Committed to getting Dale Weedlow killed. She doesn't care anything about the guy. He's just a little cog in the great world historical machine."

Lee-Lee glared at me. It took me a minute to figure out what she was mad about.

"You're annoyed because I asked all the questions," I said.

"Everywhere we go, it's like, 'Lee-Lee, set up the camera. Lee-Lee, go fetch this. Lee-Lee, go do that.' Then you ask all the questions. Dude, you're not the director of this film. I am. I'm sick of it!"

"I don't feel like arguing," I said.

"It's *my movie!*"

"Yeah, but it's Dale Weedlow's life."

"Oh, and only the brilliant investigator Sunny Childs is qualified to save people's lives."

"Hey!" I said. "For you, this is some kind of little dilettante whim, some brief interlude between NASCAR and flower arranging. Fine. But for me, this is not a notion. This is what I do. Dale Weedlow can't afford to stake his life on whether or not you'll figure out how to be a good investigative filmmaker in the space of a week."

The phone rang, interrupting us. It was Walter calling from Atlanta. "I just got off the phone with Arnold Arnold, the governor's chief of staff," Walter said. "He can give you five minutes this afternoon."

I hung up and said, "We need to go talk to Arnold Arnold up at the statehouse."

"Hey, you don't need me." Lee-Lee was wiping away tears. "You never have. Go by yourself."

Lee-Lee stomped out of the room and slammed the door.

Great, I thought. *Way to go, Sunny.*

TWENTY-THREE

"Usually it's the inmate's attorney who makes clemency appeals," Arnold Arnold IV said. "This is very irregular."

After leaving Lee-Lee to calm down by herself, I'd driven close to two hours for my meeting with the governor's chief of staff. We were seated in Arnold's office in the state capitol building in downtown Atlanta.

"I'm not making a formal appeal at this moment," I said.

"Then what are you doing here?" Arnold Arnold was a red-faced, irritable-looking man, one of those heart-attack-waiting-to-happen kind of guys, with an unusually fat neck that looked like it was about to explode out of its collar. The two pencils and the one piece of paper sitting dead in the center of his spotless desk looked like they had been laid out with a carpenter's square. I sensed this was a guy who hadn't made an intuitive leap in decades.

"Like I said, we'll have a formal written appeal tomorrow. I just wanted to go over the information we had so that at the eleventh hour you'd be able to digest whatever we have for you properly."

"Well, I sure appreciate your thinking about my digestion." He looked at his watch. "Your brother's a friend of mine, so I'll give you your full five minutes. Don't waste it."

I pulled out a folder and started to hand it to him. He held up his hands.

"I don't have time to read!" He looked at me like I'd just asked him to smell a wet dog's ass. "Give me the headlines here."

"This young man, Dale Weedlow, testified in trial that his confession had been coerced."

"Wait! Wait, hold up! He *confessed?*"

"After being tortured, yes."

Arnold Arnold IV stared at me with his little red-rimmed eyes. "Aw, come on now, Sunny. Every scum-sucking freak on death row says the cops tortured them. I don't have time to listen to that nonsense."

"The one person who testified that Mr. Weedlow was with the victims? He also happened to be the boyfriend of one of the victims—an ex-con with a history of violence, who had threatened the life of one of the victims the day before the murder. None of that came out in trial. Thanks to the dead-drunk lawyer who represented him. Furthermore, it appears that one of the victims had been stealing evidence that would have incriminated the big cheese in this town, a man named Earl Justice, and very likely lost him a huge passel of money in a lawsuit he was fighting. Finally, the GBI has determined that the autopsy in the case was falsified. This kid was railroaded."

Arnold Arnold squinted at me. "I'm confused. So are you saying the boyfriend did it? Or this big cheese, Earl Justice?"

"We're, uh, working on that."

"I'm very much heartened to hear that. Because Earl Justice happens to have been one of the largest contributors to the governor's campaign and a close personal friend of mine for over twenty-five years."

Gee, I was thinking, *kinda wish I'd known that.*

"Look, what we're hoping for is a stay of execution, that's all. We just want to have a chance to investigate this matter properly. If we don't turn anything up soon, let him die."

Arnold Arnold glared at me. "Sounds to me like you got nothing."

"At this moment, we're not asking for clemency. Just a stay. To clarify matters."

"I believe clarity is the responsibility of the twelve men and women who convicted him. Until and unless you got unimpeachable evidence that somebody else did it, I guarantee you, there will be no stay and no clemency from this governor. Thank you for stopping by. Please give my best to your brother."

I took that as my cue to leave.

When I reached the door, though, Arnold called after me. "Word of advice, young lady. You want this boy to have a snowball's chance of getting the governor's help, you better, by God, stay away from crazy accusations about a fine man like Earl Justice."

TWENTY-FOUR

The sun was low on the horizon as I headed back into Flournoy County. I called Lee-Lee on her cell phone.

I'm sorry the cell phone you are calling is currently not in service.

I'd gotten the same message four times in the past hour. Cell phones. They were great until you really needed them, then they never seemed to work.

I pulled up to the motel, parked, walked to the door of our room, and fumbled in my purse for the key. Then I noticed the door was already open.

"Lee-Lee?" I pushed the door open. As it swung in, I saw that the lock housing was smashed and the door frame split. Somebody had kicked in the door. I pulled my .38 and slipped through the door.

The place had been trashed. Our bags had been opened and our clothes were scattered across the room. The drawers were pulled out of the dresser, the TV turned over, the mattress pulled off the bed. I moved quickly through the room. No one in the closet. No one in the bathroom. I yanked back the shower curtain. Empty. The cameras, I notice, had been taken out of the cases and thrown on the mattress—but they hadn't been stolen or broken, and the tapes Lee-Lee had made of the interviews had not been disturbed.

Then I saw a note lying in the middle of the mattress. At first, I thought it was the same note that had been tacked to our door the other day. It was written in black marker on white paper. But then I realized, no, this was in a different handwriting. Besides, I'd wadded the other one up and thrown it away. I picked up the note.

we've taken her. let things run their course and she'll be fine. if not . . .

I pulled out my cell phone again, dialed Lee-Lee.

I'm sorry the cell phone you are calling is currently not in service.

I sprinted down to the hotel office. Mr. Patel sat behind the desk, watching a cricket match on TV. "Mr. Patel! Mr. Patel! Have you seen Lee-Lee?"

Patel looked up at me, then motioned at the TV. "Satellite TV. What a godsend. Cricket is a civilized game. Around here it's football, football, football—all this smashing and grabbing, it's not dignified and it doesn't make sense."

"Mr. Patel. Please! Have you seen Lee-Lee?"

"Oh, yes. Earlier, she was sunning by the pool while Sunil serenaded her. I don't know where they are now."

I glanced out the window. The cracked patio by the pool was empty.

"Odd," Mr. Patel said. "They were there not fifteen minutes ago." He pointed at a space in front of the office. "The taxi is gone. He must be transporting her somewhere."

"I've called several times, but she's not answering her phone."

"Do not, please, be agitated." Patel smiled, pointed to a radio next to the TV. "I have the CB radio. Band twenty-one, always on in the taxi." He picked up the handset. "Base to taxi one. Base to taxi one. Come in, please?" He grinned at me. "There is no taxi two, you know, but it makes Sunil feel as though he is part of a vast business empire."

The CB radio crackled once, but there was no reply.

"Atmospheric conditions, no doubt," Patel said. He keyed the microphone again. "Base to taxi one. What's your twenty? Please, come in." He frowned. "Base to taxi one. Base to taxi one."

"Somebody trashed the room and left a note," I said. "I'm a little worried."

"They what?"

"I'll show you."

Patel made a feeble gesture toward the cricket match but then followed me down to the room.

"Good Lord!" he said, when we reached the room. "This is quite disturbing."

"No kidding," I said, showing him the note.

"We had better call the police," Patel said.

My cell phone rang. I answered it quickly.

"Sunny?" A man's voice.

"Who is this?" I said.

"It's RT Miller. How about you and me have a little talk?"

"About what?"

There was a brief pause. "I think you know. Let's just say we got a subject of mutual interest to discuss."

"You son of a bitch."

Another pause. "Let's not get all excited. Meet me over at the old sawmill on Seventeen." The phone went dead.

RT Miller was a bastard, but he wasn't stupid. If he had kidnapped Lee-Lee, he was probably smart enough not to admit it on a cell phone.

I put my phone back in my purse. "Let's not call the police just yet, Mr. Patel," I said.

"But—"

"I have to go. If she and Sunil aren't here by the time I get back, we'll call the police."

•

I knew where the sawmill was because you had to pass it coming into town from the north. It was a ramshackle collection of corrugated iron sheds surrounded by a rusty fence. Sitting by the gate was a restored black El Camino with a huge hood scoop and flames painted on the sides. If RT Miller had been a car, he would have been that one–a nasty redneck with aspirations he'd never meet.

It was almost dark now and the old buildings looked like big hunchbacked animals squatting in the middle of a primeval forest. I didn't like this place. My heartbeat sped up a little.

"Miller!" I yelled.

No answer.

"Miller!"

My voice echoed off the dilapidated old buildings. I pushed open the rusted gate and walked toward the biggest building. The back side of the building was open to the air, no wall at all. I walked into the dark space. I could hear something rustling in the darkness. A rat? A bat? The mill was a little over two stories tall, with rusty chains hanging from the ceiling. Two massive rotary blades sat at the end of a pair of log feeders. It was obvious the place hadn't been used in a long time. I walked through the center of the building, between the two blades, paused next to one of the massive saws.

"Sumbitch'd cut you clean in half," a voice above me said.

I looked up into the gloom, and there was RT Miller standing on a steel catwalk that overlooked the plant. "What did you do with her?" I said.

RT Miller squinted down at me. "Do with who?"

"Stop playing," I said. "You called me out here, now tell me what you did with her."

"Put the gun away."

I fired a shot that zinged off the railing, near his hand, then plowed a small hole in the wall. "I'm a good shot," I said. "I did that on purpose. The next one won't miss. Now, where is she?"

Miller looked genuinely puzzled. "What the hell are you talking about? Where is *who*?"

"Lee-Lee."

"Who? Oh. The hot one. With the Marilyn Manson tattoo."
He smiled, showing off the teeth on one side of his mouth.
"What, did something happen to her?"

"She's been kidnapped."

His left hand rested on the railing of the catwalk. He was tapping his fingernails on the rail, making a noise like a very quiet
steel drum. "I don't know nothing about that."

I watched his fingers tapping, tapping, tapping. Something
about it seemed odd to me, but I couldn't quite place it. Then it
hit me. In my mind, I could see him swinging the baseball bat,
smashing Sunil's guitar.

I picked up an ancient piece of scrap wood and threw it at him.
He lifted his hand off the rail and caught it smoothly. "You gonna
have to do better than that, doll," he said.

"Bet you can't hit me with it," I said.

"Wouldn't want to." He sailed the two-by-four through the air.
It was close enough to me to make me nervous. But I could tell
he wasn't trying to hit me.

"You're a lefty," I said.

"Huh?"

"Left-handed," I said. "You're left-handed."

"So?"

Brittany Woodie's killer had been right-handed. The GBI medical examiner had been clear about that. Whatever game RT
Miller was playing, I was wasting my time. I'd been looking in the
wrong place all this time. I turned and started walking away.

He called out to me: "The papers!"

I turned.

"The papers you was talking about when you came by my
trailer. The ones that Brittany had stole from DCI. I'm here to discuss that with you."

I frowned. "Wait. So . . . you really don't know where Lee-Lee
is?"

"Nope."

"Or Sunil?"

"Why would I care about him? Now I'm asking you—you want these here papers or not?"

"You know where they are?"

He showed some teeth, a parody of a smile.

"Don't mess with me," I said. "I'm carrying a thirty-eight revolver and I am distinctly not in the mood. Do you have the papers or not?"

"Not on me."

"Where are they?"

He spread his hands. "You getting ahead of yourself, sweetheart."

"Look," I said. "Somebody appears to have kidnapped my cousin. I don't have time to mess around."

RT Miller sat down on the steel catwalk, started swinging his legs like a kid in a chair that was too big for him. "Hey, suit yourself."

I started walking away.

"But just for the sake of argument," he called, "let's spose that these papers have got somebody a little peeved at y'all. Let's spose that's why they want Weedlow dead. Let's spose they snatched Lee-Lee. Don't you figure that you'd be in a better position to negotiate with . . . whoever . . . if you had them papers? Hm?"

"Is there something you know that I don't?"

"I don't know nothing. I'm just a dumb country boy."

"Where are the papers?"

He just sat there, swinging his legs.

I pointed my pistol at him. "I am getting very, very, very impatient."

He looked at me without the least sign of fear. In fact, he seemed to find the whole thing kind of funny. "You ain't gonna use that." He patted the section of catwalk next to him. "Come on up here, set next to me."

I put the Smith away, walked up the stairs, sat next to him. He just kept sitting there, swinging his legs.

"Okay, okay," I said. "Enough!"

"Little towns are all about equilibrium," he said. And then he sat some more.

I didn't say anything.

"I got me a college degree while I was in prison," he said. "You the first person in this town I ever told. How about that, huh?"

I could see that he had something to say and he was going to say it in his own way, no matter what I did. The best thing I could do was shut up and let him get it over with. Sometimes the quickest way to get things done is to slow down.

"After I got out of the joint, I went up to Atlanta. Figured I'd use my shiny new degree, get me a job, live a whole new life. Up there, I wouldn't be RT Miller the crazy bastard that everybody's scared of. I'd just be some guy. It'd be like a do-over, you know. You remember that? Back in elementary school, you'd be playing some game and you'd miss the shot or whatever and you'd go, 'Do over!' And they'd just let you shoot again." He laughed harshly.

"Well," he continued, "the world ain't like that, is it? There was something on me, I guess. Some kind of stink. You got that little box—'Check here if ever been in prison.' I never checked that box." He shook his head. "Interviewed for forty-seven jobs. Started out looking for work at banks, things of that nature. That didn't last long. So I dropped back to loading dock–type jobs, heavy-equipment operator, you name it." He shook his head. "Not one job offer. Not *one*!"

"Mm," I said.

"Pretty soon my money give out, I'm living on the street. Lived in a cardboard box for six weeks. Finally one day, I said to hell with it. Come crawling back to this shit-ass little town, walked into the personnel office over at DCI, hat in my hand, asked them if they had a job. They make me sit there in the lobby for six solid hours. Finally, around quitting time, the big man hisself comes out after a while, says, 'How you doing, RT? There's a mop over in the corner. Start cleaning up, we'll see how you do, take it from there. You keep out of trouble, maybe I'll let you stay.' And then he's back in his office, making phone calls."

"Earl Justice," I said. "You're talking about—"

"I'm talking about my own father." RT Miller pawed at his eyes with the back of his hand. "Aw hell. What's wrong with me?"

The night's gloom was coming down heavy on us now, so it was almost impossible to see anything in the dark shed.

"Go on," I said.

"Hell, everybody in town knows it. Earl Justice never had no kids by his wife. But, by golly, it wasn't because his equipment didn't work. I'm proof of that." He hooted loudly, the sound clanging off the walls of the big sawmill. "You know what it's like to live in a town like this, where everybody knows your business? A town like this, can't nobody change. They won't allow it. RT Miller's got to be RT Miller forever. Loudmouth sumbitch that can't get along with nobody, can't be trusted with nothing, don't do nothing right."

"I'm sorry," I said.

"I don't give a shit if you're sorry. I didn't ask for that." Miller blew out a long breath. "Hey, forget I said that. There wasn't no need. Even if you *did* break my TV. People done worse than that to me."

We sat there for a while. After a little bit, I started swinging my legs in rhythm with his. I went to an interrogation-technique class one time where they said that synchronizing yourself physically with somebody makes them feel more comfortable. When they put their hand on their chin, you put your hand on your chin; when they breath, you breathe. I didn't know if it would work, but I figured I'd try it anyway.

"Equilibrium. Y'all come in this town and you're fixing to bust up the equilibrium. People down here see somebody like you coming, they get scared. Absolutely petrified. And they don't even know why!"

"The papers," I said. "I have less than twenty-four hours."

"My old man ain't never claimed me. Never said a word to me. I mean, it ain't like it's a goddamn secret. Everybody knows I'm his kid. He knows I know. I know he knows I know, and he knows that I.... Well, you get the point. That sumbitch acts like he done me a favor letting me make twelve-eighty-seven an hour driving a backhoe after I spent a year proving I could push a mop without peeing on the rug. The hell with him. These papers, they could use them in that lawsuit, right?"

I nodded.

"And if they win that lawsuit, it'll cost him a boatload of money, right?"

"If, yes. *If.*"

He stood. "Six years ago, Brittany and me was having problems. Like usual, I guess. But this was even worse. She was cheating on me. And I couldn't stand that, man. Anyway, one day we get in a big old fight and she says she's gonna leave me. I laugh at her. Instead of getting mad, she says, 'You ain't gonna be laughing when I drive out of this town in a Cadillac and never come back.' I'm like, 'Cadillac? On eight-sixty-three an hour? Where you gonna get the money?' And all of a sudden, she just shuts up." RT Miller looked across the big shed, an expression of anger on his face. "I figured this fellow she was cheating on me with was gonna give her some money. So I busted her one and asked her again where she was gonna get the money. She just clamped her mouth shut, laughed in my face. I knew if I stayed in that room, I'd do something bad. So I just pointed my finger at her, went 'You leave me, I'll kill you.' And then I walked out."

He turned and started walking down the stairs at the end of the catwalk.

"Where we going?" I said.

He didn't answer, just kept walking through the dark, carrying on his narrative. "I didn't think nothing of it at the time. Figured it was just something she said. Then she come up dead the next day. I thought about it and thought about it, but I never could get what she meant. Not till you walked into my trailer yesterday, started asking about these papers she'd stole from DCI."

"Okay," I said.

"When we first started dating," he continued as we walked out the back of the mill, "I was a twenty-four-year-old ex-con and she was a junior in high school. I don't need to tell you that didn't go over good with nobody. Her mama lives over that hill there." He pointed at a tree-covered rise behind the mill property. "She used to sneak out of the house and we'd meet here at the mill. Drink, laugh, fool around." He looked wistful. "We had a little secret place we'd go."

We walked toward a small cinder-block office building toward the back of the property. The door appeared to be shut with a padlock. But Miller reached out, fiddled with it, and it clicked open.

I followed Miller inside the room. It was dark and creepy. He took a powerful flashlight out of his pocket, shone it around the room. There were several desks covered with mold and dust, a table, a rotted-out couch. And a line of gray filing cabinets. Scattered on the floor were ancient file folders and papers.

"I don't know what it was," Miller said. "But Brittany was always fascinated by them filing cabinets. She'd pull out papers and say like, 'Did you know that in August of 1934, this mill sawed eighty thousand six hundred board feet of timber?'" He laughed. "Anyway, when you mentioned them papers, I got to thinking. Let's say she had them papers. Let's say she was gonna turn them into money. How would she do that?"

"Sell them back to Earl Justice," I said. "Tell him if he didn't pay, she'd give them to the lawyer in Atlanta."

RT Miller nodded. "Yep. That's what I thought, too. And I also figured she'd hide them. Where? Not in her house. Be too obvious. Brittany wasn't no fool. She knew Earl Justice could easily tell the sheriff to go over there with some kind of trumped-up drug warrant. Nah, she'd of hid them."

"Here."

He leaned over, pulled open a file drawer. There, in the beam of his flashlight, were two stacks of paper sitting in the bottom of the drawer. I pulled one out. At the top of the page was a logo: *DCI*.

"Been setting here for six years," he said. "Nobody never knew."

"And you're just giving them to me," I said. "Why?"

"Sumbitch laid me off last week. His own son, he had the assistant to the vice president of Human Resources come out there and give me this song and dance about hard times in the kaolin industry, competition from calcined carbonates, soft prices in the international market." His face was tight with rage. "The *assistant* to the vice president. To fire his own son!"

I leaned over to pick up the rest of the papers, but he grabbed my arm, straightened me up.

"I'll give them to you, Sunny," he said. "But only on one condition."

"What's that?"

"You got to tell him where they come from. You got to tell him they come from the boy who never got no baseball glove from his daddy at Christmas. You tell him they come from the boy who never got a hug or a kiss or even a smack on the ass when he acted up."

"Okay," I said. I picked up the papers and turned toward the door. RT Miller didn't move. "You coming?" I said.

"I think I'll just set here for a while." He plopped down on the rotted couch, sending up a cloud of dust.

I walked out the door.

"You tell him, Sunny!" he called. "By God, you tell him."

TWENTY-FIVE

When I got back to the hotel, I checked with Mr. Patel to see if Sunil and Lee-Lee had turned up. They hadn't. I stood in the hotel office and called my aunt, Lee-Lee's mother, to see if she had checked in with her family in the last hour or so. She hadn't. I tried Lee-Lee's cell. *I'm sorry the cell phone you are calling is currently . . .*

Mr. Patel watched me nervously as I made my calls. When I was done, I shook my head. His face fell.

"We had better call the sheriff," he said.

I was still a little hesitant. I wasn't sure whether the Sheriff's Department—or at least Deputy Woodie—was involved in trying to spook us out of town. The Sheriff's Department might well be the enemy here, I figured. But then again, they might not. It probably couldn't hurt to talk to them, though. It would give me a chance to get a read on them, see how they reacted.

"Let's go," I said.

We climbed into my car and drove over to the sheriff's office. For once Mr. Patel seemed content to be silent.

When we reached the department, something occurred to me. If Earl Justice was behind Lee-Lee's and Sunil's disappearance, and if the papers I'd just recovered were behind the killing of Brittany Woodie and Terri Ross, then maybe I could use the Sheriff's Department to bait the hook and trap Justice.

Maybe.

•

Sheriff Renice Powell didn't rise from her desk when we walked into her office. Apparently, she was working late. It was almost ten o'clock at night. She was signing payroll checks. "They got a machine down at County Administration that'll sign these checks automatic," she said, "but I like my people to know where their money's coming from."

"I want to file a missing person report," I said.

"That's what the gal out front said to me." She was still busy signing checks. I waited until she had finished the last of the checks and tossed them into her in box. She had a mannish haircut, lightly frosted, and wore no makeup. Her uniform was complicated and snappy-looking, with a Sam Browne belt and lots of shiny buttons and gold pins.

"It's my son Sunil," Patel said, his hands fluttering in the air. "He and Miss Edwards have both disappeared."

"It's well past time for me to get home to my family. You could have gave your report to the gal out front," the sheriff said.

"I'm giving it to you," I said.

She sighed heavily, looked at her watch, then pulled out a legal pad and a pen. "How long they been gone?"

"A couple of hours."

Sheriff Powell's eyes widened. "A couple *hours*!" She threw the legal pad back in the drawer. "They could be at the store buying loaf bread."

I shook my head. "You know why we're here," I said. "Dale Weedlow is about a day away from being put to death. Lee-Lee and I are here to investigate his case. I've been calling her for three hours, with no reply. Sunil's not responding on his cell phone or the radio in his cab, either. They are not at the store buying bread."

"Maybe up in Atlanta y'all got one hundred percent cell-phone coverage. This is Flournoy County. Most of this county's got no cell-phone towers. All they'd have to do is drive over some hill and they'd be unreachable."

"I don't buy that," I said. "She left all her camera and recording equipment in the room. If they'd gone out to do research for the film, she'd have taken the camera."

"Plus which, Mr. Patel, I happened to notice that Miss Edwards was an unusually attractive young gal–if you go for girls with pins sticking out of their face, anyway. I don't guess it's escaped your notice, Mr. Patel, that your boy Sunil's got a eye for pretty young white women."

"*White* women! Can Sunil help it if they throw themselves at him!" Patel looked insulted. "If there were an Indian community in this town, I assure you he would have long ago settled down with a nice Indian girl. But that being not the case, he is forced to fend off these constant unwanted advances from these immodest, scandalously dressed–"

"Yeah." Renice Powell interrupted him. "I'm sure he's resisting them girls with all his strength."

"I resent your implication! He is a highly moral boy!"

"He wouldn't be the first highly moral boy to turn up in a cheap motel over in Milledgeville with some pretty young thing."

Patel stuck his finger in the sheriff's face. "You are going to take our report. I demand it!"

"You demand it." Powell looked amused. "I don't believe you in much position to be demanding things. You ain't in India no more."

I gave her what I hoped was my most condescending smile. "I've already gotten the governor involved once this week. If you fail to take a legitimate report, I could have the attorney general breathing down your neck in a heartbeat, poking around into departmental irregularities, counting sheets and towels down at the jail, auditing your accounts, you name it. The governor has already removed one sheriff from office this year. Don't think it couldn't happen to you."

She glared at me.

"Don't you think it'd be easier to humor me and Mr. Patel, take down the information, let your people know to keep an eye out for them?"

Powell took out a stick of chewing gum, put it in her mouth, chewed for a while–all the time giving me hard eyes. I didn't break eye contact with her. Finally, she pulled out the pad of paper and the pen again.

"Full name," she said. "The girl first."

When she was done taking down all the information, I said, "You haven't asked once whether there's any reason they might have disappeared."

"I got my own ideas about that," she said.

"Like what?"

"I already mentioned the motel-over-in-Milledgeville scenario and everybody got all hot under the collar. So I'll keep my ideas to myself."

"It's pretty clear to me that Dale Weedlow's trial was a joke. Is he innocent? I can't say for sure. But I can say that somebody in this town has been extremely eager for us to leave. My conclusion is that a reexamination of the evidence surrounding the murders of those two young women is liable to show that somebody else in this town did it."

"You got somebody in mind? And don't tell me RT Miller. That rumor's been going around town for years, and I don't buy it for a minute."

"I'm not going to tell you who I think did it."

She just kept chewing her gum, looking at me with a knowing expression.

"What I will tell you," I said, "is that Brittany Woodie stole a great big pile of accounting records from DCI about a week before she was murdered. Those accounting records could have proved that Earl Justice was cheating his leaseholders out of royalty money. You may recall that he's the subject of a long-standing class action, which, if successful, could cost him millions of dollars. It might even be enough to destroy his company."

"That's a good story."

"Oh, believe me, it's not a story."

"You can prove it?"

"Absolutely," I said. "I just recovered the records myself."

She looked at me thoughtfully for a while, not speaking.

"Yeah," I said, "I'm still mulling over what to do with them. I mean, they could be evidence of a murder—in which case I ought to turn them over to you. But, of course, I'd only do that if you conceded that this case has some unresolved problems that need to be resolved."

"There are no unresolved problems in the Dale Weedlow case."

"I thought you'd say that. Which means I probably will turn them over to the lawyer for the plaintiffs in the case against DCI."

The sheriff scratched her nose. I could see her trying to figure out what to do. She knew that if I wasn't lying, then Earl Justice would be fairly desperate to put his hands on the documents. And since every public servant in the county owed fealty to Earl Justice, she knew it would be in her interest to help him get the papers.

"I better take a look at them," she said. "Just . . . you know . . . to be sure."

"No," I said. "Don't think so."

"I could charge you with impeding an investigation."

"An investigation of what? This is a closed case with a solid conviction. You just said so yourself."

Renice Powell stood suddenly, gave me a watery smile. She was in a box and she knew it. "Thank you for coming forward. I'll put the word out for my deputies to keep their eyes out for Miss Edwards and Mr. Patel."

"Thank you," I said.

We walked out to the car. I figured Renice Powell would wait about two seconds before she called Earl Justice. And if Earl Justice had snatched Lee-Lee, then the next move would be fairly obvious. An exchange: Lee-Lee for the papers.

"I do not like that woman," Mr. Patel said.

"I'm not signing up to be president of her fan club anytime soon, either."

"What are we going to do?" he said. "What *are* we going to do?"

I held up my cell phone. "My guess, this phone will ring. Very soon. And when it does, we'll find out what happens next."

"And until then?"

"We wait."

•

Mr. Patel invited me to eat a late dinner with his family. He had three sons (in addition to Sunil), four daughters, a somewhat shrewish wife, a cousin from India, and an ancient mother-in-law with racoonlike circles around her eyes who sat silently in the corner, bundled in a thick blanket, eyeing me as though I were about to steal some silverware.

The curried goat was good, the lentils were mushy and taste-less, and the vegetables were so spicy that my eyes watered. No one seemed to be in the mood to talk. The house was not air-conditioned and the heat was stifling. After the dinner we sat in si-lence, waiting for the phone to ring, while the two youngest boys played a game called Street Brawl III on their PlayStation. The bass on the system was turned up loud, so every time the two combatants on the screen hit each other, you felt a thud in your chest like it was you who had been hit.

It was excruciating.

I waited until eleven, but my phone never rang. Finally, I gave up, went back to my room, and lay in the bed, feeling exhausted and hopeless. Nineteen hours to prove Weedlow was innocent. Nineteen hours to figure a way of getting Lee-Lee back.

I called Barrington, hoping for some words of encouragement, but he didn't answer our home phone. That meant he was sleep-ing. I didn't want to wake him, so I just lay there and stared at the dark ceiling.

TWENTY-SIX

The first sign that I'd gotten through to Earl Justice was a phone call I received from a lawyer in Atlanta. It came at a few minutes past midnight.

"Ms. Childs, this is Aaron Carter with Cane and Spellman in Atlanta." Cane & Spellman was one of the largest law firms in Atlanta, and Carter was by far their most prominent attorney. A notoriously tough and effective lawyer. "I represent DCI Incorporated. I have been given to understand that you have come into possession of certain proprietary documents owned by the corporation."

I should have anticipated this. I had been assuming Earl Justice would contact me directly. But that wasn't how powerful people did things. They used minions. "Could you spell your name, sir?" I said. I wanted to slow him down, take him off his game, draw him out.

He ignored my question. "These documents are not yours. They were stolen. Your possession of these documents is in violation of Georgia criminal code sections—" He reeled off a bunch of numbers. I recognized them as the sections for receiving, theft, theft by taking, and some others I'd never heard of. "In addition, DCI has the right to file suit against you in state and/or federal court. If these documents are not returned by eight o'clock sharp tomorrow morning to the offices of DCI, the company will pursue immediate civil and criminal actions against you."

"I'm sorry," I said, "my cell phone's acting up. I still didn't catch your name."

There was a pause. "Carter. From Cane and Spellman."

"And what was it you wanted Mr. Carver?"

"Carter. C-A-R-T-E-R. Aaron Carter."

"Terrific. And the other part of what you said, Mr. Carver? Something about a free trip to Disney World? Did I hear that correctly?"

Another pause. "You may find these juvenile games to be amusing, Miss Childs, but that little smirk on your face will evaporate when you're arrested. Return those papers."

"Nice try, pal," I said. "But I have no idea what papers you're talking about."

"You have until eight o'clock sharp. And when I say eight o'clock sharp, I don't mean eight-oh-five."

"Something you may be interested to know," I said, "is that your status as an attorney does not shield you from contribution to a criminal enterprise. If Mr. Justice is—as I believe he is—a participant in a criminal enterprise, your little attempt at extortion here may have pushed you over the line from counselor to actual coconspirator. In which case, you would be liable to lose your law license." I quoted him the code sections for criminal fraud, murder, kidnapping, misprision, theft by fraud, and threw in the federal RICO statute numbers, too, just for fun. "If you have any further communications to make with me, address them to my attorney, Walter Childs, at Harris, Dunwoody and Cobb. You have a nice day, Mr. Carper."

I hung up the phone. Asshole.

It made me think, though. Was Earl just softening me up? Or what? Surely he didn't think I'd just hand over the documents. It had to be the opening gambit in his game. We'd see what came next. I considered just marching up to Justice's house and saying, 'Give me Lee-Lee, I'll give you the papers.' But I didn't know with absolute certainty that he was the one who'd snatched her. Moreover, if I went begging to him immediately, it would put me in a weak negotiating position. Better to let the deadline lapse and then let him come to me again.

TWENTY-SEVEN

The next morning, I drove over to the Waffle House for breakfast. It was the usual small-town scene—a real estate salesman in a suit that had been fashionable about ten years ago, a couple of tables full of guys with hard hats getting a bite to eat before work, grizzled old men coming in and smoking cigarettes while they drank coffee and flirted with waitresses a third their age.

I ordered scrambled eggs and raisin toast with hash browns scattered, smothered, and covered—which is Waffle House code for having grilled onions and cheese in the potatoes. I was just swabbing up the yolks of my eggs with my raisin toast when David Woodie and two other fairly large deputies came in and walked over to my spot at the counter.

"Her," Woodie said, pointing at me.

One of the other deputies came up behind me and said, "Stand up, ma'am, place your hands on the counter."

"Excuse me?" I said.

"Ma'am, please," the deputy said. "Ain't no need of a fuss in here."

I wiped my mouth, finished my mug of watery coffee, then stood. So Earl Justice was serious about having me arrested. They frisked me and then cuffed me and walked me out into the parking lot.

"What time is it?" I said.

"Eight-oh-two," Deputy Woodie said. Then to the other deputies: "Put her in the back of my car."

Woodie climbed in, waited until the other deputies were in their cars, then said, "Mr. Justice is willing to forget about prosecuting you if you turn over the items that you stole."

"I didn't steal anything."

"I wouldn't know about that. All I know is he wants something you got."

"You know this won't hold up in court."

"Hey, I'm just doing what I'm told," Deputy Woodie said. "I don't even *want* to know what this is about."

Eight-oh-two. Ten hours until they stuck the needle in Dale Weedlow's arm. I tried not to panic. The clock was running out.

•

Woodie took his time booking me in, fingerprinting me, photographing me, and so on. Occasionally the sheriff walked by the room. She made a point of not looking into the booking area, but she had a smug little smile on her face every time she walked by.

When they were finally finished, Sheriff Powell came into the booking area and said, "Well?"

"When can I get bailed out?"

"Arraignments are next Thursday. And don't think you can call in no more favors with the governor. Mr. Justice told me flat out: You're staying here till arraignment, come hell or high water. No special treatment like we done with your cute little cousin."

"I want my phone call," I said.

"Phone's broke," she said.

"I'll use my cell."

"Can't do it. It's already been logged in to the property room." She winked at me. "Don't worry, though. We'll get you that phone call directly."

The word *directly* in the rural south means *not directly*.

•

The jail had no air-conditioning. It must have been 105 degrees back in my cell. There was only one other prisoner, a squat, sad-eyed woman whose face was a road map of sorrow and alcohol abuse. There was a TV bolted to the wall on the other side of the hall from our cells. It played a country-music video silently. The woman stared unblinkingly at the video. At first I thought, *What a poor pathetic creature, staring at the boob tube like a zombie.*

But there was absolutely nothing to do, and within five minutes, I found myself converted into a zombie, too. On the screen, Shania Twain silently mouthed the words to some song while shaking around in a slinky dress that had been carefully tailored to minimize the size of her hips.

"Boy, she got it made, don't she?" the woman in the cell next to me said.

"Who?" I said. "Shania?"

"Yeah."

"I don't know. She sings crappy songs and she's married to some old rich guy she probably doesn't even love. I'm not sure I'd trade places with her."

The woman looked at me like: *Could you possibly be more full of shit?*

I laughed. "Well, come on, it makes me feel better to say that."

The woman laughed, too, a phlegmy smoker's laugh that came welling up from deep in her gut.

"What you in for?" I said.

"Solicitation," she said.

"You serious? You got prostitutes in Flournoy County?"

She shrugged. "Just me. I work the truck stop out on Seventy-five. They drag me in every six months or so, just to make sure I pay on time."

I frowned. "Pay what on time?"

"You know, my cut."

I kept frowning.

She looked at me and laughed again. "You ain't from around here, are you?"

I shook my head.

"Sheriff's Department takes a cut of everything in this county.

Video poker, drugs, dice games over in the colored part of town. You name it. Mostly they make money off the jail contracts, though. Linens, food, repairs, construction. Every businessman that's got a contract with the jail, they got to kick back ten percent to Renice Powell."

I had threatened to bring the governor down to poke around in their books—but I was just talking. It had never occurred to me that there was anything really serious here to expose. Corrupt southern sheriffs are such a cliché, I didn't figure there could be any truth to it.

Kenny Chesney came on the TV. He was wearing a shirt with the sleeves cut off and giving the camera his "Aren't I a gift from God?" look. "Man, I hate that guy," I said.

"His tour bus stopped at the truck stop one time," the woman in the cell next door said. "I done him and his whole band for a thousand bucks."

"Is that right?"

"I wish." She laughed and laughed and laughed.

She suddenly got serious, though, when Deputy Woodie came into the cell block. "Sheriff says the phone's working again," he said, a little curl of sneer hanging on the edge of his lips.

•

Normally, I would have called my brother. But I realized it was time for more serious measures, so I called Gunnar Brushwood, my boss at Peachtree Investigations.

"Gunnar," I said. "Got a little problem."

TWENTY-EIGHT

The window in my jail cell gave me a clear view of the street in front of the building housing the Sheriff's Department. At 11:25, three black SUVs pulled up and double-parked on the road in front of the building. A bunch of men and women in blue suits got out. They all had ID badges clipped to their coats, and several of them carried pistols conspicuously on their belts. The man in the lead was a tall, distinguished-looking guy with a big white mustache and a pipe clamped in his mouth. In his hand he carried a blue paper, folded in thirds, that had the look of a subpoena or a warrant.

The jail consisted of only four cells, separated from the office building by a barred wall. From my cell, I could hear everything going on in the offices.

"Let me have your attention!" A deep, drawling voice boomed through the whole building. "My name is Dudley Brashiers, Jr. I bring you greetings from the attorney general of the state of Georgia."

The big man with the white mustache came into my view now. He was holding up the blue paper. "I have in my possession a warrant from the Supreme Court of the state of Georgia authorizing me to search this entire building and to seize any and all records, computers, files, or other items that I see fit. Where's the high sheriff?" He was one of those guys who just reeked of masculine authority.

Renice Powell came out, a sick look on her face. "What is this?"

"Sheriff, I need you to instruct all of your personnel to clear the premises. Anyone interfering with our search will be subject to arrest and prosecution for impeding an investigation. That includes you. Do you understand me?"

"Let me see that warrant."

The big man with the mustache handed it to her. "Read it and weep, Sheriff," he said. "Read it and weep."

"I can't allow this," Sheriff Powell said.

"Agent Quiggly," the mustached man said, "please relieve the sheriff of her sidearm and apprise her of her constitutional rights."

"Whoa, whoa, whoa," the sheriff said. "Now hold on."

"You gonna cooperate?"

"*Mi casa, su casa,*" the sheriff said nervously. "Whatever you need."

The sheriff watched in obvious desperation as the attorney general's agents started unplugging computers, piling files in boxes. After a few minutes, she turned and walked swiftly back toward me.

"Look, Sunny," she said. "Can you make this stop? You and Earl need to work out whatever your problem is. I can't have this happening."

I shrugged. "Hey, it's out of my hands."

Sheriff Powell put her face in her hands for a moment. "Okay, okay, okay," she said, talking more to herself than to me. "I guess I'm gonna have to call Earl."

"Tell you what," I said. "Give me a minute with that guy over there. Maybe we can work something out."

"I'll make it worth your while," the sheriff said. "I guarantee it."

"You gonna drop the charges?"

"Earl would kill me. Absolutely *kill* me."

"Fine. Hey, I can sit here watching Kenny Chesney while those boys out there tear your entire building apart."

"All right, *all right.*"

She took a key off her belt, opened the door.

"Her, too," I said, pointing at the poor creature in the next cell.

"Why?"

"Because she has a sense of humor and you don't."

The sheriff blinked, then silently opened the door and let the women in the next cell out.

I walked into the main part of the building. "Could I speak to you outside, sir?" I said to the big man with the white mustache.

He motioned toward the door and we walked out into the bright sunlight.

"Dadgum, it's hot down here," he said.

"How you doing, Gunnar?" I said.

"Oh, I'm having a fine old time. You?"

"I like the little fake ID cards," I said, flicking the laminated badge that hung from his lapel. "Nice touch."

"MeChelle made them for that warehouse theft case we did for—what was that company called? The one where we pretended we were GBI agents?"

"Oh, yeah. I'd forgotten about that. What about the warrant? Where'd you get that?"

"You kidding? Jimmy pulled it off the Internet."

Our operatives from Peachtree Investigations continued to file by with boxes full of papers, sticking them in the backs of the SUVs.

"I don't know, Gunnar," I said. "Impersonating an officer? You could get in some hot water over this."

"I never said I was an officer of anything. I said I was with the AG's office. Anyway, so what? Even if we walked in there right this minute and told that woman we'd just bamboozled her, what's she gonna do? Arrest us? Shoot, Sunny, we got three trucks full of proof she's a crook."

"Mexican standoff."

Gunnar Brushwood laughed. "You see the expression on that gal's face? Priceless."

"For everything else, there's MasterCard."

Gunnar grinned. My boss and I stood out there shooting the

breeze for a while and then I said, "Well, I think we've made her sweat enough. I'm on a kind of short leash timewise."

Gunnar followed me in, made a big circle in the air, and all of our operatives walked out the front door.

"Sheriff," Gunnar said. "The state is gonna hold on to these records. If you provide full cooperation to Miss Childs in her investigation, the files will collect dust in a warehouse in one of the less pleasant neighborhoods in Atlanta, locked away for all time." He pointed the stem of his pipe at the sheriff's face. "But you give this young lady any more trouble and the governor's gonna be on you like white on rice."

He walked out.

The sheriff looked at me with a mixture of anger, fear, and wonderment. "Every time you say 'Jump,' the governor says, 'How high?'" she said. "What in the world did you do for him?"

I smiled mysteriously. "A lady never tells."

Her eyes widened. "Girl, you are not serious!"

"I'm totally serious," I said.

TWENTY-NINE

It's not natural to know when a person is going to die. Death just shouldn't be something you can set your watch by. I had been checking my watch compulsively for the past couple of days. Forty-six hours till Dale Weedlow was scheduled to die. Thirty-eight and a half. Twenty-nine. Twenty-eight. It was getting to the point where I really didn't want to look. But I couldn't help myself.

Six hours and a few minutes.

I had been procrastinating, but I figured I had to make some calls now. Lee-Lee's mother—my aunt—is a sort of nervous, flighty person to begin with and I dreaded talking to her. I figured I'd better let my mom triage things a little.

I dialed Mom's number. "Mom," I said. "I need your help. Lee-Lee's missing."

My mom is one of those people who always knows what to do. Frequently what she knows to do is entirely the wrong thing—but at least she's calm and purposeful. "Missing in what sense?"

I filled her in on the whole story.

"You need the FBI," she said. "Kidnapping is a federal offense. Call Barrington. Fill that town with men in blue suits until whoever snatched her cries uncle."

"I don't think so," I said. "Look, we've got two possibilities here. Either she's dead. In which case, it really doesn't matter what happens. Or she's alive and somebody wants to use her for leverage. If the feds show up, it's liable to spook them, and maybe whoever has them will just say, 'We don't need the aggravation; let's just go bury these two people out in the swamp somewhere.'"

"Call Barrington."

"Mom! I'll *handle* Barrington. Okay? The reason I called you was because I wanted you to call May and let her know about Lee-Lee. You can keep her calm."

"Oh, I see," Mom said. I could see her smiling brightly into the phone. "You don't want me to *solve* things. You just want me for damage control."

"Truthfully?"

"Don't let me take up any more of your time," Mom said lightly. "I'm sure you're very busy. I'll call May. Don't you worry your head about it."

She hung up on me. Maybe Lee-Lee was right about my always having to get in the last word. But believe me, I learned at the foot of the master. After I talk to my mother, I always seem to hang up the phone feeling guilty.

I sighed. Now what? I was running out of time. And options.

•

There was one last thing I could think of. I still felt sure that Earl Justice would call. But in the meantime, I needed as much ammunition as possible for whatever negotiations ensued. I had a few more questions for Ervin Kindred.

I drove by the lawyer's office, but it was locked and the lights inside were turned off. I called information, got his address, and headed to his house.

It was just a few blocks from his office, a nice little white Victorian house with a tin roof and broad porch. I knocked on the front door. No one answered. I tried the handle, walked in.

"Mr. Kindred? Mr. Kindred?" I don't know why, but I was sure he was there. Maybe it was the smell of the place, or something I heard. Whatever the case, I walked through the house until I found him. He was sitting in a dim room, the walls completely covered by bookshelves, reading a book under a small lamp.

He looked up at me when I walked in.

"I intentionally didn't answer the door," he said. "One of the fine things about self-employment is that on occasion you can just close up shop and come home to read."

He was freshly shaved and immaculately dressed. He wore pressed pinstripe pants, a crisp white shirt, and a bow tie with the Harvard colors emblazoned on it in diagonal stripes.

"You're sober," I said.

"I am. I don't enjoy reading while intoxicated," he said.

I sat in the chair opposite him without being asked. "I talked to Aimee," I said. "She told me a funny story. She said you were all set to give Dale Weedlow a vigorous defense, then Earl Justice came by and you had a fight, and then after that you just chucked in the towel."

"She said that, huh?"

"I mean, come on. I read the transcript. You didn't defend that kid."

He held up the book he was reading, a tattered Penguin paperback. "I'm reading Xenophon," he said. "He leads a mercenary army of Greeks in service to Darius, the Persian king, in a fight against Darius's nasty brother. The nasty brother wins a big battle—just north of what's now Baghdad. Xenophon and his Greeks have to retreat to save their skins. They spend months fighting their way free of the Persians, up through all these mountain tribes who are busy trying to kill them, and finally they get over the mountains in what's now Turkey, and from the front of the army comes this big cheer: 'The sea! The sea!' The Greeks, of course, they're a seafaring people, and so it's a great moment for them. They think, All right, boys, we've got this thing licked. We've survived and we're all going to make it home." He smiled at me. Then the smile faded. "Only . . . they're wrong. Took them another two years. And there was a lot more dying along the way."

"Earl Justice convinced you to throw the trial, didn't he?"

"The sea! The sea!" Ervin Kindred said to me, an odd sort of smile on his face. And for a moment, I could see past the broken-down old drunk to the man who Aimee Wallace had fallen in love with all those years ago.

"What's your point?" I said.

"You've made it pretty far," he said. "But you aren't home free yet. Not even close."

"I'm well aware of that. Earl Justice kidnapped Lee-Lee yesterday. But I have something Earl Justice wants. I'm going to use it to get her back. And with any luck, when I do that, I'll get something from Earl Justice that will help me spring Dale free."

"Earl did come to me while I was preparing for that trial. We did have a fight. Amy was right about that. And her Christian name *is* Amy, by the way. Not a soul in this town calls her Aimee. That's something she made up. Did she tell you about her grandmother from Louisiana, how she was French on that side of the family?"

"Uh-huh."

"Her grandmother was a sharecropper about two miles from here. Never left Flournoy County in her life." His eyes got hard for a moment. "She's got a gift for making things up, for making the world fit her little rose-colored notions of humanity."

"What are you saying?"

"I'm saying she thinks I'm some kind of noble creature beaten-down by the mean old world." He shook his head. "But I'm not. I'm just weak."

"We're all weak."

He looked at me for a long time without speaking. "Young lady, if you were weak like I am, you'd be sitting in an easy chair up in Atlanta, reading a book." He tossed Xenophon on the floor next to his foot. "Yes, Earl and I had a fight. Amy was sitting on the other side of the door. I'm sure she heard shouting. But she didn't hear the words. No, Miss Childs, our fight didn't have anything to do with him asking me to throw the trial."

"What was it, then?"

"Brittany came to me about six months before her death. She

told me that she wanted my help. She was concerned that DCI was cheating their lessors. She said it was a very complicated scheme and she needed to know what her legal position was if she sneaked documents out of DCI's files and passed them to this lawyer up in Atlanta who had filed a class-action suit."

"Diggsby."

"That's him, yes. Now, at that time, I would say that sixty percent of my income derived from work I did for DCI. I told Brittany that advising her would put me in a conflict of interest situation, and so I couldn't help her. She seemed real disappointed. Now, you had to know this young girl to understand what happened next." He looked thoughtful for a moment. "Brittany was a very ambitious young woman. And she had about had enough of living in this little town. She saw bigger things in her future than being a secretary at DCI. I think she saw that lawsuit as her ticket out of here. I don't think she had the slightest interest in giving those papers to that fellow Diggsby up in Atlanta. She knew the score. Diggsby wins that lawsuit, it won't change things for the lessors. All the money in kaolin is in the processing, not the mining. That'll never change. So she figured she'd pull all this evidence together and sell it to Earl."

"Okay, I've already heard this story," I said.

"Yes, but there's a part of it that I'm quite sure you haven't heard yet. Like I say, I told Brittany I couldn't help her." He waggled his head back and forth for a moment. "Back in those days, I was still in my forties, reasonably vigorous, capable of a certain windy charm when I was sufficiently aroused. Brittany was an attractive young girl. And she knew it. I won't say she was out-and-out using me. And I won't say I was using her. But . . . have you ever heard that old country song, 'Third Rate Romance'? It's about a couple renting a room at a cheap motel, pretending that the whole thing is not the tawdry, sad affair that it so obviously is."

I sang part of the chorus. " 'Third rate romance, low rent rendezvous.' "

"Don't quit your day job, darling."

I laughed.

"But, yes, I think that song sums up my relationship with Brittany. It was all a little pathetic. She aspired to be something more than a secretary at a mining company, married to an abusive redneck—which was the path she was headed on if she'd stayed in this town—and she needed my help to get there. And I wanted to feel like I was more than some aging country lawyer with a drinking problem." He looked at the floor morosely.

"It is what it is."

"I suppose. Anyway, she got me to more or less warehouse the documents here in my office. It was a black box kind of notion. She would give me some papers, which I would secure in the safe in my office but never look at. That way I would have no specific knowledge that would ethically oblige me to talk to Earl or to report her theft to the police or anything of that nature. And in turn, she would get to shelter the papers from any legal action Earl might pursue by virtue of attorney-client privilege. That was her theory anyway. I don't know why she didn't just bury them in a hole. But that was typical Brittany. She was one of those people who loved intrigue for its own sake. She was just a little too clever for her own good."

"So what was your argument with Earl about?"

"Well, Brittany was killed and the papers just sat there. I didn't know what to do with them. Figured I'd let them sit there forever. At any rate, the trial was about to start, and one day Earl came to me, said he knew I had these papers. How he found out, I don't know. Maybe the lawyer, Diggsby, in that class action knew about them. Maybe RT Miller knew about them from Brittany and he told Earl. Maybe the papers came up missing and he was just guessing. I don't know. Whatever the case, he'd figured it out somehow." Ervin Kindred blew out a long breath of air, making a slight whistling sound with his teeth. "The proper thing to do, of course, was to just sit there and say, 'Attorney-client privilege prevents me from disclosing any information.' Blah, blah, blah ... Just repeat that till he went away, then call up Brittany's mother and ask her to haul them away. But, of course, Earl wasn't having it."

"What did he do?"

"He told me flat out that he'd pull all the business he gave me, take every scrap of his business to a lawyer up in Atlanta. Well, you've seen me at my worst. I don't really care about much of anything anymore. But at the time, I was still concerned about my"— he smiled cynically—"my *standing in the community. My welfare. My reputation.* All the rest of that baloney."

"You gave him the papers."

"I said, 'I'll leave the building unlocked tonight. The safe will be open. If somebody were to break in and steal them, well, what could I do about it?' And that's what I did." The lawyer kept looking at the floor.

"Funny thing," he said finally. "It wasn't until he had walked out of my office that I put the whole thing together. I had been pretty much convinced that RT Miller had killed Brittany and Terri. I mean, the case against Weedlow, as you have repeatedly said, was not terribly strong. Absent his confession, the case was extraordinarily weak."

"What about the tools?"

"To me, that almost makes the case. Anybody who was organized enough to kill them in the manner that this person did would never have left the murder weapons there with their fingerprints all over them. It's totally nonsensical. Anyway, like I say, I'd been thinking it was RT Miller who killed them. In fact, I was a little concerned he was gonna come after me—given that I'd been fooling around with his fiancée. But anyway, when Earl walked out of my office, that's when it hit me. It wasn't RT Miller. It was Earl who'd killed them. It had to have been. I don't know if he did it personally . . . but he was behind it. Sure as the world.

"I mean, I wouldn't pretend that I loved Brittany or anything. But she was somebody I cared about. And I was selling her memory down the river. For what? For Earl Justice's money." He shook his head. "I just pulled out the bottle and started drinking. It was so clear what a worthless man I had turned out to be. Worthless. Worthless!" He smiled sadly at me. "After that, I just caved in. I was half in the bag through the whole trial. That poor Weedlow boy got sentenced to death in a case that any kid six months out of law school could have won."

He leaned over, picked up his book. "So today I decided I would read all day long, right up until six o'clock. And when they throw the switch on the poor boy, I intend to take out a bottle of my finest scotch and get stinking drunk."

"I have one last question," I said. "I found the documents. If she gave them to you, why did she keep a separate set elsewhere?"

"Insurance?" He shrugged, then opened his book and said, "I wish you luck, young lady. I don't expect I'll see you again. But if you would, when six o'clock comes, say a prayer for me and Dale Weedlow both. Meantime, I'd be obliged if you'd get out of my light."

THIRTY

As I walked out of Ervin Kindred's house, a Sheriff's Department cruiser slid up to the curb and the window rolled down.

"Get in." It was Deputy David Woodie, looking at me through a pair of wraparound glasses.

"I don't think so," I said.

"I'm doing you a favor."

"Somehow I doubt it."

"Suit yourself," he said.

He started to drive off.

"Wait!" I called. I figured if he was this unconcerned about talking to me, maybe there would be some benefit in it for me. He stopped about thirty feet down the street, made me trot over. "What. Tell me what it is."

"Not here."

I thought about it for a minute. Was this some kind of trap? Was he here on behalf of Earl Justice? Maybe he would lead me to Lee-Lee. There was only one way to find out. I put my hand in my purse, my palm nestling the butt of my .38. Then I climbed in and set the purse on my lap.

He drove for a while. "You wearing a wire?" he said.

"Why?"

"Them guys from the attorney general's office," he said. "I don't give a damn who you are, who you know, the attorney general don't send three cars full of GBI agents down to Flournoy County just because somebody like you makes a phone call. And they especially don't go to all that trouble to seize a bunch of accounting records just so they can stick them in a warehouse."

"What are you getting at?"

"You're GBI, right?" he said.

"Nope," I said.

He cleared his throat nervously. "Don't tell me you're a *fed*."

I gave him the slightest little shrug. It could have meant anything. I'd let him think whatever he wanted to.

"I *knew* it!" He said, slamming his fist into the steering wheel. "I knew it. A *fed*!"

We were heading out of town. Pretty soon we were out in the trees.

"Where are we going, Deputy?" I said.

"We're going somewhere that I feel safe," he said. "Somewhere that I feel confident there's nobody with no microphones. And that's all I'm saying till we get there."

Was this some kind of act? Was he suckering me off into the woods so he could bury me in a hole? Or not? My sense was that he was genuinely afraid. It was a risk. But at this point I didn't see that there were any risk-free options.

Eventually we came over a rise. There in front of us was a huge factory with several slender chimneys sticking up hundreds of feet into the air. A small sign at the edge of the road said DCI. He turned off at the next exit, passed a guard shack, waved to the guard, who waved back without expression, and headed toward the DCI plant.

"You taking me to Earl?" I said.

He looked at me curiously. "Why would I be doing that?" he said.

"You tell me."

"No!" he said derisively. "I ain't taking you to Mr. Justice."

"Then why are we here?"

We stopped dead in the middle of the huge parking lot. There wasn't a car within a hundred feet of us. He got out of the car and surveyed the scene in all directions.

"Because this is the biggest piece of open ground I know of. I can see four hundred yards in all directions. I don't want nobody sneaking up on us, or recording what we say with some kind of parabolic microphone or something."

"I see," I said.

"I'm gonna frisk you," he said.

"Forget it," I said.

"You want what I've got," he said, "then you let me frisk you. I'm not talking if you got a wire."

I thought about it for a while. "Fair enough," I said finally.

He gave me a thorough pat-down, made me pull up my shirt, hooked his finger into my bra, and probed between my breasts. There was nothing creepy or sexual about it, though. All he was interested in was whether or not I was wearing a wire.

"Talk to me," I said.

"Are you empowered?" he said.

"Empowered to what?"

"I want to know if I'm talking to the right person."

I figured it couldn't hurt to play along. "I'm the right person."

"I want to know if you can make me a deal. If not, I want to talk to your superior."

"That depends."

He laughed angrily, jabbed his finger in my face. "Do not," he said, "do *not* think you can play me."

I smiled coldly. "Who do you think you are?" I said. "You wouldn't be standing here if you weren't very, very sure that you were standing in it, and I mean hip-deep. If you've got something real, something that can help us, then I'll do what I can to help you."

"Who was the guy with the mustache? Was he really working for the governor? Or is he a fed, too?"

"Forget him. I told you I'm the right person. You talk to me."

"You'll keep me out of jail?"

"At a certain point, it's out of my hands," I said. "But if you give me something real, then I'll talk with the U.S. attorney." I wasn't lying. What he didn't know was that my help wasn't worth a plug nickel with the U.S. attorney. But that wasn't my problem. "But make no mistake, Deputy, this is the moment of truth. You got something to say, you better say it now."

"I want guarantees."

"I give you my word," I said. "You give me something that'll help me, I'll do what I can to help you."

"All right," he said finally. "I can see the handwriting on the wall. Sheriff Powell's got her hand in the till seven ways to Sunday. I guess y'all are fixing to take her down. Right?"

"My question to you," I said, "is this. We already have the computers. So why do we need you?"

"I'll testify. I been in law enforcement long enough to know—you need somebody inside who can tell you what all that stuff in the computers means. If you don't have somebody who can get up there on the stand and say, 'This code means this, that account stands for that,' then you still got no case."

"We can get a clerk. Why do we need you?"

He surveyed the tree line again, like he was expecting men in black suits to start crawling out of the woods. Suddenly the whole thing struck me as so absurd that I almost burst out laughing. I managed to control myself, though. I knew that the second he suspected I wasn't a federal agent, I was in big, big trouble.

"You know it's not just the sheriff, right?"

Again I shrugged.

"I mean, Flournoy County *is* Earl Justice. You understand that, don't you?"

"Keep talking."

"I can give you Sheriff Powell. Jail contracts, kickbacks, corruption, you name it. That part's easy."

"Okay."

"Just so you know, y'all didn't fool me for a minute. Who'd want to see a movie about some moron like Dale Weedlow? The minute your so-called cousin showed up in town, I knew something wasn't right. I mean—Dale *Weedlow*? A movie about Dale

Weedlow? Gimme a break. What kind of fool would believe a story like that?"

I smiled in what I hoped would be a mysterious way. I really could not figure out quite where he was going with this. So I'd just keep my end of the conversation as vague as possible and see where it went.

"It's just I never figured y'all for being feds." He shook his head. "Well, anyway, the point is this. The corruption in the Sheriff's Department is just the tip of the iceberg. There's road contracts, there's any kind of shenanigan you can think of. Hell, the coach of the football team at Flournoy High gets a cut of the concession money at the football stadium. I can give it all to you."

"We already know about that," I said. "Do you honestly think we put fourteen federal agents in this jerkwater county so we could take down some coach because he skims a dime or two every time they sell a Mountain Dew at the football game?"

For the first time since I'd gotten in his car, David Woodie smiled. "You want Earl Justice, don't you?"

"You better believe it."

He kept smiling. "This fall, Sheriff Powell is up for reelection. I'll give you Earl Justice. But I want the whole ball of wax. I want to run as the reform candidate. I can't even be *charged* with a crime."

"Two minutes ago, you were just happy to stay out of jail," I said. "I think you may be getting ahead of yourself."

"Two minutes ago, we was talking about Sheriff Powell. Now we're talking about Earl Justice."

"Tell me what you got."

"Here's the big picture. There's four kaolin producers in the state. Three of them are big international companies. They got a lot of money, so they can afford the latest technology. DCI is the little guy. The kaolin business has been in the crapper for about ten years. The only way DCI stays in the game is by keeping costs down. Earl Justice uses every trick in the book to keep down the cost he pays for the mud."

"All of which is terribly fascinating. But it's not helping me."

"Listen. I'm telling you. A leaseholder starts bitching how he ain't getting paid enough, Mr. Justice sends out a deputy sheriff to tear up the guy's house looking for dope, sends the extension agent out to make sure he's not using illegal pesticides, sends out the tax collector to reassess the value of his property and jack up his taxes. All the money that changes hands in this county—it's all about keeping down the price of that white mud."

He looked thoughtful. "Here's where I'm going, Sunny. See, I kept racking my brain. Why is it that y'all kept looking at the Weedlow case? It's got nothing to do with corruption. And then finally when I saw you in that evidence room, counting all the trial exhibits, it hit me. You're using Weedlow as leverage to get to Mr. Justice. And that's when it finally started making sense."

"Now *you're* not making sense," I said. "Draw me a picture."

"The missing exhibit," he said.

"It was never introduced in trial. There's no record of what it is."

David Woodie smiled. "Uh-huh," he said.

"Quit wasting my time. Just tell me what you've got."

"This is a small town. We're just normal folks around here. There's only a couple people here who dress real nice. I bet there ain't fifty people in Flournoy County that wear a tie every day." He paused dramatically. "Much less French cuffs."

I narrowed my eyes. French cuffs. What was he getting at?

The deputy reached in his pocket, pulled out a plastic evidence bag. In the bottom was a small gold object. A cuff link. With a diamond sparkling in it. It was the mate to the cuff link that Lee-Lee and I had found.

"We found this at the murder scene. Must of come off when he killed them girls."

I stared at it.

"All you got to do is get somebody to testify that Earl owned this cuff link. Hell, I guarantee you somebody will remember it. His secretary, one of his employees—somebody. It's real distinctive."

"Yeah," I said. "That's true . . ."

"So," he said proudly. "There you are."

I stared at him. "Do you have a hole in your head?" I said finally. "Earl Justice owns DCI. The mine where the bodies were found was run by DCI. All he has to say is, 'Gosh, yeah, I lost that cuff link when I was over inspecting the mine a couple weeks before the murder.' That doesn't tell me squat."

David Woodie seemed to deflate. "He told me and Deputy Powell to make sure Weedlow ended up in jail."

"He said that? Out loud? Well, why didn't you say so? And you'll be willing to swear to that in front of the governor? Today? That you framed Weedlow?"

"How come you keep talking about Weedlow? I thought this whole thing was about Earl Justice."

"It hasn't escaped your notice, has it, that Dale is an innocent man and that he's going to die today?" I said. *"Has it?"*

He looked slightly puzzled. "Yeah, but . . . Dale *Weedlow?* That boy ain't no use to nobody."

"He's a human being!"

David Woodie shrugged dubiously. "Yeah, I guess."

"All right," I said. "Let's march right into his office and start asking his people about that cuff link. Maybe somebody will recognize it."

"The main office is back in town," Deputy Woodie said. "But the gal who was his secretary back then, she works at this here plant now. Her name's Jan Fleming. Let's go talk to her."

"Okay," I said. "Lead on."

•

We walked in the front door of the plant and spoke to a receptionist, who spoke briefly into a phone. After a few minutes, an attractive woman of about my age came out and looked nervously at the two of us.

I let Deputy Woodie do the talking.

"Jan," Deputy Woodie said, "I've got a lost item I think you might be able to identify." He took out the cuff link and held it up to her.

She squinted at it blankly. "Me?" she said.

"What?" Woodie said.

"You want me to identify it?"

"Yeah."

"I've never seen it in my life."

Deputy Woodie gave her a hard look. "I ain't fooling around, Jan. We got to know where this come from."

"I don't know where it came from."

"It's not Mr. Justice's?"

"Why would I . . ." She looked around nervously. "Oh, I see. You mean from back when I was his secretary. You're saying it went missing way back then? And you only just now found it?"

"Uh-huh."

She squinted even closer, finally shook her head. "No, that's not Earl's."

"How would you know?" I said. "Surely you didn't see every piece of jewelry he ever wore."

"He never wore cuff links, not even with a tuxedo. Didn't even wear them at his daughter's wedding. He always said he thought they were fruity."

"You're sure of this?" Deputy Woodie demanded.

"What, you think I'm making it up?" she said sharply.

"We just need to be sure," I said.

"Well, I'm sure," Jan Fleming said.

Deputy Woodie stared for a long time, then finally said, "All right, then." Jan Fleming walked back into the hallway behind the receptionist's desk.

"I don't know about that," Woodie said.

"Why would she lie?" I said. "We're wasting time. Forget the cuff link." I walked out of the plant. Deputy Woodie followed me.

"Where you going?" he said.

"You just wasted my time," I said. "The cuff link is a dead end. Right now, my main job is making sure that Dale Weedlow doesn't get executed. And what you've given me isn't enough. Earl

Justice is close to the governor and his people. Your word that he told you to frame Dale Weedlow is just not going to be enough."

"My *word*?" He stopped and blinked. "Well, hell, I got it on tape, Sunny. I got a tape of our whole conversation, him telling me and the sheriff to make sure Weedlow went down."

"You have a tape?" I stared at him, eyes wide. "Why didn't you say that in the first place?"

"I didn't know if it was important."

"You must be the dumbest person I've ever met," I said.

"Hey!" he said. "There's no need to get personal."

THIRTY-ONE

We drove to Deputy Woodie's house, retrieved the tape. I looked at my watch. It was 1:45. That gave me an hour to go to Earl and trade the papers for Lee-Lee. Then I'd have a drive of almost two hours to get to Atlanta, an hour to sit down with Walter and draft a clemency appeal, a few minutes to get from Walter's office to the governor's office.

It was doable. Close, but doable.

•

With the tape and the two cuff links in my purse, I drove to Earl Justice's office. I figured a guy like Justice might be working even though it was a Saturday afternoon. The headquarters of DCI weren't much to look at. It was an undistinctive one-story brick building that could have been a very small high school. I parked in the parking lot and walked up to the reception area.

When I told the receptionist I wanted to see Mr. Justice, she said that he was home, that he came into work on Saturday mornings but that he always left work in the afternoon to go riding.

"Riding what?"

"His horse."

"Oh," I said.

I went back to my car and drove to his house. I found him in the barn, feeding oats to a beautiful black gelding.

"Well!" he said. "If it isn't the woman of the hour. I was wondering when you'd get here."

RUTH BIRMINGHAM

"Let's just get this over with," I said.

"Do you ride?" he said.

"I took riding lessons when I was a girl."

"You better find a horse and a saddle, then," he said. "Because I'm going for a ride."

He led the black horse out of the barn, then swung onto its back.

I looked around the big space. There were six more horses in the stalls around the barn—all of them large, powerful thorough-breds. Great, I thought. They were all twitchy, explosive-looking animals. Back when I'd ridden, it had always been on listless old horses that were unlikely to give problems to thirteen-year-old girls.

I decided that the bay mare in the corner was the least dangerous-looking horse, so I approached the stall, fed it a carrot, and patted it on the nose. It didn't exactly seem overjoyed to see me, but at least it didn't try to bite me.

A few minutes later, I was gingerly riding the mare out of the barn. Earl Justice was already several hundred yards down a trail that headed off across the pasture behind his house and into the woods. I tried to get the horse to go at a gentle trot, but it took off like a rocket—probably testing me out. I managed to hang on, reining it in when we reached Earl Justice.

He looked amused. "I hope Scheherazade's not a little too much horse for you, doll."

"Where is she?" I said.

"Who?" He looked at me innocently.

"I don't have time to screw around, Earl," I said.

He grinned. "You cannot imagine the panic they are in down at the sheriff's office," he said. "Who were those people that showed up down there? They weren't from the governor, I know that much."

I figured trying to bluff Earl Justice was probably a mistake. "They were private investigators from my firm in Atlanta," I said.

"My my my. That was ballsy—if you'll forgive the expression."

He picked up the pace a little, just enough to make me uncomfortable. He knew the trail and the horses. I didn't. He was just trying to rattle me.

"I just want my cousin," I said as calmly as I could.

"So let me ask you this," he said. "If you're not really a filmmaker, what are you doing down here?"

"I never said I was a filmmaker. Lee-Lee's the one making the movie. I just came down to help out."

He closed one eye thoughtfully. "So y'all really just came here to make a documentary about Dale Weedlow?"

I nodded.

"Not a very interesting story, I would say."

"It is if he turns out to be innocent."

"You probably should have worn a helmet," Earl Justice said. "A fall from that horse could really put a hurt on you."

"And he *is* innocent, Earl. As you well know."

"How would I know that?"

"I have a witness who puts your car at the scene of the crime that night."

"Terri's car broke down that night. I loaned my Jaguar to her. I'm sure she drove it out there herself."

"You ever known Terri to smoke pot?"

He looked at me curiously.

"I mean, that was Dale's official story. He lured them out there with the promise of free dope."

"Mm," Justice said. "I always thought that was a little implausible. Terri was kind of straitlaced."

"They're going to uncover the truth," I said. "It's all over now. You might as well give her back before things get worse for you."

"Let's say I have, ah, detained your cousin. What then? What could induce me to hand her over to you?"

"Brittany's papers. She made two sets of copies. The first set was the one she gave to Ervin Kindred. You got those back. But the second set has been sitting around in an abandoned sawmill for the past six or seven years. I don't care about your lessors and whether you're cheating them or not. You give me back Lee-Lee, I give you the papers."

"So you really have a second set of papers?"

I reached into my back pocket, pulled out a sample accounting document that I'd brought along, handed them to him.

He unfolded them, glanced at them, then laughed. "Did you actually look at these?"

"Not all of them."

"Well, I hate to tell you, but this is nothing. It's an accounts receivable report. It's nothing." He tossed the papers over his head. They swirled around my horse's head. The horse shied a little, whinnied loudly. I finally got her calmed down, but it was a frightening moment. He was right: This was *way* too much horse for me.

"There are a lot more papers," I said.

"It doesn't matter," he said.

"Why not?"

"We played it straight in the lawsuit. I produced every scrap of paper that lawyer up there in Atlanta asked for. Truth is, they got no case."

"Then why are Brittany and Terri dead?"

"You have to understand the economics of this business. Any fool with a front loader and a bulldozer can mine kaolin. There's no trick to it. Cut down to it, start digging. Hell, it's just dirt. The trick is taking all that mud and turning it into a high-value mineral. And all of that happens at the plant. Blunging, degritting, centrifuging, brightness enhancement, delamination—all these processes take a lot of skill and knowledge. And more important, they cost a lot of money."

"Then why the double booking?"

"Who said there was double booking?"

"Brittany did."

"Brittany didn't know jack about accounting. She was a data-entry clerk who liked trumping up a little drama in what was actually a very dull and colorless life. She may have called that lawyer and told him she had evidence of double booking. But that doesn't mean she *actually* had it."

"Then why did you feel obliged to bully those papers out of Ervin Kindred?"

He raised one eyebrow. "That's his story?"

"That's his story."

He shook his head sadly. "Poor Ervin. What a sad case. Smartest man I ever met in my life. Decent fellow, too. But somewhere along the line, he just fell apart. I still don't know why."

I wasn't sure what was going on here. Was he trying to lead me off track? Trying to bluff me? He wasn't somebody who was easy to read–a natural poker player. He might have been lying, he might not. But somehow I just couldn't quite sniff out the lie–if it was there at all.

"You know Dale Weedlow is innocent, right?"

"Wouldn't be surprised."

"Did you bully Ervin into throwing in the towel on that case?"

"Absolutely not. If Ervin threw in the towel, he did it for his own reasons."

"Deputy Woodie says you went into the sheriff's office and said for them to put Dale Weedlow down. He has this conversation on tape."

"Does he now?"

"Tell me why you would have wanted Dale Weedlow in jail if you knew he was innocent."

"I didn't know he was innocent. Not then. Matter of fact, I still don't."

"And yet you told the sheriff to frame him."

"I told the sheriff to make the case quick. I didn't specifically say 'frame.' I wouldn't have done that."

"Your whole story sounds cockeyed," I said.

Earl Justice rode for a while, and then finally said, "Do you like history?"

"I read historical novels sometimes," I said. "That's about as far as it goes."

"Reason I bring it up is because I was always fascinated by the early kings of England. Aethelred the Unready, Canute, Harold Hardrade, William the Conqueror, Edward the Confessor–all those guys. See, I'm like one of those guys. Here in Flournoy County, I'm the king. Being a king's a tough job. You got to defend your turf all the time, from enemies inside and out. *L'état, c'est moi.* I *am* Flournoy County. Why? Because I seek glory? Hell no. Grand scheme of things, my little kingdom don't amount to a hill of beans. See, DCI is the smallest kaolin producer in the world. There are four kaolin companies in this state–three of them owned by big international outfits with all kinds of money. And me. My competitors are billion-dollar companies that own mines and plants all over the world. They got other businesses to help them ride out the tough cycles. Not me. I got a little company that my granddaddy built. We got kaolin mines in three Georgia counties and we got one plant. Period. My company made about two hundred million dollars last year.

"I'm not asking you to feel sorry for me. My point is this: My payroll accounts for almost half the total income in this county. Half! Kaolin prices have been under pressure for a decade. There's overcapacity in the industry. What happens if DCI folds? Some lawyer from Atlanta's gonna come down to my factory, give everybody thirty minutes to collect their belongs and leave; then he's gonna slap a padlock on the door. And that will be all she wrote. Average wage in this industry is forty-six thousand dollars a year. You think anybody else in this benighted part of the world is gonna take up the slack? Hell no! We'll be talking welfare, suicides, life savings down the toilet, kids who'll never get a chance to go to college, house foreclosures. If DCI craters, it'll take down the grocery story over in Hamlin, it'll kill the Flournoy Bank and Trust, it'll put six or eight real estate companies out of business, and it'll bankrupt between ten and twenty of my local suppliers. The county budget will go south. Schools will have to fire teachers; the art and music programs will disappear. It just goes on and on and on. The human cost will be terrible."

"That's all very sad."

"Keep your snide comments to yourself till I'm done. My company is a fragile, fragile thing. I've kept it afloat for thirty-five years through thick and thin by doing whatever it took to keep it going. If I had to intimidate lessors to keep costs down, I did it. If I had to get a little physical with union organizers, I did it. If I had to fight a lawsuit for ten years, I did it."

"If you had to kill Terri and Brittany . . ."

He shook his head. "No. See, that's the point. This whole county, it's like a balloon, just waiting to pop. One pinprick and the whole thing goes. A double murder in a place like this—it gets people nervous and worried and discontent. I can't afford nervousness and discontent. Brittany came to me, said she had papers proving I was cheating some leaseholders. I looked at the papers. They were crap. Has my company cut a few corners, interpreted some accounting rules in fairly liberal ways? Sure. But anything illegal? No.

"Still, I figured, *Fine, I'll pay her off.* It's like a personal-injury lawsuit against a grocery store. Whether the grocery store is at fault or not, they pay off the plaintiff just to be rid of the nuisance. I deposited a check for ten thousand dollars in her bank account the day before she was killed. I expected her to be gone by sunup."

We rode in silence for a while.

"That's who I am," Earl Justice said finally. "Anybody around here will tell you. I'm a tough bastard. But I don't take mulligans on the golf course, I don't shoot pen-raised quail, and I damn sure don't hang women up from the rafters and gut them like hogs." He seemed angry suddenly. "It's wrong and it's unmanly. What kind of person would do a thing like that?"

"Not Dale Weedlow."

"I don't know that."

"Help me, Earl. An innocent man's gonna die."

"I'll tell you the plain-out truth," Earl said. "If he gets out, it'll bring the spotlight on this whole county. All the corruption, all the kickbacks, all the shady stuff that the Sheriff's Department and the county administration is involved in, it'll fall on me—even though I'm not directly involved. I'm the king here, so I'll take the brunt of it. Which I don't mind—in principle. That's my job. Problem is, it'll suck DCI down with it. And I can't let that happen."

"Jesus Christ," I said.

"Sometimes a goat has to be sacrificed to the gods," he said. "For the good of the realm."

I mulled it over. Was this all some kind of clever ploy to draw me away from the truth? It didn't feel that way. It was too raw, too close to home. There was a sadness about him as he told the story that just seemed inconsistent with fraudulence. We rode some more, circling around to the bottom of the hill that led up to the house.

I was starting to feel panicky. Why couldn't Earl Justice have just been guilty? I was virtually sure by now that he wasn't. First, the cuff link apparently wasn't his. Second, he'd offered a plausible reason for the presence of his car at the crime scene. And finally, it was a safe bet that it was the killer who'd snatched Lee-Lee. If Earl were really the killer, he'd have offered to trade Lee-Lee—if not for the papers, then for our silence.

So if it wasn't him, who was it? We were coming out of the forest again, Justice's mammoth house visible at the top of the hill.

"Race you," Earl Justice said as we came out of the trees. Then he snapped the reins and his big stallion took off.

Competitiveness is a curse, I guess. I felt angry at the guy. Maybe because I wanted him to be guilty. He was a son of a bitch—but probably not a killer. I leaned over and urged my horse, Scheherazade, to follow. It didn't take much effort to get her moving. She was born to run. As soon as I started to race, though, I realized I had made a stupid, stupid mistake. I had no business galloping on a horse like this. But by then, it was too late. We thundered up the hill. I was terrified. The hill seemed endless.

And then, suddenly, somewhere in the middle of the hill, the ter-ror evaporated and I decided, *Okay, if I'm going to get killed, I might as well die a winner.*

Earl Justice knew the horses and could outride me with one hand tied behind his back. But I had an advantage. He was a big man—well over two hundred pounds. I, on the other hand, barely clear five feet and weigh about 105 soaking wet.

Halfway up the hill, my horse started gaining. I don't think Earl expected me to win, so he probably wasn't pushing his horse the way he could have. When he caught a glimpse of me out of the corner of his eye, he cursed and slapped his horse on the neck. We rode literally neck and neck for about two hundred yards.

"Come on, baby!" I yelled. "Come on, Scheherazade!"

Then the toll of Earl Justice's weight started preying on his big stallion, and my mount edged in front. A yard, a yard and a half, then two.

"Go, baby, go!" I was yelling like a banshee.

And then we crested the hill. What possessed me, I do not know—that stupid competitiveness gene, I guess—but I raised my arms in triumph.

Scheherazade felt my hands release the reins and took it as her cue to plant her feet and give me a little shimmy. Suddenly, I was no longer a rider—I was a wingless bird suspended in the air. And that was it. Lights out.

THIRTY-TWO

When I came to, I was lying on the leather couch in Earl Justice's trophy room. "That was a fairly acrobatic fall you took," Earl said. He had two glasses of whiskey in his hands.

I sat up slowly, my head throbbing. "You were hoping I'd fall and die, weren't you?" I said.

"The thought crossed my mind," he said.

I looked at my watch. 2:43 P.M. I felt a surge of panic. I was way behind schedule. And I still had absolutely no idea who had killed Terri Ross and Brittany Woodie.

"So you really don't have Lee-Lee, do you?" I said.

"Nope."

He held a whiskey toward me. "Drink."

"Can't." I stood unsteadily. "I gotta go."

"I find you very attractive," he said. "I don't suppose–"

"Not a chance," I said.

He looked at me wistfully for a minute, then smiled broadly. "I had to ask."

I walked to the door. "Wait a second," I said. I reached into my purse, pulled out the cuff link I'd found on the floor of the murder site. "Recognize this?"

His eyes narrowed. "Why?"

"Never mind," I said.

•

When I reached the car, I saw that the trunk of my car was wide open. The box of Brittany's documents was gone.

I looked back at the house. Earl Justice was standing on the balcony under the big neoclassical portico, sipping his glass of whiskey and looking down at me.

"You son of a bitch," I said.

"Okay, so maybe those papers were a little more damaging than I let on," he said.

"And what happened to all that 'I never take mulligans on the golf course' stuff?"

"I don't," he said. "But still. Golf is just a game. This isn't, darlin'. I couldn't let you keep those papers."

"How did you know they were there?"

"I didn't. But you were lying on the couch and I figured, Hey, why not check your car? Voilà, there they were."

I stared at him. "So why should I believe anything you said today?"

"Go ask Ervin about that cuff link you just showed me. Then you get back to me with that question." He finished his whiskey in one big gulp, made a sour face, and went back inside.

"Are you saying..."

"This is a small rural community. Not a lot of fancy dressers. I only know one man in this town who wears cuff links. Ervin Kindred."

A wave of horror ran through me. Had Ervin Kindred been playing me all along? There was only one way to find out. I jumped in the car and floored it.

THIRTY-THREE

I knocked on the door of Ervin Kindred's house, but it was locked and nobody answered. Next, I walked over to his office, where I found Aimee Wallace sitting at a computer trying to look busy.

"I need to see Ervin," I said. "It's urgent."

"He's taking the afternoon off."

"I know. Do you know where I can reach him? He's not at his house."

"Is there some kind of urgency?"

"Aimee, Dale Weedlow is going to die in a matter of hours. I would call that urgent."

"You don't actually think you're going to be able to stop it."

"Yes, I do. I've found evidence indicating that someone besides Dale Weedlow was at the crime scene."

She studied my face for a while. "Who?"

"I'm afraid I can't tell you that."

Her tongue poked thoughtfully out of her mouth for a moment. Then she said, "He's probably out at his hunting shack over on the other side of Hamlin."

"Give me directions."

"I better go with you," she said. "It's a little hard to find."

"Hop in," I said.

She did. I took off, letting her point the way as I drove. It took about twenty minutes to get to the other side of the county. Then we had to work our way down a series of increasingly small and decrepit roads, eventually ending up on a gravel track that barely qualified as a footpath.

I was feeling increasingly nervous. Time was getting seriously short. And what if Ervin didn't know anything?

My gas gauge was down around the *E*. If I took a wrong turn coming back, I was liable to run out of gas. There were stretches out here where there was nothing but woods for miles and miles. A lot of things could go wrong. And there wasn't time for even a single hitch now.

"You're sure we're going the right way?" I said, looking at my watch.

Aimee Wallace nodded.

Finally, the road ended. I couldn't drive any farther. "Aimee . . ." I said.

"This is it," she said.

"Where's his car?" I said.

"There," she said. She pointed. And sure enough, just a few hundred feet away, seemingly sprouting from the middle of the forest, was an old four-wheel-drive pickup.

"We'll have to walk the rest of the way," Aimee said.

She got out and started walking gingerly through the weeds. "I guess I'm not really dressed for hiking." She held up one of her pale, stocky legs, showing me a three-and-a-half-inch heel. "Don't let me hold you up. Just follow the trail. You'll see it. I'll wait here."

"Great," I said.

"Plus, with this hole in my shoulder . . ." She gently touched the dressing, which was just visible under her blouse.

"Hey, don't even think about it," I said. "If I don't get back within half an hour, drive out and call the GBI. Not the sheriff's office. The GBI."

She frowned, a curious expression on her face. "I don't understand why that would be necessary."

"Just do it!"

I jogged quickly up the hill and found myself standing on a low ridge, looking down toward a cabin. Between the cabin and the ridge was a large pit about a hundred yards wide and maybe twice as long. At the bottom of the pit were a few pools of stagnant water. The water was bone white. An old kaolin mine. There was no indication anybody had been mining there in a great many years, though.

I trotted through the pit, avoiding the pools of water, and eventually reached the cabin. When I looked through the door, I saw Ervin Kindred seated on a chair, his palms resting flat on his thighs. He was still dressed for the office—white shirt, bow tie, wool pants. The only incongruous thing was his footwear—a pair of boots stained with white mud. An unopened bottle of Johnnie Walker Black sat in front of him.

When I knocked on the door, he jumped.

"Good gracious!" he said. "You about scared the fool of me." He stared at me, puzzled. "How did you find me? And what are you doing out here?"

I decided it was time for a big entrance. I walked in, unscrewed the cap of the whiskey bottle, walked over to the cabinet, pulled out two Dixie cups, set them on the table, and poured a couple of fingers of brown liquid into them. Then I took out a pocket recorder, slapped it down on the table, and hit the record button.

"This is Sunny Childs. Today is the thirteenth of May. Flournoy County, Georgia. Present with me is Ervin Kindred, trial lawyer for Germind Dale Weedlow. Mr. Kindred, you might as well start drinking now. Dale Weedlow is not going to die today."

Kindred eyed me curiously.

"Come on," I said. "What are you waiting for? You've ruined your life already. Go ahead, drink."

His hand went out to the whiskey, but he didn't pick up the cup. "Why do you think Dale Weedlow isn't going to die today?"

"Because he didn't do it."

"Oh. Yeah." He snorted slightly.

"For God sake!" I shouted. "I'm sick of this. You've lied to me every time I've seen you. Now just . . . please, cut it out. Tell me the truth."

He looked at the whiskey. His hand had a slight tremor, which caused little circular ripples to rise on the top of the whiskey.

What was it going to take? I had a hunch he'd been waiting to confess for years. There was a part of him that was a decent, normal man. And that decent, normal man had been eaten up with guilt for a long, long time. I just hoped I could get past whatever demons had seized control of his mind so long ago, and get the decent man to talk.

I took out the gold cuff link that Deputy Woodie had given me. It was still in the little plastic bag with the evidence control number inked on it.

Ervin Kindred stared at the bag.

"Remember this?" I said. The gold gleamed in the dark room. "A missing piece of evidence? It was found on the floor of the shed where those girls were found. It's yours, Ervin."

Ervin looked at it for a long time.

"You took them off so you could roll up your sleeves before you did all those things to Brittany and Terri. And in the heat of the moment, you forgot them."

He took a slow, deep breath.

"Are you alone?" he said finally.

"Yes," I said.

He just kept looking at the cuff link.

"The clay on Terri and Brittany's feet," I said. "That didn't come from the mine where Dale Weedlow worked, did it?"

He hesitated, then finally picked up his drink and downed it. Then he looked at the wall for a while. When he finally spoke, his voice was louder and more certain than I'd expected. Like he'd come to some sort of decision. "No," he said.

"We're sitting in your hunting cabin. There's an old abandoned kaolin pit next to your cabin. They got the clay on their feet from walking through there, didn't they?"

He nodded.

"Say it out loud, please, Mr. Kindred."

He poured another whiskey, downed it quickly. Then he sat up straight. "It was a warm night. I had come out here by myself. Brittany Woodie drove out to the cabin. As I told you before, we had been having a relationship. She had recently extorted some money out of Earl Justice, and now that she'd gotten her money, she was going to be leaving town the next day. She came out here to say good-bye to me. She was intending to have a night on the town before she left, and so she'd gotten all dolled up. She liked to wear heels. Didn't think about it until she got here, I guess, but this is kind of a rugged area. She wasn't dressed for it. She took off her heels and she walked barefoot through the old mine pit next to my cabin. I could hear her cussing the whole way. It had just rained, and by the time she got here, her feet were white halfway up her calves."

"And what happened then?"

He stared at the bottle, poured some more but didn't drink it. "I don't want to get into that."

"Mr. Kindred, you have to say it. Dale Weedlow will die if you don't say it."

He sat for almost three minutes. Finally, he said, "I don't want to get into the rest of it. Suffice it to say that she was dead a few minutes later. After it was over, I dragged her body back down the path, up to her car. Well . . . actually not to *her* car. That was where the problems started. What I found when I got up to the car was that Brittany hadn't been alone. Her friend Terri Ross was sitting in the car at the top of the hill. It was getting dark, so I didn't see her until I had gotten right up to the car. She jumped out of the car and started screaming, 'Oh, my God, what happened?' and all that sort of thing. Of course nobody heard her. We were miles away from the nearest house. I told her there had been an accident. I said Brittany had fallen. I finally got Terri calmed down. We got back in the car."

"*Her* car?" I said.

"Actually, the car belonged to Earl Justice, Terri's boss. I learned later that her car had been in the shop, and Earl had loaned his to her. Anyway, Terri drove. And as she drove, she kept asking me questions about how this could have happened. I guess she didn't buy my explanation. We were just driving along and suddenly she looked over at me, and I could see. I could just *see*. She knew.

"She slammed on the brakes, got out of the car, and started to run. We were still in the middle of nowhere. I was in my late forties at the time. Not exactly spry. But in my day, I'd been a pretty good athlete. I was bigger than she was and I was desperate. I grabbed her, pulled her off her feet, got her into the trunk of the car. There was duct tape in the back, so I wrapped duct tape around her hands and around her mouth.

"After that, I just drove around for a while. I knew Terri was going to have to die. But I couldn't . . . I just . . . I couldn't face actually *doing* it."

"Killing her."

He looked up at me. "Killing her. Yes. I didn't want to kill this girl. I knew her and I liked her. She was an admirable person. But still. I knew how it had to end." He sighed loudly. "And once it ended, there had to be a suspect. Whether their bodies were found or not, the police would try to find out who the last person to see them was. For all I knew, Brittany might have told twenty people she was on her way to see me. There was blood on the floor of my cabin. There were drag marks in the clay. There was clay on her feet. My fingerprints were in the Jaguar she'd borrowed from Earl. There was a huge amount of forensic evidence. If I was suspected of any involvement, we were sunk. So I was going to have to come up with a scenario. I had to come up with a viable suspect for the crime.

"We drove around and around and around. Eventually, it came to me. I had this client. He worked in a kaolin mine. I'd defended him recently for charges related to a scuffle he'd gotten into at a bar. He'd been in and out of trouble for years. It was perfect. It was a weekend night. I thought, If we could sneak Brittany into the mine where he worked, we could make it look like he had done it."

"You're talking about Dale Weedlow."

"Of course I'm talking about Dale Weedlow." He drank some more. "So the idea was that we would make it look like some kind of sex crime. I had a friend in Maryland, a prosecutor, who'd mentioned a case he'd had where a woman had been hung upside down and eviscerated. There were some details of the crime that had never been released. I figured if we copycatted the crime, we could make it look like Dale Weedlow was the obvious suspect. But then late in the trial, I would be able to pull things out of my hat about this crime in Maryland, suggest that it was some serial killer passing through town who had really done it. Enough to buy reasonable doubt for Dale.

"I had another client—I think you're familiar with RT Miller—who'd been arrested recently for organizing a cockfight. I figured that if I offered to defend him for free in that case, he would be willing to testify against Dale. And given that RT was Brittany's boyfriend, I was pretty sure that if he believed Dale was guilty, he'd be more than happy to say that Dale did it. All he had to do was put Dale with Terri and Brittany that night. And again, I would seed his testimony with some kind of detail that would be demonstrably false. The prosecution would put him on the stand, and I'd pull out this lie of his and make it crystal clear that his testimony was not credible. In fact, because of my affair with Brittany, I knew all about Miller's abusive behavior toward her. I could put him on the stand—'Isn't it true, Mr. Miller, that you threatened Brittany's life last week?' *Blah, blah, blah*—and suddenly the jury would see him as the perfect alternate suspect. His credibility would be shot, there'd be more reasonable doubt, and"—Ervin Kindred snapped his fingers—"the jury'd let Dale walk. Furthermore, by then the morons in the Sheriff's Department would be done with the investigation and any evidence connecting us to the crime would have long disappeared."

"You weren't counting on the confession."

"I wasn't counting on the fact that they'd torture him, no."

"But they did."

"It all seemed perfectly reasonable on the spur of the moment. But frankly, I hadn't counted on how the . . . death . . . of those two girls would affect me. I just fell apart. Maybe if I'd been a little more vigorous in trial. But they had that confession. And I just couldn't rally. I was drinking throughout the trial. So Dale Weedlow was convicted."

"Of a crime," I said, for the benefit of the tape, "that he did not commit."

Long pause. "Yes." He poured another whiskey, then drank it.

"And that's why you're talking to me right now, correct? Because it's fish-or-cut-bait time. If you don't tell the truth now, he dies for a crime he didn't commit."

Kindred nodded.

"For the record, please, Mr. Kindred. Yes or no."

"Yes." His voice was barely audible. Tears had begun to run out of his eyes, streaming down both sides of his nose. "I don't want it on my conscience."

"All these years, you could have spoken out."

He sighed loudly. "I had my . . . reputation to protect. My freedom. My livelihood," he said. "I guess it's easy to keep fooling yourself that, oh, maybe he'd win his appeal on a technicality or something and I wouldn't have to step forward."

"But that's not going to happen."

"Obviously not."

"Why'd you come out here today? You planning on drinking yourself to death? Shooting yourself? What?"

He stared at the wall. His palms lay flat on his thighs. "I'm past planning for anything," he finally said. "None of it matters anymore."

I looked at my watch. Did I have everything I needed to get Dale's sentence commuted? Maybe, maybe not. I needed details. "Mr. Kindred," I said, "you were a little soft-focus when it came to the actual perpetration of the crime. It's time for you to stop dodging responsibility."

Kindred said nothing.

"Come on. Be a man here. For once. Did you notice that the whole time you were talking, as soon as it came to the things you actually did, you kept saying *we*? Step up to the plate. Say it. I! *I!* Not we. *I* did it. *I'm* responsible."

But Kindred said nothing.

"Come on. First person. Not the royal we. Say it."

Kindred picked up the bottle and drank.

"Why, Mr. Kindred? What happened? Why did you suddenly snap and kill this young woman?"

I looked at my watch. It was going to be *so* close. I was barely going to make it at all—and for sure there wouldn't be time for me to help draft a petition for clemency. I was just going to have to sprint into the governor's office like some maniac, waving the tape recording and shouting.

"I'm responsible," Kindred said finally. "Isn't that enough?"

I wanted more. But I figured this should be at least enough to get a stay. "All right, then," I said. "I'm going now."

"Honey . . ." a voice said. It took me a moment to process the voice. Aimee Wallace. "Honey, no, I'm afraid you're not."

I turned around and Kindred's secretary stood in the doorway, her fat bare feet covered in white up to the ankles. In her hand was a pistol. Which was pointing at me.

My first reaction was just to stare at her. But then I reached into my purse.

"It's not there, honey," Aimee Wallace said. She waggled the pistol in her hand. "I took it out of your purse while you were concentrating on driving."

She was right. It was my gun that she was holding.

Instinctively, I jumped up.

"Oh no, no," Aimee said. "I'm not so good with guns, but if you don't sit down, I'll do my best to shoot you."

I sat back down slowly. I must have looked terribly confused.

Aimee walked into the room, came around, and put her hand

on Ervin Kindred's shoulder, then kissed him on top of the head. "Nobody understands him," she said to me. "Nobody understands his suffering like I do."

Ervin Kindred didn't move. He might as well have been a statue, slumped over in the chair.

"Some of us are built strong," she said. "Others of us are just built to lie there and suffer. It's up to us strong ones to protect the ones who can't do it for themselves."

"Shut up, Amy," Ervin muttered.

Aimee smiled sadly. "Look at him. He can't even raise his voice at me. Poor sweet Ervin."

"I don't understand," I said.

"It doesn't matter if you understand," she said. And then she shot me. Well, she tried anyway. Like she said, she wasn't so good with a pistol. The shot went wide, missed, and broke a window.

"Jesus God, Amy," Ervin said. "This has to stop!"

Aimee fired again. This time, she hit me. I felt it in my stomach, not so much a pain as a horrifying shock that just drained me of all will and all clear thought. I fell over on the floor and rolled up into a ball.

She stood over me. I squeezed my eyes shut. I could hear her pulling the trigger again and again, firing until the .38 was empty.

The room was dead silent. My ears were ringing from the noise.

"Is she dead?" Ervin said finally.

"I don't know," Aimee Wallace said. She poked me with her bare white toe.

And suddenly something flooded into me, a rush of anger. *No, I'm not dead, you fat cow! You shot at me from five feet away and you only managed to hit me once!* I stomped her in the knee. There was a loud pop, and I felt something give. She fell backward, screaming.

"What did you do?" she howled. "What did you do to my leg?"

"Where's Lee-Lee?" I shouted. She was on the floor now, looking up at me and clutching her broken leg.

"What?" she said.

"Where's Lee-Lee?"

"Lee-Lee? Why would I know where she is?" Then she doubled over in pain. "Oh, my leg. You broke my leg!"

I stopped paying attention to her. If she didn't know where Lee-Lee was, I had no use for her. Too many other things to think about.

I pulled up my shirt, knowing there was something bad wrong with me. I found a small round hole three inches to the left of my navel. It was leaking blood. I reached around to my back. Couldn't find an exit wound. There was something very disorienting about the whole thing. I felt faint and my vision had narrowed to a small tunnel. Suddenly, I had an incredibly strong compulsion to get out of that cabin.

I grabbed my pocket recorder and my purse, banged through the door, and began running. Ervin Kindred ran after me. "Wait," he yelled. "Wait, Sunny, I'll tell you everything."

Aimee Wallace screamed after us. "Don't you leave me here! I need help! My leg! Oh God, my leg! Ervin, please, don't leave me!"

In the movies when people get shot, they always fall down and lie there placidly on the floor. Believe me, as somebody who's actually been shot, I can tell you it doesn't work that way. I just had this feeling, like *I gotta get outta here!* Fight or flight, as they say. I was done fighting, so now I just ran and ran. Soon, Aimee Wallace's cries had faded to nothing. Every footfall made pain shoot through my abdomen. But still, it felt better to run than to stand there. It was like something in the back of my mind believed that if I just ran fast enough, I could outrun my injury. The pain was starting to come on now, sharp and piercing. But pain was better than that disorienting shock I'd first felt. I got to my car and climbed in.

Kindred reached the car just as I got it started. I tried to lock the doors, but he wrenched open the door and climbed inside before I had a chance.

"I'm not going to hurt you," he said. "Let me get you to a hospital."

"Get out!" I screamed. I kicked him hard. He dragged me

across the seat, then climbed over me as I pummeled him with my fists. He seemed not to notice as I hit him. In my frenzied state, I probably wasn't hitting him very hard. Like I say, I'd had one moment of fight, and now my brain was totally focused on flight. A wave of exhaustion rolled over me and I just couldn't seem to struggle any longer. I slumped back in the seat.

Ervin Kindred pushed me into the passenger's seat, put the car in reverse, and began backing rapidly down the dirt road.

"Just don't torture me," I said. "Okay?"

"I'm not going to kill you."

"It's been a bad day. I'm not really up for getting my guts cut out."

"Oh for God sake, just turn on the tape," he said. "I'll tell you everything."

THIRTY-FOUR

I sat there as Ervin Kindred backed the car rapidly out of the woods. Finally, it got through my thick head that, no, he probably wasn't going to kill me.

"The tape," he said, looking at his watch. "Hit the button. We've got to get it all on tape."

For a moment, I could see through the broken man to somebody he might have been once before—somebody stronger, somebody more capable, somebody who didn't just sit around letting misfortunes tumble on top of him.

"It's already on," I mumbled.

Kindred hit pavement, dropped my car in drive, and floored it. The car fishtailed wildly. It struck me that he'd just drunk an awful lot of whiskey.

"Are you sure you're okay to drive?" I said.

He looked at me for a second, and then we started laughing and laughing.

When we finally stopped laughing, he spoke. "It was all like I said. What I left out was who actually killed Brittany and Terri. And why."

I was feeling strange now. The reality of my injury had set in. It hurt like crazy, but I wasn't dead—and probably wouldn't be for a good while.

"I was in my cabin and Brittany came out to say good-bye. Just like I told you before. But it got a little more complicated than that. Within a few minutes after she got there, Amy Wallace arrived. There was a court filing that needed to be FedExed that day. I had to sign the papers. So Amy came out to the cabin to get my signature.

"When Amy walked in, I was with Brittany. Like I said, she was saying good-bye to me, saying that she was leaving town the next day. I was a little bit out of my head, I guess, and I was pleading with Brittany to stay. Pleading in just the most abject, miserable way. In retrospect, I don't even know why. I had always known that Brittany didn't care all that much for me. But I guess I just felt lonely. And she was telling me that she was going to get this money from Earl Justice and that she had to go—that if she didn't leave town now, she'd probably never leave.

"So there I was, humiliating myself in front of this woman that I didn't even really have all that much affection for—when Amy walked in. Well, Amy sized things up and she started in on Brittany, telling Brittany how she didn't sufficiently appreciate me and how unfeeling she was. It was all a bunch of hooey."

"In what sense?" I said.

"Oh, come on. It's obvious to anybody who's around Amy Wallace for ten minutes, that she's been in love with me forever. And I've never had the slightest attraction to her. I've just taken advantage of her doglike loyalty all these years and never given her anything in return but a paycheck. So when Amy started in on her you-don't-truly-understand-Ervin-Kindred speech, it was obvious to me that she wasn't angry at Brittany so much as she was mad at me for neglecting her.

"Most people would have understood where Amy was coming from and would have found her whole speech so pathetic that they would have humored her and let her ramble on. But Brittany had no patience for it. She was leaving this town, you see. Leaving all this petty small-time business behind. So she had no stake in keeping things tranquil, in maintaining the peace. She just laughed at Amy. She said something to the effect of 'Amy, you've wasted your life on this man. He's never going to love you. And furthermore, he's not worth it. You're both nauseating losers and you deserve each other.' I'm putting it a little stronger than she did, but that was the gist of it."

He laughed hollowly.

"It was all so completely obvious and true. Well, Amy got very mad. She went into her wet hen routine, scolding and clucking and so on. And Brittany just laughed at her. Laughed and laughed. Of course, Amy was really mad at me. For not caring about her. But she took it out on Brittany. She picked up an ash spade from the fireplace and hit Brittany with it. Brittany went down, just like that. *Pow!* Hit her head on the floor and didn't move. Amy was so worked up that she started hitting Brittany as she lay there on the floor. I had to drag her away. When Amy finally calmed down, it was obvious that Brittany was dead.

"From there, it went more or less like I told you earlier . . . except that Amy was with me. I guess I felt responsible. I figured it was all my fault that Amy Wallace was so full of anger. So instead of calling the police on her, I helped Amy cover up the crime. It started out as a little thing. All I did at first was help Amy drag Brittany out to the car. I didn't have any clear idea in mind as to what we were going to do. Maybe bury the body somewhere else. I don't even know. But then when we got to the car, there was Terri Ross sitting there in the front seat. We told her Brittany had fallen, but she didn't buy it. It was obvious from those wounds that she hadn't just tripped on the rug and banged her head or something. So Terri started screaming and carrying on. Amy started yelling at me, 'Put her in the trunk! Put her in the trunk!'" He drove for a while in silence. "So I just did it. I grabbed Terri and put her in the trunk.

"Then we drove around for a while, trying to figure out what to do. Amy was the one who came up with the plan for pinning it on Dale Weedlow. She worked it all out. We drove the car to the DCI mine and we dragged Brittany into the shed and hung her up. Then I said, 'I can't do this, Amy.' So she said, 'Go back in the car.' About ten minutes later, she came back out and her hands were all covered with blood. She said to me, 'Take Terri inside. You'll know what to do.'

"I walked Terri in, and Brittany was already hanging there. Amy and I had discussed in very vague terms what needed to be done. But this! My God, I couldn't believe what Amy had done. But I was in a sort of daze, like a zombie. So I hung Terri up on this hook, and she was struggling and crying, and then I hoisted her up. Once she was hanging, I took off my cuff links and rolled up my sleeves, then put a trash bag over her head because I couldn't stand the look in her eyes. Finally I just walked out of the shed."

He drove for a while in silence.

"I went back to the car and told Amy that I couldn't finish it. Amy said, 'Of course you couldn't. I didn't expect you to.' Then she went back in and I heard the most horrible noises. I got back in the car so that I wouldn't have to hear it. After a while, she came back and I said, 'What did you do?' And she said, 'Can we just not talk about this, Ervin? Ever again?' And we never have."

"One last question," I said.

"Okay."

"Where's Lee-Lee?"

"Huh?"

"Lee-Lee and Sunil Patel disappeared last night. Where are they?"

He squinted curiously at me. "I don't have the faintest idea."

I turned off the tape recorder. If that wouldn't get Dale Weed-low off the hook, nothing would.

"What time is it?" I asked.

"Three-forty-five."

"You need to start driving to Atlanta," I said.

Ervin Kindred looked at me as if I were crazy. "You're going to a hospital."

"The execution is at six o'clock. It'll take between an hour and a half and two hours to get to the governor's office. It's rush hour. These days, Atlanta traffic makes Los Angeles look tame. There's just no time to piddle around."

"I can't do that," Ervin Kindred said. "You're going to the hospital."

"No, I'm not."

"You could be bleeding internally. What if that bullet nicked a major artery in there?"

"I would already be dead," I said with a bit more confidence than I really felt.

His face was getting white and sweat was breaking out on his face. He looked like he was about to faint. "I'm not feeling so hot," Ervin Kindred said. He pulled the car over, climbed out, and stood on the edge of the empty road, bent over like he was going to throw up. But then he just stood there.

I could feel the time ticking away.

"We don't have time for this, Ervin!" I said. I slid over behind the wheel. "Let's go, Ervin!" The lawyer was still busy deciding whether he was going to throw up or not. I could see he would only slow me down.

"Do you have a cell phone, Ervin?" I said.

He nodded, still looking at the ground.

"Call the sheriff, tell them to pick up Amy. Then find Lee-Lee."

"But . . . what are you—"

I drove off and left him there, hunched over on the roadside in the middle of the empty forest. The time for dawdling had run out.

THIRTY-FIVE

I stopped the car at the Star Mart outside town, started filling up my bone-dry tank, then walked in and got two bottles of water and four packs of BC powder. Caffeine, painkillers, water–I figured that would keep me going for a while. It was a sort of surreal thing, standing there paying for my gas and my BC powder and my water while the clerk rang up the order and chatted with me about the weather. When we got done, she pointed at my belly. "What happened to *you,* honey?"

I pulled up my shirt, showed her the bleeding hole. "Got shot," I said. Then I tossed a twenty on the counter. "Keep the change."

●

I hit the interstate ten minutes later, got in the far left lane, and drove as fast as I could. My car maxed out at a squirmy, juddering 105. I didn't feel nervous or scared. I had an odd sense of distance from the world, as though I were drifting slowly away from myself.

At the same time, though, my perceptions were oddly acute. I could tell I wasn't about to lose consciousness. Whatever blood loss I had suffered, it was still a ways away from killing me. It wasn't that I wasn't concerned. I just didn't feel scared. It was more this clinical thing going in my head, like I was measuring blood loss against how much time it would take to get to the governor's office. If I lost a pint an hour, I'd probably die before I made it. If my plumbing was leaking blood at the half-pint-an-hour range, I might well make it. Dale Weedlow's life, my life—it all depended on a simple question of hydraulics.

I drank both bottles of water, trying to pump as much liquid into my body as possible. Hydration was the key. If I could replace enough of the missing blood fast enough to keep my blood pressure up, maybe I could buy an extra half hour. The BC powder started to kick in after a while and the pain receded to the level of bad cramps.

I pulled out my cell phone, tried Lee-Lee. No answer. I called Karen Spruel, Dale Weedlow's pinko appeals attorney. An assistant from her office said she was in her car, driving down to Jackson for the execution. I punched in her cell number, but there was no answer. After that, I called Walter.

"I need a clemency appeal," I said, "and I can't reach Weedlow's appeals attorney."

"By when?"

"An hour?" I said. "It's got to be at the governor's office before six."

"I'm in a meeting," he said. "Let me get one of my associates on it."

He put me on with an earnest sounding young woman who seemed a little nervous about the idea of doing a death-penalty appeal in an hour. "Find an old appeal," I said. "Surely somebody in your firm has done one before. Then we'll fill in some facts. Put a good typist on the phone and I'll dictate." She seemed happy at the prospect of getting off the phone.

I decided that I couldn't afford to concentrate on the road, so I just got in the emergency lane and didn't even bother with the normal traffic. The typist came on the phone and I dictated all the salient facts of the case. I felt like I had never been more clear in my thinking than I was at that moment. The words came out in a logical order, every sentence polished and sure, with long dependent clauses and parenthetical phrases and semicolons inserted in all the right places. It would all be just perfect, I had no doubt.

At 4:45, I was hitting the southern outskirts of Atlanta. I hung up the phone. The clemency appeal would be done and it would be in the governor's office on time. But the appeal itself was useless without the recording I had sitting on the seat next to me. In some distant corner of my brain, I felt an odd sense of satisfaction—maybe even awe—at my own performance. *I'm shot, and look at me go!* Maybe it was the caffeine from all that BC powder that I'd swallowed. Whatever the case, I was feeling exceptionally pleased. *What an amazing chick I am! I'm indispensable! I'm saving a man from death row! I'm . . .*

. . . busted.

As I crested a rise near Old Dixie Highway in Morrow, I suddenly saw something appear in the emergency lane. I swerved, tires screeching, saw a state patrol car flash by, a trooper standing there with his radar gun balanced on his hand. As I tore by, nearly sideswiping him, the trooper scrambled into his car. The blue lights started swimming up in my mirror immediately, the siren getting louder and louder. I looked at my watch. I couldn't stop. But then if I didn't . . . I started imagining roadblocks and choppers and other extreme inconveniences.

I slowed. When the patrolman got behind me, I waved to him to pull around next to me. As the trooper slid in next to me—siren and lights going full blast—I rolled down my window. The trooper was a hard-eyed, skeptical-looking guy with three chevrons on his sleeve.

"I've been shot!" I yelled.

He waved angrily at me, indicating that I should pull over, and shouted something that I couldn't hear. He shouted again, and all I heard was his siren.

"I've been shot!" I yelled again.

He kept yelling and motioning me to pull over. This was going nowhere fast. I realized with a sinking sensation that if I couldn't hear him, he couldn't hear me.

"I've! Been! Shot!"

He responded by pointing a pistol at me.

I pulled over. Getting shot once in a day is plenty.

The cop took his time walking up to my car. He still had his pistol out and he was talking into the radio on his shoulder. When he got to within fifteen feet of my door, he yelled, "Take your keys out and drop them out the window."

I thought about it. That seemed like a really bad idea. Once I gave up the keys, I'd lose control of the situation. I could be stuck here for the duration.

I put my head out the window.

"Keys! Now!"

"Uh, Sergeant?" I said. "I really don't have time to discuss this with you. I've been shot. I'm taking a death-row clemency appeal to the governor right now and I'm slowly bleeding out. I really kind of have to go."

He looked at me with the sort of expression that a hungry pit bull gives to a piece of meat. Unless I was very much mistaken, that was not a sign that he was giving my story a sympathetic hearing.

"Keys!" he yelled. "Out the window!"

I left the keys in the ignition and the engine running as I said, "Sergeant, I'm getting slowly out of the car. I have a bullet wound that I'm going to show you."

"Don't you move, ma'am." He had the gun aimed at my head.

But I got slowly out of the car anyway, lifted my shirt. The blood had run all the way down to my knees by then.

His eyes widened.

"What I want you to do, Sergeant, is radio your dispatch back at Post. Tell them to contact the governor's office. The governor's people are aware that I'm driving to the capitol building to hand-deliver a death-penalty appeal. They'll give you instructions. Do it now, please, because I'm really not feeling so hot and I don't have time to argue with you."

I slumped back into the car, put the car in drive, and floored it. The trooper was yelling frantically into his microphone as I headed back down the highway. I grabbed my cell phone and called Walter.

"Sorry to get you out of your meeting again," I said. "But could you call the governor or one of his people. I just got pulled over for speeding down in Morrow. I need them to tell the trooper to escort me instead of shooting me."

Walter said, "You are *so* gonna owe me when this is over with."

"I'll buy you dinner at Seeger's."

"You better believe it."

"Oh, and speaking of shooting people? I just got shot a few minutes ago."

"Sunny?" he said. "Did you say what I thought you said?"

"I'm fine," I said. "Just make the call."

"Sunny—"

"And don't tell Barrington. He'll get all nervous over nothing."

I could see the trooper coming up fast in my mirror. He had a lot more horsepower than I did. He was still yelling into his microphone as he came up even with me again. Cars were peeling off in front of us, trying to get out of our way. Fortunately, the traffic going in our direction wasn't too bad, since we were heading in toward the city. It was past five o'clock now, dead in the middle of rush hour.

I looked over at the trooper. Once again, he was motioning me to pull over. At least now he wasn't pointing the gun at me. He was waving and yelling into the microphone. Then suddenly, his expression changed and he barked something into the mike. Then he yelled something at me.

"What?" I yelled back.

He turned off his siren and yelled again. This time, I could hear him. "The governor says no police escort!"

I frowned.

"You're. On. Your. OWN!"

The blue lights went off and the trooper slowed, receding into the rearview mirror. On my own. Well, so be it. I'd been on my own since Lee-Lee disappeared.

The traffic was thickening. I got back into the emergency lane, nudged the needle back up to a hundred. My big old car was shimmying and complaining again.

I looked at my watch. 5:15. In a perfect world, I could make it to the exit for the state capitol in another five minutes. Another five to get to the capitol building. Plenty of time. In a perfect world.

Problem was, this was Atlanta. Rush hour. Anything could happen.

And as I crested the rise next to Turner Field, it did. In front of me were six lanes of traffic, six lanes of red brake lights, six lanes of cars stopped dead in the road.

Far off in the distance I could see a tractor-trailer. It was sideways, overturned and burning. And it was smack in the middle of the 75/85 corridor, the highway that led toward the capitol building.

I felt a groan come out of me. This was really, really bad. I kept racing down the emergency lane. But then even that clogged up and I had to slam on my brakes. I skidded to a stop.

The cars in front of me were obviously trying to get off at the University Street exit. But they weren't moving at all. I got out of the car, stood on the roof, and stared. There were cops stopping everybody up ahead, even on the off-ramp going down to University. No one was getting through. No one.

I called Walter again. "Sorry, sorry, sorry for interrupting again," I said. "There's a tractor-trailer burning in the middle of the corridor. I'm stuck. I'm not gonna make it."

"What do you want me to do about it?"

"Can you call the governor's office and–"

"Sunny, you need to make the call this time. I'm starting to lose traction with those people."

"Who should I talk to?"

"Your buddy Arnold Arnold the Fourth is the point man on this thing."

"Great."

"Now, did I hear you correctly that you'd been shot? Are you okay?"

"I don't have time," I said.

I hung up, called the governor's office. It seemed to take forever to get through to the switchboard and then the various sec-
retaries, but finally I reached Arnold Arnold, the governor's chief
of staff.

"Delay the execution!" I said.

"Can't do it," Arnold Arnold said.

"For God sake, I've got a tape right here in my car. It's a confession that tells exactly what happened."

"Don't be telling me it's Earl Justice."

"It's not Earl Justice."

"Glad to hear it."

"Look, there's an overturned tractor-trailer on the highway,
I've been shot, and I'm not going to make it by six. Just push it
back to seven."

There was a long pause.

"Can't do it," Arnold said finally.

"You son of a bitch," I said.

"Taking a tone ain't helping your cause, Sunny," he said.

"Half an hour," I said. "Stay the needle till six-thirty."

"Get here by six," he said. "If it takes a few minutes to listen to
what you've got, the governor will stay the execution till we can
get through it. But the governor ain't gonna hold off a lawful execution on the basis of some hysterical phone call."

He hung up in my ear.

I was still standing on the roof of the car. I weighed my op-
tions. If I stayed where I was, Dale Weedlow would die. I knew
Atlanta traffic–burning semis did not get cleared in half an hour.
We would be sitting there for the duration. And putting aside
Dale Weedlow, I could die, too.

Rising up in front of me–maybe two miles away–was the gold
dome of the capitol building. Two miles. On a normal day? Sure,
no problem, I could run two miles in thirty-five minutes. With a
bullet in my belly? There was no knowing.

A woman leaned out of a car nearby and said to me, "Um, ma'am? I don't know if you realize it, but you're bleeding."

"No shit," I said.

Getting shot makes you a little grumpy.

I jumped off the roof of my car, reached through the window, picked up the tape recorder. And started to run.

THIRTY-SIX

I couldn't tell you exactly what happened next. I remember heat on my face, so I must have passed close to the fire. But whether I ran straight up the interstate past the burning truck, or whether I got off at University and ran through the slummy neighborhoods south of the capitol building, I couldn't tell you. I just remember excruciating pain and a sort of drumbeat in my head that kept me going, telling me, *Just one more step, just one more step, just one more . . .*

I remember running into the capitol building through the front door and into the rotunda, where a state trooper stood operating the metal detector. I remember getting into a little bit of an argument with the guard because I wouldn't put my tape recorder through the X-ray machine. I remember some shouting and then the governor himself coming out from his office–which was only a few feet away–and saying, "Let her through, Sarge, it's okay."

I remember seeing a clock. It said 6:02. I remember the sick feeling I had, like everything I'd gone through had been a total waste.

And then a voice saying, "Don't worry. That one's a couple minutes fast."

The governor took my arm and led me back to his office.

"Get a doctor in here," he said. Then: "Who's got the phone? Make the call. Tell the warden to hold everything till we see what she's got."

There was a roaring sound in my ears, I couldn't seem to catch my breath, and my vision was narrowed down to a thin black tunnel.

Somebody pressed play and then the tape started playing, but there was nothing but a hiss. I remember a long silence with nothing but hiss. And then another voice–Arnold Arnold's, I think–saying, "She's got nothing. She's been jerking our chain."

Then the governor: "Hold up, hold up, Arnie. How do you work this thing?"

Then another voice: "Maybe there's a rewind button."

Then my own voice, off in some distant place. "This is Sunny Childs. Today is the thirteenth of May. Flournoy County, Georgia. Present with me is Ervin Kindred, trial lawyer for Germind Dale Weedlow...."

Someone else said, "Catch her! She's falling!"

And another voice: "Be careful, sir. That's my wife."

THIRTY-SEVEN

When I woke up, Barrington was sitting next to my bed, holding my hand. My hand looked ghostly white next to his brown skin.

"What happened?" I said.

"You're in the hospital," Barrington said.

"Duh," I said.

"Oh . . ." Barrington smiled. "You mean what happened to Dale Weedlow?"

"Yeah."

"It's all over. The governor pardoned him. Ervin Kindred and Amy Wallace are in jail. The governor has sent the GBI in to take over the Sheriff's Department in Flournoy County."

"What about Lee-Lee?"

"She's fine," Barrington said.

"Who kidnapped her?"

Barrington got a funny expression on his face. "I think I'll let her tell you." He got up and went to the door.

Then my mom came in the room and it was the usual fountain of tears and melodrama. Her hair was perfect and her handbag matched her shoes. She managed to subtly imply that I had gotten shot with the express purpose of scaring the life out of her. We almost got in a fight but didn't. Situation normal.

"You're still a smart-ass, so I guess you're going to be fine," she said finally, dabbing at her eyes with a Kleenex. Then she patted me on the leg and said, "You make me so proud. I'm going out to find Walter. He's downstairs getting coffee. I know he'll want to see you."

Barrington and I sat there for a while without speaking.

"Damn it," he said finally. "I hate this."

"I'm fine," I said. "I'm *fine.*"

"That's not what I'm talking about."

"What, then?"

"In case you're wondering how I found you at the statehouse," he said, "Walter called me. He told me you'd been shot."

"I told him not to tell you! I didn't want you to worry."

Barrington looked at me incredulously. "What do you think I'm here for? I mean, seriously."

I didn't say anything.

"I knew you were heading for the governor's office. So I just went there." He stared out the window. We had a nice view of a huge air-conditioning unit. Finally, he said, "It just hit me as I was tearing down the street toward the statehouse: What are we messing around for?"

"Messing around?"

"You and me. We said we'd get married—what, eight months ago? But we still haven't even set a date. We're just lolling around in limbo, like we've got forever. But the second I heard you'd been shot, I just realized, You know what? We don't have forever. Let's just do it."

"Okay," I said.

"Three months from today. Isn't that enough time?"

"Mom will howl."

"Yeah, but look on the bright side. It'll give her something to obsess about for the next three months. Wouldn't that be better than having her obsessing over your health?"

"Good point," I said.

We sat quietly for a while.

"That *was* you, wasn't it?" I said finally.

"Me, what?"

"When I was kind of fading out in the governor's office. I heard someone say, 'That's my wife.'"

Barrington gave me a small, odd smile. "Yeah," he said. "It just came out."

I gave his hand a squeeze. "Say it again."

"What?"

"Say it again."

"That's my wife."

I closed my eyes and smiled. Wow. Wife. I liked the way it sounded. Suddenly, I felt very tired.

I said, "I think I'm gonna sleep a little bit."

THIRTY-EIGHT

But back to Lee-Lee.

It turned out there was no kidnapping at all. As she put it later, "Dude, it was like there was too much pressure! I just couldn't deal."

Amazing. In the middle of trying to save somebody from death, she just bailed. Her justification for the whole business was as follows: "I wrote the kidnapping note just to give you a little motivation. I knew if you had enough pressure on you, you'd fix everything. It's what you do. I was just getting out of your way."

Turned out she and Sunil had driven up to Nashville in his cab. They went to the open-mike night at the Bluebird Café, where Sunil met a producer who knew some guy, who had a friend, and so on and so on—all of which ultimately resulted in Sunil getting a development deal with RCA Nashville and a publishing contract at Tree Music. He's working on a CD now with the tentative title *Hot 'n Spicy*. Only in America.

But, again, back to Lee-Lee.

Who'da thunk it? Lee-Lee—the girl who never finished anything in her life—actually completed her film. She turned out to have a gift, not only for filmmaking but for self-promotion.

Her movie—which was called *Feet of Clay*—won Best Documentary at Sundance last month. If you happened to have been out there sitting next to Robert Redford at its world premiere, you would have thought my involvement in the freeing of Dale Weedlow was limited to playing straight man to Lee-Lee. She managed to get the most unflattering exchanges between the two of us on film, ones where I was telling her she was wasting her time, that Dale Weedlow was probably guilty, that she was a fool, and so on. I came off as a slightly eccentric, heavily armed naysayer with a smart mouth.

And my heroic run to the capitol building? My last-second save? The bullet in my belly? The film managed to glide over these facts in a way that—without quite lying—suggested that it had only been Lee-Lee's steadying presence and nerve that had kept me on track to do what needed to be done. In fact, you might have even left the theater with the impression that it was Lee-Lee—rather than I—who had arrived at the governor's office two minutes before they were scheduled to put the needle in Dale Weedlow's arm. I'm telling you, the movie was brilliant. It was southern gothic in its purest form, every character in the movie coming off weirder than the next, Flournoy County converted into Lee-Lee's own personal version of Faulkner's Yoknapatawpha.

She moved to L.A. a month ago, where she's sitting in an office on the Universal lot, deciding which of the many scripts being thrown at her she should deign to direct.

And Dale Weedlow?

He launched a civil suit against Sheriff Powell and other local worthies. He then settled the suit, using the proceeds to buy up leases throughout Flournoy County. If Earl Justice doesn't rob him blind, Dale will probably end up being the second-richest man in Flournoy County.

Me, I'm doing nicely, thanks.

I have a gold ring on my finger and I'm happy as a clam. It only hurts when I laugh.